BRAGG
FOR HIRE

BRAGG
FOR HIRE

JOHN B. CHEEK

For my family, all of them.

CHAPTER ONE

The contract had been sold to Atticus as an easy one: pick up an Imperial diplomat from the failed mining talks with the Repsians, and ferry him by scout car to a drop pad to catch a ship off-planet.

It's a taxi job, Bragg. Easy money. Put your thumb here to accept.

But it was a lie—it was always a lie. Every job thrown to mercenaries was unhealthy. The truly easy jobs, the safe ones, were given to someone more reliable and less expendable.

So Atticus wasn't the least surprised by the Repsian troop carrier that had appeared suddenly in the scout car's rear-view monitor. The failure of negotiations over Imperial mining rights on the planet meant war with the native Repsians, and now the only question was when the troop carrier would open fire. Probably soon, since the planet's large yellow sun had risen to give the carrier's turret gunner good light for shooting.

If it hadn't been the troop carrier, it would have been something else, because there was no such thing as easy money.

Atticus steered the scout car down a steep slope into what looked like the dry bed of an ancient river that had once wound through this now arid plain. The bottom was flat but full of rocks and the wheels stuttered, throwing Atticus against his restraints. He heard the diplomat's helmet hit the open frame of the car with a sharp crack.

"What are you doing?" the man shouted.

"Getting low, sir," said Atticus. "I don't want to get shot and neither do you." The man had been an ass from the beginning and Atticus had taken a strong dislike to him.

"What if you destroy the car?" said the diplomat. He was gripping the seat with both hands. "What then? Do we hide under a rock and hope they don't find us?"

"That's where you come in, sir," said Atticus. "You're the diplomat, aren't you? You can lull the beasts with soft words and I'll shoot'em in the ass when they're not looking."

"Very funny. I really doubt you know what you're doing."

"Damn," said Atticus. "You got me, sir. I'm just a grunt. All the real drivers are ferrying the important people."

It was a good line—pithy and well-delivered—but the man didn't rise to the bait. Atticus decided he'd been too subtle and ran the right side of the car over a tall rock. The vehicle tilted high on its left wheels and the diplomat shouted in terror. That was better.

The car fell again, bouncing hard, and Atticus studied the arrow of red dust in the rear-view. The carrier was coming up fast. The Repsian gunner would fire a ranging shot soon and it might get lucky.

"How far back are they," said the diplomat. He sounded breathless now.

"Five klicks, give or take," said Atticus. "But no worries, sir. We're faster."

"Are we? How much faster?"

The bastard had to ask. "A lot," Atticus lied.

"A lot. How reassuring. They really did reach down a long way to find you, didn't they?"

Atticus turned the steering grip and the right side of the car slammed against the wall of the riverbed. The diplomat's helmet bounced from a frame pillar to strike the safety bar behind his seat.

"Shit!" Atticus said. "Sorry!"

"You did that deliberately!"

"No, sir. It was the booze."

"Good God! Are you drunk too?"

"No more than usual," said Atticus. "Don't worry, the doc says I'm high-functioning."

"You're a disgrace!" shouted the diplomat. "I'll be reporting your misconduct to the Clearinghouse!"

"You wouldn't be the first, sir."

The diplomat said nothing else but tucked his head low between his shoulders, and held tightly to his seat. Atticus wouldn't mind being reported, since it would mean they'd survived this mess. There was nowhere to hide the scout car on this flat plain except in the lower spots like this riverbed, and he could see the end of it coming up. What they really needed was more speed, but the throttle was set to the stops already. Shoving out the diplomat remained an option, but Atticus wanted to get paid.

Soon the riverbed ended and the car rose to the level of the surrounding plain. Immediately a spout of shattered rock erupted twenty meters to their right. There was the ranging shot; and it was a damn nice one from five klicks. Atticus admired professionalism. He craned in his seat to look for more cover ahead.

"Are you lost too?" said the diplomat, a bit wanly now. Some of the starch had come out of him.

But Atticus didn't relent. "Maybe," he said. "I wasn't going to say anything."

The man moaned. "We won't survive this, will we?"

"Fifty-fifty, sir. Sixty-forty if I can get rid of this headache. You don't have a flask on you, do you?"

There was a loud metallic bang and the diplomat screamed again. The car jerked forward violently and bits of something very likely important spun away into the distance, glittering in the strong sunlight.

There was that lucky shot.

Atticus spied several low hills, ahead and to their right. He would have to veer away from the direct line to the drop pad to reach them, but they were cover and cover was the one thing they needed most right now. He turned the steering grip but the car refused to change direction.

Uh oh.

Atticus bent to look for a loose connection beneath the dash panel. The car's unguided right wheels now slammed over something unyielding and the little vehicle tilted up to ride again on its left wheels. The diplomat shrieked. Atticus ignored him, searching for control, but the steering grip spun freely in his hands. The right wheels dropped back to bounce violently.

The diplomat let go of the seat to wave his arms. "Stop! Stop! I can drive better than this!"

"Not in this car you won't," said Atticus. "The hydraulics are trashed. You do speak bug, right?"

The man pounded the air with his fists. "You idiot! Do you have any idea what they would—"

He never finished. The rear of the car lifted behind them, and the entire vehicle vaulted forward in the air. A gout of bright blood hit the windscreen and Atticus hoped it wasn't his. It was a lot. He braced his feet against the floorboard and grunted as the front end slammed into the ground. The dying car bounced twice, then careened to skid sideways on two wheels before falling back, stopping forever against a ridge of plowed soil.

Atticus blew out a breath. *Well, shit. This isn't good.*

He scanned himself for obvious injury, then checked the display on his pancake, the ultra-thin bio-monitor built into the forearm of his exo-suit. Respiration up. Heart rate up. Blood pressure up. But no angry red lights. It wasn't his blood.

That left the diplomat.

The man's forehead now rested against the inside of his helmet and his eyes were closed. Unconscious, but probably alive. Well, maybe: his right arm was severed at the shoulder. Atticus peered around the inside of the car, looking for the arm and wondering whether his contract required delivery of an entire diplomat. But there was only bloody mud on the floorboards.

No matter. They had to move.

Atticus released his restraints and climbed out. The damage to the car was extreme: a heavy caliber round from the carrier had entered the left rear quarter of the vehicle, destroyed its small engine, and exited through the right side of the passenger seat, taking the diplomat's arm with it. Atticus walked around the car, scanning the ground, but it seemed the arm had taken a ride.

He examined the diplomat, confirming the fabric of the man's exo-suit had crimped properly around the shoulder socket. That would stop the worst of the bleeding, and also protect his atmo supply. Atticus pushed the diplomat back against the seat and pulled the protective tab from the back-up pancake affixed to the man's chest. This unit was far less functional than the one now only monitoring a right arm, but it did indicate the diplomat's vitals weren't critical. Not yet, at least. He certainly needed medical attention far sooner than he could reasonably hope to get it.

Atticus moved back to the driver's side to retrieve his plasma rifle from behind the seat. The weapon wouldn't stop an assault carrier but it would give the bugs inside it something to think about while Atticus did his own thinking. He slung the rifle on his shoulder and went back around to pull the diplomat from the wreckage. He draped the man over his other shoulder, and set out at a shambling run for the little range of hills. He didn't bother to look back for the carrier. If it was close enough to shoot him, it would, and there wasn't a damn thing he could do about it.

The hills turned out to be crumbling mounds of rock, but they did offer concealment, and Atticus carried the diplomat up a narrow, steep-sided hollow. Somewhat miraculously, they had cleared the plain without being shot at again. Perhaps the Repsians had stopped at the ruined scout car to admire their handiwork. Maybe they had found the arm.

Atticus stopped to catch his wind. After five minutes he moved on, now at a walk. Seventy-five meters into the hills, a slope above him kicked up and shards of rock fell to rattle on his helmet. *Shit!* They were after him. More rounds struck the ground near his feet, throwing up debris.

He tried to run again but his legs were heavy. Another round passed over his shoulder, just missing the diplomat. Fear rose in Atticus for the first time. To his left, up a hillside not too steep to climb, was a jumble of large rocks. Maybe he could get lost in there. Atticus turned to climb the slope. His legs trembled under the weight of the diplomat.

Suddenly a heavy mech-gun began firing from the jumble of rocks.

Son of a bitch! How did they get around me?

Rounds from the gun zipped over Atticus's head. He dumped the diplomat and dropped to the ground, but there was no cover here. He closed in on himself, expecting to be hit at any moment, but the gunner in the rocks ignored him.

Red tracers from the gun whipped through the air to enter the hollow from which Atticus had just emerged. He turned to look. Two Repsians lay on the rocky ground there, dead or dying. The mech-gun dismantled a third as Atticus watched. The creature's long black arms fell away in gushes of yellow fluid, and its thick black legs crumpled, dropping a heavy, insectile body to the red dirt. Behind it, the head of a fourth was sheered away, and its decapitated body danced awkwardly across the slope for several seconds before collapsing. The scene was violent and brutal, but Atticus felt nothing but relief.

The heavy gun uttered a final burst before falling silent. Then a voice called to Atticus on the emergency channel: "Come on up, friend! They won't be back for a while!"

Atticus nearly laughed: he had been lucky—damn lucky. "Copy that," he said. "Coming up."

He dragged the diplomat the last fifty meters to the rocks. The man's helmet bounced over the stony ground, but there was no clause in Atticus's contract that said this had to be pretty.

* * *

At the edge of the rock pile, a short, wide man in a battered exo-suit knelt behind a flat-topped boulder. An old style mech-gun was laid over the boulder and the man was wiping out the weapon's feed chamber with a rag.

"How do?" he said. "Pull that poor bastard over here and let's have a look at him."

Atticus dragged the diplomat around the boulder and let his boots fall to the dirt.

"Well now," said the gunner, "they won't want him in the band anymore."

Atticus knelt to examine the seal around the diplomat's shoulder socket. It was imperfect, but the med-lights on the auxiliary pancake still burned yellow. He was stable.

"The name's Walt," said the gunner, poking out a hand.

Atticus stood and took the hand briefly. "Atticus."

The man repeated this to himself quietly, then said, "Atticus Bragg?"

"Yes."

"Well now, ain't that something? Proud to meet you, sir!"

"Likewise," said Atticus.

"I'm a merc too, you know. Sixteen years now."

"Let's do this later, friend. How far to the drop pad?"

Walt pointed in the direction of a forked mountain. "That way. About three klicks from this spot. I was heading there myself when I saw you. Me and another fellow, a friend of mine, had a dust-up of our own. We were walking security for the pad and bumped into a bug patrol. Back that way." He turned to point in another direction. "About an hour ago. We weren't expecting a fight, you know, and he got hit right off."

"Yeah," said Atticus. "I didn't get any warning either. Sorry about your buddy."

"Me too. So who's the slot machine?"

"A diplomat," said Atticus. "There's a ship waiting for him at the pad."

"Where's the arm?"

Atticus shrugged. "We left the bugs a souvenir. Who's at the pad?"

"A security platoon," said Walt, "plus a maintenance squad. The usual. They do put those things back on, you know—arms. He ain't gonna be your best friend when he wakes up."

"He was already testy," said Atticus. "Do they have anything heavy there?"

"Nope," said Walt. "A couple of hours ago this wasn't a war. That arm couldn't have gotten far."

"You'd be surprised how they carry. Let's move, friend, before the bugs come back."

Walt laughed. "No hurry on that account. Those ugly bastards are down there telling each other they won't take this shit in their own house, but no one wants to go first." The man lifted the gun from the boulder and looped its cradle sling over his shoulders. "I wouldn't!"

Atticus lifted the diplomat again. Three klicks and he would be rid of the man. He wondered if the arm would turn out to be a problem after all.

"Ready, Major," said Walt.

"I'm not a major anymore. 'Atticus' will do fine. Lead on."

* * *

Walt did, setting a quick pace through the hills, and soon they looked down from the top of a steep slope to a drop pad made from hastily poured temp-crete. There, a group of Imperial soldiers were firing light weapons up at five Repsian assault carriers that had just come over the crest of a low ridge that overlooked the far side of the pad. Behind the soldiers, a small scout ship lifted from the pad. The ground shook as it accelerated out.

"Was that your ride?" said Walt.

Atticus grumbled and pulled a transponder from a pouch on his web belt. He pressed the transmit key and a red light on the unit flashed three times before going dark. He tried again, getting the same result. He shook the transponder at the departing ship. "Goddamn chickenshit pilots! He's bugged out on me!"

"What now, boss?"

"Down to the pad, I guess. What else can we do? That bastard pilot had better hope I die here."

They moved down the slope and jogged onto the pad. Atticus dumped the diplomat in a yellow-painted landing circle before trying the transponder again. The red light flashed again and went dark. He threw the device at the ground and stepped on it. "He's gonna get it."

"They have the right idea," said Walt. He was pointing to the security platoon, which had now moved to the edge of the pad to shelter behind tall piles of rubble pushed up by the construction engineers. It wasn't a bad position but without heavy plasma or close air support the platoon would be overrun and destroyed by the carriers no matter what they did.

Atticus shook his head. "A valiant but doomed last stand isn't in my contract."

"Nor mine," said Walt, "but we're short on options just now."

Atticus growled. He bent to pick up the diplomat. "I'm tired of carrying this bastard but he's got a mouth on him awake."

"Leave him," said Walt. "He'll be all right. He looks dead already."

It was a good point. Atticus dropped the man back to the pad and followed the gunner to a pile of rubble on the security platoon's left flank. At the top Walt set the barrel of his mech-gun into a notch formed by two broken stones. He shrugged off his ammo pack to lay out long belts of heavy slugs. Atticus took a position on the other side.

"On came the beasts!" said Walt, adjusting the gun's sights. "To fight! And fire! And fear! One hour before, no thought of death was near!"

Atticus looked at him and laughed. "A hell of a time for verse."

"That one came easy. There ain't enough poetry in the world, my friend. I aim to fix that."

Fire from the Repsian carriers increased as they approached the pad. Their guns scoured the rubble, blowing clouds of dust and shards of rock back on the defenders. Walt sighted over the barrel of the gun and fired a long burst in reply. The rumble of the weapon vibrated in Atticus's chest, and he felt the dread of heavy combat return bright and fresh, as if it had never left him. Maybe there weren't enough years to live some things down. He lifted his rifle and played blue plasma on the lead carrier, trying to pop its undercarriage welds, but the vehicle advanced unimpeded.

"This is no good," said Walt. "I can't penetrate."

It wasn't good at all. The defenders' weapons were simply too light to penetrate the carriers' tung-steel and electro-field armor. The lead vehicle had stopped short of the tallest rubble pile and it now sat enduring point-blank plunging fire while waiting for the others to come up. Its turret gun raked the piles, turning soldiers who exposed themselves into red rags. Soon Repsian infantry would emerge from the vehicles to climb the piles and finish the business.

A shadow passed over the ridge line and Atticus looked up to see a mid-size troop transport circling the pad. The pilot seemed to be deciding whether to land or report everyone dead.

Atticus called to the ship on e-channel. "Pad to ship, pad to ship! Do you copy?"

There was no response. Now he could hear the whine of hydraulics as the carriers dropped their ramps to spit out infantry. The ship continued to orbit, pulling fire from the carriers onto itself.

"Pad to ship," Atticus called again. "You're Plan A, and there's no Plan B. Do you copy?"

"I copy," said a female voice. "I'm coming in."

"Fall back!" said a panicked voice on the channel.

The banging of ramps hitting rocky ground echoed between the two ridges. Walt pulled his gun from the notch and swept up what remained of his ammunition. "Let us exit stage rear, good sir!" he said, then he turned to move briskly down the slope toward the pad.

But Atticus paused to watch. What emerged from behind the carriers was a nightmare. The Repsians were tall, three meters or more, and they scuttled over the ground on six legs that were thin and hairy like a spider's. But they had an erect torso and four arms, long and muscular, that ended in three fingers of hard, chitinous material; and they had a long sickle thumb that could spike a man's skull to stir his brains. Worse, they were intelligent, and masterful engineers, fiercely jealous of what they had scraped from their barren planet. Their chief flaw, perhaps fatal in time, was a lack of space-faring capacity: they had never left their planet.

If all other things had been equal, the Repsians would have been dismissed by Imperial planners as provincials, and left to enjoy what little they had in peace. But things weren't equal: Repsia was rich in the rare-earth elements for which the Imperial war machine eternally hungered. But now it seemed the Repsians had asked too dear a price for what lay beneath their feet, and the Emperor would simply come and take what He wanted at the point of the sword.

Atticus turned to follow Walt, and they jogged to the center of the pad, where its defenders milled in confusion, waiting for the ship. A few soldiers fired on the Repsian infantry coming over the rubble, but most had their helmets tilted back uselessly to watch the ship descend. Atticus didn't know where the platoon's leadership was—maybe dead—but someone had to step to the wheel, or this would go bad, fast.

I guess that means me. Atticus grabbed an idler, and pushed him down to lay on the temp-crete. "On the ground, soldier! Put some fire on those bastards!" He moved across the pad, pushing others down to fire on the advancing aliens. Heavy slugs buzzed past him and blasted ragged chunks from the temp-crete, and from the soldiers who lay on it. This extraction couldn't happen fast enough.

The ship dropped straight down now. Its rear loading ramp was extended, allowing fire into the interior of the ship. As Atticus watched, several slugs plowed shiny gouges in the hull. This was some crazy-ass pilot, and she wouldn't stay long.

He knelt to key command channel on his pancake. "Listen up, folks! This will be a tap-and-go extraction! When you feel it, move your ass to the ship! I want covering fire from everyone still on the ground!"

The ship's skids hit the pad with a double clang, thirty meters away, and Atticus tapped the two nearest soldiers. "Go!"

They scrambled to their feet and ran for the ship. The first one to the ramp was hit from behind halfway up, and thrown forward. He slid back down to the pad on a slick of his own blood and didn't move. The second soldier disappeared into the ship.

The Repsians were seventy-five meters away and pressing hard. Atticus ran among the survivors, tapping steadily and trying to leave a good pattern of covering fire. But the bugs chewed up most of the platoon. Soon he tapped the last two soldiers left alive, a man and a woman lying together, and knelt to cover their dash to the ship.

Now there was one last item of important business.

Atticus ran to where the diplomat lay in the yellow circle, dangerously close to the ship's hot exhaust vents. He slung his rifle and picked up the man's remaining arm to drag him across the pad to the ship. Something punched Atticus's shoulder and he stumbled, spinning on one foot. The black ship, the gray pad, and the tan sky whirled around him. He found himself on his knees, dazed, no longer holding the diplomat's arm.

I'm hit.

He reached up to touch his shoulder and pulled back a bloody glove. *Damn.* The fabric should crimp around the wound, but the suit was old and patched in places long forgotten, so who knew.

Walt appeared beside him. "On your feet, Bragg, and grab a boot!"

Atticus pushed himself up to stand. The air around them sang with passing rounds, but the pain in his shoulder faded as adrenaline carried it somewhere else. He would pay for the rush later, crashing into twelve hours of bourbon-fueled sleep. He bent to pick up the diplomat's left boot. Walt got the right, and together they dragged the man across the pad to the ship, struggling to get him over the pile of bodies now clogging the foot of the ramp. The man didn't protest the rough treatment and Atticus frowned. The bastard had better be alive to redeem for cash: there was a hard limit on the number of bar tabs Atticus could ignore.

They dropped the diplomat's feet to the deck in the troop compartment as the transport lifted away and rotated to find its departure vector. Rounds clattered against the hull. Atticus suspected the wounded who lay on the pad below were doomed. With the collapse of the mining talks and the start of hostilities, the Repsians would work to scour all human presence from their planet.

There were twelve survivors in the troop compartment, all huddled into one corner: Atticus, Walt, the diplomat, and nine soldiers who had gotten up the ramp. With Walt's help, Atticus shoved the diplomat into a med-cocoon and cinched the restraints. He removed the man's helmet and keyed the cocoon's anti-shock program. Within seconds, the man opened his eyes and raised his head. He looked at Atticus absently as he adjusted himself in the cocoon, then he grunted in surprise and snapped his head around to look at his shoulder.

"Where's my arm?" he said.

"Shot off," said Atticus. "In the car. It was a lucky shot. A nice one, really, from five klicks. You're lucky to be alive."

The man stared at him. "It's here, right? In the ship? My arm?"

Atticus gazed off toward the cockpit hatch. "I looked around for it."

The man blinked in confusion. "You looked around?"

"Yes," said Atticus. "Some."

"It's not here?"

"I'm sure it was in bad shape," said Atticus. "That car was trashed. You should have seen it."

"You don't have my arm?"

"Well, not—no."

The diplomat surged against his restraints. "Fool!" he spat. "All I needed was a driver to get me to my ship! Instead, I got a lack-wit grunt without sense enough to pick up a man's arm!" The man glared at Atticus until his strength failed, then he collapsed back against the cocoon, coughing. "You won't get paid for this," he said, "whoever you are. I can promise you that."

Atticus lifted a finger to him. "Stop right there! You'd be down there with that ugly face planted in the dirt if I hadn't dragged your fat ass out of that car and hauled it around with me! You're lucky to be alive!"

The diplomat shook his head. "Nope, you screwed up. You screwed up and I lost my good arm! I'll see you broken for this. That's another promise."

Atticus cocked his arm to smash the man's nose. Instead, he

slammed the fist into the console of the cocoon, prompting the machine to extend a thin arm and jab the diplomat with a sedative shot. The man's eyes closed and he slipped under, still wearing a snarl on his lips.

Atticus fumed. This easy taxi job had turned all kinds of bad. Worse, the man was right: Atticus had screwed up. But it had nothing to do with the arm. He should have weaved the scout car. That was protocol when pursued under fire. But they had been late, and he had been cocky and stupid.

Son of a bitch!

"What an ungrateful bastard," said Walt.

"No shit. I should have left him in the car for the bugs to find."

The wheel on the cockpit hatch turned and the door swung open. A slender figure in gray flight coveralls stepped over the coaming to take in the scene in the bay. She noticed the diplomat in the cocoon and turned to the survivors. "Who else needs medical attention?" she said.

When no one spoke, Atticus gestured to his shoulder. "I guess I'm next."

She walked over to inspect the wound. "You're just grazed. A few stitches from the med-bot at the station will fix you up."

Atticus shook his head. "Naw, you got a staple gun handy?"

She blinked. "Seriously? Are you a masochist?"

He wasn't, or he didn't think he was. He did know he couldn't afford the services of a med-bot, but she didn't need to know that. "Two minutes," he said, "and I'm good."

The pilot shrugged. "Suit yourself." She opened a metal cabinet near the cocoon to rummage inside.

Walt frowned. "I guess I'll have the honor, huh?"

Atticus nodded. "You're Johnny on the spot, my friend."

The gunner made a face and poked at the hole in Atticus's suit. "She's right. It doesn't look so bad."

Atticus took the staple gun from the pilot and offered it to the gunner. "In that case, zip me up tight, Walter."

Walt accepted the gun reluctantly. "It's not Walter," he muttered.

But Atticus had turned his attention to the pilot: "That was a neat piece of flying, ma'am."

"Thanks, but I wish I had gotten more of you off the pad."

"Not your fault. I'm Atticus."

"Agrippina, but call me Grippa. We dock at Repsia Station in thirty."

"We'll need a med-cart," said Atticus. "For the asshole in the cocoon." He flinched as Walt shot a staple into his shoulder, closing the wound.

Grippa stepped to the cocoon to look more closely at the diplomat, then she gave Atticus a look. "Racine Wince? He's too rich and important for a med-cart. I'll comm for a full team."

Atticus squinted. "Wince of Centaurus Major?"

"That's the one."

"Son of a bitch!" said Atticus. He looked at Walt. "I'm screwed. There's no bucking him."

"At least he's not dead," said Walt.

Atticus pointed an angry finger at the diplomat. "You heard me tell him that! But there's no pleasing the bastard." He jumped in his seat as Walt hammered another staple into his shoulder. "Goddammit, man, you use that thing like a stun club!"

The gunner sniffed. "There's no pleasing you either."

Atticus wondered if all this could get fixed, somehow. "Who's the station commander?"

"General Warren," said Grippa.

Walt drove another staple, now giving it something extra. "Okay, that's enough," said Atticus thinly. "I don't know Warren. What's he like?"

Grippa gave him an odd smile. "Tough, fair. Demands results and pushes hard to get them. Doesn't tolerate failure."

"So not likely to buck Wince."

"No, not likely. Belt in for arrival." She turned and left through the hatch, dogging it behind her.

Atticus made a frustrated fist. This contract was a total loss, with a hole in his suit and a busted shoulder in the bargain. He scowled at Wince.

"I know what you're thinking," said Walt. "But that cocoon won't let him die, even with a knife in him."

This made Atticus laugh. "Naw, he ain't worth it. Let's dump the bastard with the medics and drink up whatever cash I got left. That might take a minute or two."

"I'm in," said Walt. "Hot food and sleep are for the weak and the timid."

The troop compartment of the transport had no windows to show the universe beyond itself, so only a small tremor in the deck plates told Atticus the ship had been grappled by the station to be pulled into one of its enormous hangars. An Imperial Command Station was the hub of every planetary action, housing the command, support, and logistics staffs, and any ground troops not down-planet. There were also civilian and R & R sectors, and massive hold spaces containing enough booze to power a field army through a campaign. Finding alcohol would be the easy part. Affording it, and finding a bed later, would be the rub.

When the ramp dropped to the hangar deck, Atticus and Walt yanked Wince from the cocoon and dragged him from the ship. Atticus took a moment to key the diplomat's chest pancake to tell the medics he was deathly allergic to pain-block. Who knew, maybe he was.

They dropped the limp man in front of a tall android sheathed in plasti-skin to approximate a human. It wore a white lab coat and held its arms in a position that may have been intended to suggest compassion. To Atticus it made the thing resemble a street preacher. Two humans in white coveralls flanked a gurney behind the robot.

"Hello, sir," said the android. "I am Med-Bot 10 Dash 6. What is the nature of—"

Atticus gestured to the diplomat. "Just look at him. The man's less one arm."

"Do you have—"

"No."

"Where is—"

"Down on the planet."

The android let a beat pass. "I see, sir. How did—"

"Does it really matter?" said Atticus. "Fix him up. Or not, I don't care. Just don't let him die. At least not until tomorrow." Maybe Atticus could set things right by then.

He turned to stride back up the ramp, gesturing for Walt to follow. In the troop compartment, they collected their weapons and ammunition, and said goodbye to the remnants of the security platoon. They seemed stunned, and Atticus patted shoulders and helmets as he passed. His own shoulder throbbed, but he had no money to fix it the easy way. Bourbon would have to do, and soon.

"Let's go find The Hole," said Walt. "Somebody'll have locker space for our stuff."

"Fine," growled Atticus, waving a hand. "Lead on." On the ride up, he'd decided maybe he shouldn't have been so cavalier about the man's arm, and it pissed him off. This whole operation pissed him off, and he knew he would act on it, sooner or later, one way or another.

They strode down the ramp and entered the station, ignoring the android and the two men carefully strapping Wince to the gurney. In the station corridors, they were passed by squads of soldiers bound for the fighting below and waddling under the weight of their full kit. Atticus wished them well, but found no envy for them. He felt like a civilian again, and he liked it—most of the time.

The station itself was a dump. Unsecured cabling hung low from the overheads, and many hatch doors screeched on their hinges. Corners were brown with dirt, and new pipes and fresh repairs shone brightly from grimy bulkheads. As always, nothing but the best from sixty years ago for The Emperor's Finest.

The Hole was the mercenary space in every comm station. It was always jammed in next to the engine compartments, where heavy vibration and the smells of fuel and lubricants made sobriety the poorest option. The Hole here was the worst Atticus had ever seen. It was brutally hot and mold draped the walls. The bunks—opened with credits he didn't have—had filthy mattresses and graffiti. Half a dozen mercs wearing little but tattoos idled around a battered table, smoking and passing a bottle.

"Charming," said Walt, holding a finger to his nose. "We're in the wrong line of work, my friend."

"Don't I know it," said Atticus. He raised his voice to call to the mercs. "Hey! Anybody got locker space?"

Heads turned at the table, curious, but only mildly so. A key chit was flung at them. Atticus snatched it from the air.

"Twenty-one," said a heavily muscled blond with a cigarette dangling from his lip. "But just 'til tomorrow. I'm blowing out."

"Right," said Atticus. "Thanks."

They found the man's locker and crammed in their weapons, ammo, and suits, and leaning against the door to get it shut.

"Now," said Atticus. "The second order of business. Let's get hammered."

They went into the first bar they found. The man behind the counter was slow to notice them, exercising a practiced eye for poverty.

"Bourbon!" called Atticus, stifling an urge to reach for the bottle himself. "Tall glass, three cubes. The middle-shelf stuff, not the swill you pour on the grunts."

Walt asked for a beer.

"So what's your story?" said Atticus.

"Well," said Walt, "sixteen years a merc, like I said before. But I was never in the service like you. My older brother started taking contracts when he got out, so I gave him a hand here and there. Nothing else to do."

"Then he bought it."

"Yeah, he did. He was my only kin at that point, and working contracts was all I knew, so I stayed at it. It's easier to do what you know, even when it sucks, than start fresh on something new. I guess you know that as well as anybody."

Atticus grunted and took a sip of his drink, thinking how he might head off the topic of himself. But Walt had already wandered off in his own direction: "You know what I want to do?" the man said. "You're gonna laugh, but I'll tell you. I got plans, you know. Someday I'm gonna quit thumbing contracts and write."

"Write?" said Atticus.

"Yes, holo-mances. You know, kissing and fluttering and swooning, and all that. There's money in it, you know. Wives and whatnot on the core worlds, bored out of their heads, they eat that shit up. I'll have to stuff my mattress first, but then I'm out, my friend—well and truly out."

Atticus smiled indulgently. The whiskey had softened the edges, and the gunner was a kindred spirit, despite his eccentricities. Atticus raised his glass. "Amen, brother! Here's to getting the hell out."

Walt raised his beer. "I try every day!"

They laughed and drank, and Atticus signaled for another round. "I'm getting out too," he said, "but between now and then I need another contract. I got a suit with a hole, a shoulder with a hole, no place to crash, and this might be my last drink. I'm flat busted."

"A sad story, friend, but something will turn up with this new war fired up down below."

Atticus pounded a fist on the bar. "Goddamn diplomats! They screwed it up again. And that son of a bitch Wince is screwing me!"

"Matsya-nyaya," said Walt.

"Eh?"

"A Hindu saying. The big fish eat the little fish."

"Ain't that the goddamn truth!" said Atticus. He drained his glass. "How do we get to be the big fish, Walt? Tell me that."

"Not thumbing contracts, that's for sure," said the gunner. He slapped a credit sleeve on the counter and told the barman to leave the bottle. "But to hell with that! Let's roar, my friend!"

Atticus reached over the bar to lift another glass, and he poured from the bottle for both of them, shoving a glass at Walt. "Commencing to roar, my friend! When we find the bottom of this bottle, we have a social call to make. You'll like it."

They found the scout-ship pilot in the R & R section. He had a girl on his lap and a drink in his hand. The other hand was pulling on a slot lever. Atticus didn't miss the irony. The girl had the glassy eyes of a narc freak, and Atticus tapped her on the shoulder.

"Clear out," he said. "We got business."

She gazed at him vaguely, but the pilot didn't turn his head. "Find your own," he muttered.

Atticus planted a scarred fist on the man's ear, spilling the drink and the girl.

The pilot grabbed his head and ducked away. "What the hell?"

"It would have been better for you," said Atticus, in a conversational tone, "if the bugs had killed me down there." He grabbed the man's shirt and swung him off the stool. The girl skittered away. "But they didn't. It ain't that easy, you know. I'm hard to kill."

"Who the hell are you?"

"I was one of the passengers on your manifest," said Atticus, "and I'm not satisfied with the service I received."

The light, and fear, dawned in the man's eyes. "They were shooting at me, man! I had to leave! How did you find me anyway?"

"I know people," said Atticus. "People who know things." He

pulled the pilot closer. The liquor hummed in Atticus's head. He felt strong and he was still pissed.

But the man went limp in his hands. "Look, I'm sorry! The bugs were shooting at me!"

"You mentioned that," said Atticus. He fumbled for the pilot's name. It was something stupid. Fa—yeah, that was it. "Listen up, Mr. Fa Pilot Man! You don't leave soldiers on the ground! Ever. And certainly not when the shit's flying thick and fast, and the squeeze is on!" Atticus grabbed the man's balls. "Have you ever been squeezed, Mr. Pilot Fa Man?"

"Ahh, God!" the man screamed. "Stop!"

Atticus knew he should, but there had been a lot left in the bottle. The fear in the man's eyes was gratifying. "I bet you look down on us ground-pounders, don't you?"

"No! No! I don't—"

Atticus lifted a fist and smashed his knuckles into the pilot's nose. Bright blood washed over the man's mouth.

Walt stepped closer to them. "Hey, man—"

Atticus pushed the pilot toward him. "You want a lick at him too?"

"Naw, At," said Walt, "you've made your point." He pulled the pilot from Atticus's grasp and shoved him away to safety. "C'mon, friend, let's hit the rack. It's been a hell of a day."

Atticus turned a hard stare on the gunner, but already his rage had dimmed to something more melancholy. Maybe he was getting better. "You were right, Walter. I do need to get out of this business, but I ain't got poetry in my soul like you. What'll I do?"

"Not drive, it seems. And it ain't Walter."

Atticus wagged his head. "I ain't fit for anything else. I'll be pulling contracts 'til what's left of me is zipped up in a bag and fired out a tube. I'm ruined for the gentler arts."

"A man can always change," said Walt.

"So I've heard," said Atticus. "Do you think I was too hard on Mr. Fa Man Pilot?"

"He'll think twice before doing that again."

"Good," said Atticus. He pointed a finger at Walt. "That Grippa, she's the one with balls, you know."

"Indeed, she is," said Walt. "You watch yourself."

Atticus grinned. "Where's the fun in that?"

CHAPTER TWO

Something nudged Atticus's shoulder, waking him.

"You Bragg?" said a voice above him.

Atticus's tongue seemed swollen and his eyes were gummed shut. He could only nod.

"Message for you."

Something settled lightly on Atticus's back, and heavy boots walked away. He pulled his eyes open to find himself lying on the deck in The Hole. His head was pillowed on his arms.

Jesus, I have more self-respect than this—or I did once.

He explored on his back with his fingers, wincing at the pain in his shoulder. He found a communications flimsy that rattled in his hand as he struggled to focus on its words:

ATTICUS BRAGG, MERCENARY, WILL REPORT TO THE COMMANDING GENERAL AT 1145, THIS DAY.
// WARREN/GEN/COMM/VA095B
— NOTHING FOLLOWS —

Shit.

He was being called on the carpet. That damn pilot in R&R had connections here, and he was working them to get even with

Atticus the easy way. Atticus would be tried as a civilian now, and there wasn't much protecting a civilian on a military post at war. Atticus groaned and closed his eyes again. "Well, son of a *bitch*!"

"Not so loud," said Walt, from somewhere above. "My head's thumping." The bastard must have bought a bunk and laid Atticus on the floor next to it, like a dog.

"The Comm Gen wants me," said Atticus

"It's that pilot in R & R."

"No shit," said Atticus. "Maybe I can get a shuttle off the station. What time is it?"

"1123. How much time you got?"

"Not enough."

"That pilot's sure got some pull," said Walt. "On the other hand, no station MPs are standing over you."

It was a good point. Atticus wasn't currently in mag-cuffs, which could mean he wouldn't be strung up right away. "Fine," he said, "I'll go take my beating from the General."

"Good luck," said Walt. "I'll bring coffee to the brig later."

There was only enough time for Atticus to comb his hair and run a dry razor over his face. A general was a general, even if Atticus was a civilian now, and showing up muss-headed and hungover was not a good way to start a plea for mercy. He snarled a good-bye at Walt, and walked out of The Hole to meet his fate.

Atticus didn't need to ask directions to officer country: every planetary comm station was like every other one, at least in physical layout. He climbed up-station through the crew spaces, then walked by the squad bays and the chow halls to the command levels. He passed with a glance the door to the small corridor office that had been his, long ago, on another station, and in another life. That office had been the domain of Atticus Bragg, Major of Infantry. That Atticus was responsible for the pilot's beating. He had charged far too hard into far too much before the end had come, trying to find something for himself. He no longer knew what that was. He knew only that he hadn't found it, and he had stopped looking for it long ago.

"State your business, merc," said a voice.

Atticus dragged his head up to see a young soldier sitting at the Podium, the flag officers' bulwark against the riff-raff. The man had a suspicious eye, and no battle ribbons on his tunic.

"Atticus Bragg. The General sent for me."

The man didn't blink at the name. He held out a hand. "Your orders?"

Atticus passed the flimsy. The man pondered it with a supercilious eye, then sniffed. "You didn't put yourself out, did you?"

"I shaved."

The soldier handed back the flimsy. "General Warren is at the end of the hall. You're two minutes late."

"Aye, Lieutenant," said Atticus, giving the rank a slight emphasis. He moved past the man to walk down the hall, stopping at a metal door to knock three times.

"Enter!" called a voice.

Atticus opened the door to find a gray-haired man sitting at a simple metal desk clogged with coffee mugs and data pads. A younger man, thin and pale in an admin tunic, sat on a stool next to the desk, looking territorial. Atticus knew the type: vindictive, and exercising power and influence by controlling the flow of information to his boss. He could have put the report about the pilot near the top of the General's morning stack.

"Major Bragg!" said General Warren, waving him into the room. "Welcome!"

Atticus paused at the doorway. This didn't have the air of a dis-hearing. "Good morning, General," he said, before moving to stand in front of the desk.

"I had no idea you were on-planet, Bragg," said the General. "The dip-dips don't keep me informed. They like to run their own shop, you know. But it's my planet now that this thing has come to blows. What happened to you?"

"I was running a dip out from the talks, sir, and the war started en route. We lost the car to a carrier gun, and the dip lost an arm. A damn lucky shot. Not for him. I carried him to the pad, but there wasn't a ship to take us out by then. The bugs were assaulting the pad and there was a nasty firefight."

The general grunted. "I heard that."

"I thought surely we'd snuff it in heroic fashion," said Atticus, "but this crazy pilot dragged her ramp and got a few of us off. Not many."

"Nine that survived," said the admin. "Plus the Major and another merc. And Wince. Thirty-six dead or missing."

The General scrubbed a hand over his mouth. "Your ride bugged out, you say, Bragg?"

"Yes, sir."

The General grunted again. "I'd punch that bastard right in the nose, if it was me." The admin made a negative noise, and Warren straightened his tunic. "But, yes, well, that'll be dealt with through proper channels, of course. As it should be."

Atticus said nothing.

Warren leaned back in his chair. "Wince made trouble for you, as I'm sure you expected. But I don't have authority to order you paid. It was the diplomats' contract."

"I understand, sir."

"The worthless bastards made a cock up of negotiations, lording it over the Repsians and dangling a cheap price for mining rights. Now they want us gone, but we still want what's in the ground down there. The problem is, we don't have enough force in this sector to roll them over, at least not yet, and they know it. It'll be a grind to push the creepy bastards under."

"It always is, sir."

"Ain't that the truth," said Warren. "Jorn, give me that flim. Bragg, there is something we can do for each other, since you seem to be here at loose ends."

"A contract, sir?"

"An easy one."

Atticus frowned.

"A captain arrived last week by private shuttle. A noble. Rail is his name. He's the heir to the Sirius System seat in the House of Lords. Not some village chief, you know. He's doing his service time, and I have to do something with him."

"I understand, sir," said Atticus. He did: he would be babysitting. It wasn't the worst kind of job and he might make a valuable connection in the bargain. Atticus needed some kind of break to go his way, and this might be it.

"So here's the job," said Warren. "This Rail has a platoon, and you have him. Not officially, of course, but you're to keep him out of trouble." The General waved the flimsy. "These orders attach you as an advisor, guiding the good Captain with a firm but gentle hand in the direction of his duty. Lord knows whether he knows it or not. Your own paramount duty is to keep the man alive for his glorious future, toward which this lowly service is merely a necessary way post."

"I understand, sir."

"Good, so you accept?"

"Sleeping on the deck is hard on my joints, sir."

The General stared at Atticus. "You're a damn shame, Major. War chews up men without mercy." He handed Atticus the flimsy. "You'll be happy to know I can do a little better than the standard rate on this one, to make up somewhat for Wince."

"Thank you, sir."

"Tread lightly, Bragg, this is a powerful family. But don't hesitate to act to protect him from danger—especially the danger of his own stupidity. He's to serve honorably, if without distinction, and be returned from whence he came." The General flicked his fingers toward the universe beyond the station.

"What's the op area?"

"A quiet one," said Warren. "The quietest I could find, in fact. Well back from the lines, which have firmed up in the last twelve hours. Both sides are pushing in everything they've got, to get a leg up early."

"Yes, sir. One suggestion."

"That is?"

"Another merc came out with me. A good man. I'd like him to come along—as extra eyes."

The General rubbed his lips. "Well, I suppose so. Better to lay it on thick now then explain why I didn't later. Who is it?"

The admin picked up a data pad.

"Walt," said Atticus. "I don't know his last name."

The pale man typed on the pad. "Waltham Whist," he said.

"That's surely the one. Heavy weapons and dems. Sixteen years and change taking contracts, mostly in the Rump Systems. Four battle ribbons, and a rep letter for—" He tapped on the screen. "AWOL. Came back later."

"He'll do," said the General. "Write him up. You sure he'll go, Bragg?"

Atticus nodded. "Whether he likes it or not."

The General laughed. "Go grab your man, Major, and meet Captain Rail in his squad bay."

"Bay eighteen," said the admin.

"Yeah," said Warren. "You drop in four hours."

"Yes, sir," said Atticus. "Thank you, sir."

"My pleasure," said Warren, "and this time I believe you'll have a pilot you approve of."

Atticus hesitated at the door, but the General had already dropped his eyes to sift through the mess on his desk. Atticus let himself out. This did sound like an easy one—a laugher even.

But they never were.

"We almost didn't get off that planet," said Walt later. He wasn't happy. "I remember it very clearly, almost like it happened yesterday."

"It's a decent job," said Atticus. "Easy, and a bump up from standard. You'll like it."

"But that thing down there just got started, At. It'll be a mess until it settles down. I like my hot zones tied up neat."

"Quit your bitching, Walter," said Atticus, "and bring our stuff down here. Bay eighteen." He hung up the receiver before the gunner could respond. The man just needed a kick in the pants. Most did.

Squad bay eighteen looked and smelled like every other bay Atticus had ever prepped in. The seats were polished to bare metal by years of use, and the deck was grimy with gun cleaning oil and the dirt of a hundred planets. Soldiers were scattered around the bay in small groups, cleaning their weapons, or arguing over cards and nonsense. Their empty exo-suits hung on the bulkheads, ready to don.

"Stop!" said a firm voice behind Atticus.

He did stop, and he turned to find a tall man wearing worn but well-pressed utilities. His close-cropped hair was iron gray, moving toward white, and he had a firm-set mouth and discerning eyes. This was clearly the platoon sergeant, guarding his territory.

"What's your business here, merc?" he said.

"I have orders, Sergeant," said Atticus, holding out the flimsy.

The man accepted it and dragged a pair of spectacles from his chest pocket. He donned them and read the paper carefully, glancing up at Atticus twice. He returned the flimsy and offered a hand. "Welcome, Major. You weren't expected. My apologies, sir."

Atticus took his hand. "I don't wear the gray anymore, Sergeant. It's just Atticus. Where's the Captain?"

The Sergeant pointed deeper into the bay. "In the weapons shop, s—." He frowned. "I'm Thorkin. Anything you need, you let me know."

"There is one thing. Another fellow will show up here soon, piled with gear. Make a place for him pleese."

The Sergeant nodded. "Will do."

Atticus walked down the central aisle toward the back of the bay, studying the men and women of the platoon. There was nothing unusual about them: they were common soldiers, spit from the mil-houses operating on the less desirable planets. Some were fresh-faced, but most wore the deliberate indolence of veterans. None of them met his eye for more than a moment. Atticus wasn't one of them, and they had a soldier's wariness of the unknown.

But Thorkin's worth as a platoon sergeant was evident. It showed in the way the troopers stowed their gear, neatly and uniformly, even while they themselves sprawled on the seats and across the deck like lazy children. And it showed in their cool manner. They had confidence in their NCO, and confidence in themselves. The Captain was coming into a good situation, likely by the General's design.

The weapons shop was an enclosed space with a large dura-glass window, through which Atticus could see a young man in a pressed, well-fitting uniform with captain's bars. He stood over a weapons tech, watching the man weld the shoulder stock of a plasma rifle. The purple light flickered on their faces. Behind the Captain, two soldiers carefully examined flamethrower units. Weapons check was one of the sacred rituals of deployment.

Around the corner from the window was an open doorway. Atticus placed himself outside of it, waiting to be recognized. He could see now that Rail was of average height, and wore a close haircut that had passed out of military fashion some thirty years before. Perhaps it had been urged on him by an insistent grandfather who had served. After a moment, the Captain noticed Atticus and turned toward him. His face was sharp-edged and patrician, accustomed to privilege and the casual use of power.

"Yes?" Rail asked.

"General Warren ordered me to report to you, sir," said Atticus. "Attached as an advisor." He offered the flimsy.

Rail made no move to take it. "I've heard. I have no need of an adviser. I do—"

"Sir, the Gen—"

"Do not interrupt me again, mercenary. As I said, I have no need of an advisor. I do need more riflemen, however. You are assigned to Third Squad—that's Pickett's squad. I want to hear nothing more from you." Rail turned back to the welder.

Atticus didn't move. He had expected to meet resistance: no man liked to think he needed minding. Atticus himself would have bucked off the babysitting. The situation needed finesse.

"Sir, I under—"

"You are dismissed, mercenary," said Rail crisply.

Atticus frowned, and turned away from the doorway to walk back to the front of the bay. This thing wasn't off to a good start, which wasn't entirely unexpected. He would have to wheedle his way into high councils, probably stepping on a few toes in the process, but Atticus intended to get paid this time, whatever it took.

"Pop says you're Major Bragg," said a voice behind him.

Atticus stopped to look around, finding two male soldiers who had moved into the central aisle. They were bare-chested and heavily tattooed.

Atticus shook his head. "No, man, I'm not Bragg. I did meet him once though. Scary dude."

The shorter of the two laughed and punched his compatriot on the shoulder. "I told you Pop was full of shit!" he said. He turned back to Atticus. "You're way too small to be Bragg. He's a big, brutal son of a bitch that doesn't take shit from anybody."

Atticus nodded. "Yep, that's him."

The soldiers wandered away, dismissing him. Atticus smiled at his own joke, but felt the usual sadness that his reputation still preceded him, even now. It was a burden he carried, his reputation. He was The Hero Turned Rebel, The Man Who Refused, and The Big Brutal Son of a Bitch That Took No Shit From Anybody. But it was all wrong—every bit of it. He was a good soldier, or he had been, and honorable. Maybe he still was. He didn't know anymore.

At the front of the squad bay, Atticus found a seat away from the others to lean his head against the wall and sleep.

The end for him had come on Gliese 5c.

He'd had a battalion then: five hundred soldiers honed to a gleaming edge, only to be thrown with a ham hand against a rebellion army no one really wanted to fight. But soldiers never chose their enemies. They could only kill them, and Bragg's Bunch was good at that.

That day they were the bait in a trap, dragged through a coastal rain forest by orbital command, hoping to flush out two regiments of rebel infantry concealed in the trees. To Atticus's surprise, it had worked. They had made enough noise, and caused enough nuisance, to pull the enemy into a fast-moving chase toward three regiments of Imperial mechanized infantry, dug in and waiting. It was perfect.

Until it went wrong.

Atticus watched the operation with his executive officer in the battalion command post, a gray tent erected beneath a tree that dripped something that wasn't water. The tent contained only a wobbly table over which the comm gear projected a crooked holo-map. The map showed the terrain and the position of his three companies, but little else. The rebels' satellite jamming was working too well.

"Whiskey 43," said a voice on the circuit. "This is Romeo 4 Actual."

It was Blake, the CO of Charlie Company. He had been assigned the trickiest job of the day: pretending to lag the others, like a bird faking a broken wing.

"This is Whiskey 43," said Atticus. "Go."

"Sir, we got drops on our flanks."

"Drops?"

"Yes, sir. We're taking fire from three sides."

Atticus looked at Charlie Company's position on the holo. It had suddenly slowed, and now it was much too far behind the others. "Understood, Romeo 4," he said. "Pick up your speed. Is the main force still pursuing?"

"Yes, sir. We're still in contact to our rear, but the drops may cut us off."

"Understood. Hang in there, Blake. Speed up, but maintain contact to your rear. Report in ten minutes."

"Aye, sir."

Atticus pulled up the orbital command channel. "Whiskey 43."

"Go, Bragg," said a voice. It was the ops officer—not who Atticus wanted.

"Let me have the Comm-Gen, sir."

"He's listening."

"Sir, we got drops on both flanks of the drag company. They're getting pinched. Permission to stop and support."

"Negative, Bragg," said a new voice—the Comm-Gen now. "This thing is nominal. We can end this nonsense right now and go home."

So you can strut for your fourth star? thought Atticus. "Sir, there's one hundred and two men and women in that company. The drops are unexpected."

"You have to expect the unexpected in war, Major Bragg," said the General. "Right now, the iron is hot and you will carry out your assignment. Continue to your objective. Comm-Gen out."

The circuit went dead. Atticus keyed to c-channel. He couldn't wait ten minutes. "Romeo 4 Actual, this is Whiskey 43. Sit rep."

The Captain sounded breathless now. "We're still receiving heavy fire from three sides, sir."

"Can you speed up?"

"Negative, sir. Not now. We're carrying wounded and fully engaged. I'm leap-frogging forward."

Shit. That would slow them down even more, especially with wounded to haul out. This thing was going to Hell fast. Atticus keyed to the other companies. "Romeos 2 and 3, what's your status?"

"We're clear, sir. No contact."

"Same, sir. But I can see Romeo 4's incoming fire. It's a light show."

Atticus swore. This operation was suddenly looking like a catastrophe. He kicked a leg of the table and the holo-unit fell off. The exec scrambled to pick it up, but the damn thing was worthless. Atticus looked around for his plasma rifle, but they had taken it away from him and hidden it, on the Comm-Gen's orders. Atticus was no longer allowed to go forward to fix things himself. He had to rely on his officers.

He keyed c-channel. "Romeo 4, sit rep."

"Bad, sir," said Blake. He sounded stressed. "We can't move fast enough to keep the bad guys on our flanks from bounding ahead. We'll be surrounded soon. We have seventeen KIA and twenty-three wounded." There was a pause. "Twenty-four, sir."

"Understood. Move as fast as you can, Blake."

Atticus keyed orbital command again. "Whiskey 43."

"Go, Bragg." It was Comm-Gen, probably expecting his call.

"Romeo 4's in the shit, sir, and lagging hard. Permission to engage the drops on their flanks."

"Still negative, Major. A pitched battle in that green feature will slow the rebels' momentum. I got three heavies waiting to end this. You will not move a meter back the way you came, Bragg. Proceed to your objective. War is hell. Let's finish this and get out." The channel went dead.

Son of a bitch! Atticus kicked the table again, but this time the exec didn't move.

"To hell with him," said the man. "Let's go get Charlie."

"That's exactly what we're going to do," said Atticus. He keyed c-channel again. "Stop where you are, Romeo 4, and form a defensive perimeter. Hang tight, Blake, we're coming to get you."

"Aye, sir. Stopping."

Atticus considered calling the Comm-Gen again, but it was pointless. Orders were orders, and insubordination was insubordination. He keyed the circuit. "Romeos 2 and 3, swing around to 342 and 018, respectively, and move to engage the enemy on your fronts."

They acknowledged.

There it was: the end of a long career. Atticus felt oddly numb to it. His father had been angry at the news of his enlistment, insisting Atticus had traded his immortal soul for a regular paycheck. That had been sixteen years and eight campaigns ago. As Atticus listened to his company commanders coordinate their movements, he reflected that maybe the old man was right. Maybe he was just a cog in the machine, and it was time to slip loose and spin on his own.

His court-martial had been a public spectacle. The news-holos led with each day's testimony, followed by analysis and speculation. Until then, Atticus hadn't realized how much the Imperial propaganda machine had ginned up his exploits to motivate a new generation of citizens to enlist and chase the fighting reputation of Major Atticus Bragg. There were even protesters demanding he be freed to continue his rampage across the galaxy.

But the result had been a foregone conclusion. The failure of the trap that day had extended the action on Gliese for another nine months, far beyond the most pessimistic predictions. So someone's head had to roll. Two heads, actually. The Comm-Gen was soon recalled, and to Atticus's knowledge, he never got his fourth star.

Now, to the universe, Atticus was the tainted hero. A soldier's soldier, equal to all comers, but hot-blooded, pugnacious, and defiant of authority. It was a reputation that ignored the sixteen years of unblemished service that preceded his hard fall from grace. Atticus was still trying to find his feet, five years later, suffering the pity of men like Warren, who valued him for what he had once been, but who kept his distance in case what brought Atticus low might be catching. He longed to shed that ill-fitting skin.

Someone shook his bad shoulder. It was Walt.

"You sleep and I work," said the gunner. "Is that how this thing is gonna go? I want out already."

Atticus looked around. "Where's our stuff?"

Walt jerked a thumb over his shoulder. "Laid out on the deck, nice and pretty. That iron-ass platoon sergeant looks like he wouldn't have it any other way."

"Stay on his good side," said Atticus.

"He doesn't have one. That's not a pretty face. Have you met the boss? What's he like?"

"A noble," said Atticus. "He doesn't need help from anybody, but I'm supposed to keep his nose clean and his ass wiped."

"I bet that General told you this would be an easy one," said Walt.

"Yep. They always do."

"And they're lying bastards."

Walt helped Atticus up and they walked to their gear. The gunner had spoken truly: their weapons and kit were laid out on the deck in good order, and their suits were hung neatly with the helmets polished. Walt had even contrived to have Atticus's suit repaired while he slept.

Atticus bent to pick up his plasma rifle. It was an older model, less efficient than the weapons line soldiers carried now, but the rifle was an old friend—maybe his oldest, and certainly his most trustworthy. There was dirt on the stock and around the sights. The red grit of this planet seemed to get into everything.

While they were picking through their gear, Sergeant Thorkin strutted closer to stand over them. "How are you set for plasma, Bragg?" he said. "I think we got a few packs for that model in the back."

"I'd love a couple to top me off," said Atticus.

"Go kit yourself out from the stash," said the Sergeant. He pointed to the back of the bay, then glanced at Walt. "You too."

"Much appreciated," said Atticus.

The Sergeant nodded. "What do you know about this op, Bragg?"

So it was give-some, get-some with this Sergeant. Atticus pulled a rag from the pouch on his web belt and worked it over the stock of his rifle. "I don't know a lot," he said. "Mainly that it's make-work for His Greatness in there. A nice quiet sector, well back from the lines."

"And you're babysitting him," said Thorkin. It wasn't a question.

"That's about the size of it," said Atticus.

"You and me both, and that man's already shit in my front yard trying to change things that don't need changing. Maybe he'll be worth a damn, but it's not looking good so far."

"Let's give him a chance," said Atticus. "We were all green once."

Thorkin ran an appraising eye over his squad bay. "I heard he's a noble."

"You heard right," said Atticus. "He's just passing through."

"I figured. Not worth my time. I also heard you don't like pilots, Bragg."

Walt laughed.

"I got nothing against pilots as a group," said Atticus, working at a dark spot behind the rifle sights. "Just a disagreement with one in particular."

Thorkin chuckled. "You two go get fitted out. We'll load in 110 minutes." He strutted away as he had come.

Atticus laid his rifle aside and stood. "Come on, Walt! Let's go plunder the Emperor's stores."

* * *

The supply clerk was surly and skeptical, but in the end they took what they wanted and carried it back to lay on the deck with the rest of their gear.

Walt surveyed his fulsome kit with evident satisfaction. "Happiness," he said, "is plenty of ammo."

"Is that poetry too?" said Atticus. "If so, it ain't Shakespeare."

"He never carried a mech-gun," said Walt, "or he would have said the same." He lifted a finger to the ceiling. "Hear my ode to twelve hundred meters per second!"

"Shakespeare wrote sonnets, not odes."

"Aren't you the learned one," grumbled Walt.

Sergeant Thorkin's sharp voice echoed from the bare walls of the squad bay: "Platoon! Fall in!"

The men and women of the platoon rose to form two ranks that bracketed the bay's central aisle. Atticus ambled to the end of the nearest rank and placed himself next to Walt. As he waited, he wondered where Third Squad might be in this assembly, and whether the Captain had informed the squad leader of his new additions. He decided probably not, and that General Warren would want Atticus to ignore this reassignment. So he would.

When the bay was still, Rail emerged from the weapons shop to walk down the central aisle. His hands were clasped behind his back. "Good afternoon, soldiers," he said. "I am Captain Marcus Rail. Since this is our first op together, I will cover the ground rules for my command. First and foremost, I expect everything to be done by the book. There's a war down there now and we've been ordered to a hot sector."

Atticus exchanged a glance with Walt. This wasn't a good

start. Rail's credibility with the platoon would hit zero when they landed in a dead sector with no bugs for a hundred klicks. This young Captain needed a lot of work.

"We have important work to do," continued Rail. "Dangerous work, and we will do it by the book. At the drop point we will disembark quickly—no more than twenty seconds—and spread out in a square-delta perimeter, terrain permitting. We will then move to our assigned position under Condition Five security. We will engage and destroy any enemy unit we encounter. We are on status red now, and I want everything buttoned up, tightened down, and done—"

"—by the book," said Atticus, together with Rail. Walt sniggered.

"I will be watching each of you carefully," said Rail, "and evaluating your performance as His Majesty's soldiers. I expect nothing less than perfection. You will deploy with haste and spacing. You will observe comm and fire discipline. You will listen carefully to myself and Sergeant Thorkin. You will gear up, maneuver, and bivouac with military precision. Do I make myself clear?"

The platoon responded to him in unison: "Yes, sir!"

Rail scowled. "Not good enough! Am I clear?"

This time their shout thundered from the bulkheads: "YES, SIR!"

While this was going on, Atticus's mind had wandered away to consider his empty stomach. He returned to find Rail standing in front of him, but facing the bay door still.

"Sergeant Thorkin!" the Captain barked.

"Sir!"

"Why isn't this man standing at attention?"

Atticus frowned at this. He hadn't been a by-the-book

commander, nor had he demanded his subordinates follow the book slavishly. It was a security blanket to be held close until it wasn't needed anymore. But Rail needed it now, so Atticus drew himself up fractionally.

Thorkin hustled to Rail's side. "He's a merc, sir."

"I'm aware of that," said Rail, still facing the door. "But the rules apply to everyone in this outfit, Sergeant. Even sell-swords." He sneered the words.

"Yes, sir," said Thorkin. He aimed a pleading look at Atticus, who pulled himself straighter.

Rail now turned on his heel to face Atticus squarely. "I'm not a fool, Bragg," he said softly. "I know why the General sent you, but I don't need a nursemaid. I do not want your opinions and I will not tolerate interference. But I know I can't get rid of you, however much I'd like to, so I will allow you to earn your money in Third Squad. Am I clear?"

Fat chance, sir, thought Atticus. "Yes, sir," he said aloud.

"Good, don't forget it." Rail turned away from him. "Sergeant Thorkin!"

"Sir!"

"Gear up the platoon, and move to the hangar. I will inspect them at 1400 sharp, immediately before we load."

"Aye, sir," said Thorkin. He lifted his chin to address the platoon. "Suit up!"

"Holo-mances don't have to be that good," said Walt. "That's the beauty of it." He and Atticus were pulling on their exo-suits. "There's a formula, right? Girl meets boy, girl likes boy but can't get boy, girl pines for boy, then finally gets boy after all. Boom, you're done."

"I see," said Atticus. "What if boy is a disgraced former infantry officer turned mercenary with no pot to piss in, and a taste for cheap bourbon?"

"No," said Walt. "It has to be believable."

"Says you, but all those fluttering ladies will be swooning on you and knocking you down. You'll need a bodyguard."

"You're hired," said Walt. "Hey, there's that easy one for you!"

"Well, that's ruined it," said Atticus. "There's no such thing." He tested the integrity of his suit and the functioning of his pancake. His blood pressure was up. It could be the hangover, or the Captain, or the op—or all three.

"That suit is older than me," said Walt. "You look like you fell out of the Scorpius Wars."

Atticus shrugged into his web belt. "Actually, I did catch the tail end of that one."

"You're older than I thought! Plus you can't drive. Forget the bodyguard thing."

"That mech-gun ain't exactly spec either," said Atticus. "These kids think you're here to give them a history lesson."

"Scurrilous heathen!" said Walt. "Plasma's got nothing on a tungsten slug moving at twelve hundred meters per second!"

"Maybe, but you'd better kill what you shoot at, because you won't outrun it." Atticus pointed to Walt's heavy bandoleers.

Walt grinned. "I always get my bug. Lucky for you."

Atticus laughed. "You win."

Geared and suited up, they followed Thorkin and the platoon from the squad bay. The soldiers were boisterous, and most seemed to know what they were about: their suits were folded and tucked properly, their web belts carefully balanced, and their plasma rifles held in positions of least effort. Whatever the platoon might come up against down below, there was experience to handle it—at least among the troops.

Thorkin led them through the station to a hangar bay cramped with materiel bound for the fighting below. Atticus saw pallets of weapons and ammunition, vehicles, plasti-tents, field kitchens, pop-up command posts, sacks of temp-crete for pads and bunkers, bladders of water, pallets of fuel tabs, comm gear, generators, crates of spare parts, and the thousand other items brought by an Imperial Expeditionary Force to support a planetary action. All of it was being moved, and moved again, by an army of hangar monkeys in an overwhelming clamor of shouting, banging, beeping, and overworked loader engines.

But somehow Thorkin found a route through it all, stopping at a small troop transport much like the one Atticus and Walt had ridden up to the station the day before. Its loading ramp was down and waiting.

"Form up!" shouted Thorkin.

Again, the platoon formed into two ranks that faced each other, this time extending out from the foot of the ramp. Atticus counted heads while they waited. There were forty-six soldiers ready to load, plus Rail, Thorkin, and the two mercenaries. They were a full strength platoon. That was common at the start of a campaign. Later, as the fighting wore on, it would be a different story.

Walt elbowed Atticus and pointed to the ramp. In its shadow, Grippa leaned against the hull of the ship, watching the platoon assemble. The General had been right: Atticus did approve of their pilot this time. He wondered if Grippa knew Mr. Fa Pilot. He hoped they weren't friends.

* * *

Rail made them wait a half hour. This told Atticus the man had doubts about his authority: making others wait was the oldest power play from insecurity in the book. It seldom worked with veterans, however, and it didn't now. Atticus saw the eye-rolling in the opposite rank, and heard the muttering in his own. Rail was not getting off to a good start with his troops.

Thorkin hurried to the foot of the ramp and drew himself up. "Pla-TOON! A-ten-SHUN!"

The troops pulled themselves to attention with the barest flicker of insolence. Atticus lifted himself a little straighter. He put a finger in his ear, then pulled it out again, deciding to play by the rules. It might be the way to get to this Captain.

"Present arms!" Thorkin bellowed.

The platoon pushed its weapons forward for inspection. Captain Rail, wearing an absurdly well-tailored exo-suit, began stepping down the opposite rank. His hands were again clasped behind his back, and Atticus noticed for the first time the Captain steadfastly refused to engage the soldiers in front of him. When he stopped, it was only to turn his head slightly to murmur to Thorkin, who trailed behind. Atticus frowned. To Rail, the men and women who made up his platoon were the Sergeant's responsibility, and the Sergeant's problem. It was even possible it didn't occur to Rail to speak directly to individual soldiers.

Reaching the end of the opposite rank, Rail stepped across to stand in front of Atticus. The Captain frowned, and his eyes wandered over Atticus's gear. "Sergeant Thorkin, what model exo-suit is this?"

Thorkin leaned this way and that, taking in Atticus's suit.

"Well, sir, I'd say its a well-patched Mark 4, with synth-muscle bracing and a few other mods."

"That's precisely what it is," said Rail, "and it disgraces this platoon. General Warren has seen fit to send us disreputable vagabonds in thirty-year-old exo-suits." The Captain's eyes wandered to Walt. "And carrying ancient weapons."

Thorkin looked uncomfortable. "But sir—"

Rail held up a hand to stop him. "I'm well aware who this man is, Sergeant. But it's no excuse for his outdated gear, or his slovenly appearance. And he smells of cheap booze. I'm not at all certain he's sober."

"He wouldn't be the only one, sir," said Thorkin with an indulgent smile. "But the drop straightens them out quick."

"These two are yours, Sergeant. Their failures are your failures. Their disrepute, yours."

Thorkin's smile faded and died. He had been solicitous of Atticus until now, even deferential, but his eyes narrowed, and he gave Atticus a look that was half pleading and half suspicion.

"He gets our glory too. Right, sir?" said Walt.

Rail gave the gunner an acid glare. "There's no glory for mercs," he said, "only the vulgar lure of profit." He turned to move toward the ship, followed by a subdued Thorkin.

Atticus settled in to endure another speech from the Captain, but Rail merely ordered Thorkin to load the platoon.

"Aye, sir!" said the Sergeant. "By your files now! My right first! Load!"

Walt and Atticus waited while the soldiers in the opposite rank filed into the ship, their boots clanging on the ramp. The noise in the bay was giving Atticus's hangover a hangover.

"Well, look who's back for more," said a voice behind them.

Atticus turned to find Grippa standing behind them. She wore a gray flight suit, and her hands rested on her hips. Strands of brown hair had fallen from a tight bun to frame her face. She was lovely—better, she had balls. Atticus thought he might be in love.

"Yeah, it was fantastic," he said. "Warm, not too crowded. Are you dropping us?"

"I'm your driver," she said. "But I'll be careful. Rumor is you're hard on pilots."

"Word gets around here," he said.

"It's a small station."

"Don't leave me high and dry," said Atticus, "and we'll get on fine. Where are you from? I can't place your accent."

"Everywhere," she said. "I'm a mil-brat, raised in every rusty station and shit-posting between here and the Edge."

"Yet you bought into the adventure."

She shrugged. "A girl's got to do what she knows. I'll tell you, I don't like that Captain of yours. He's not happy about where he's going and he's barking up the tree to get his orders changed."

Atticus glanced at Rail, who was stabbing a long finger at Thorkin. "Any chance of that?"

"I have it on the best authority, no," said Grippa. "Absolutely not."

Atticus raised an eyebrow. "The best authority?"

Grippa laid a fingertip next to the name strip on her chest. It read "Warren."

"I see," said Atticus.

Walt chuckled. "The plot thickens."

Atticus glanced at the ramp, where the front of their file was now boarding. "So the good General decides to send Atticus

Bragg to shepherd the Captain on the planet, and he assigns his best, most trusted pilot to make sure we get there. I see the plan."

Grippa smiled. "Yes, something like that."

"It's a good plan," said Atticus, "but it's hard to fault the man for resenting the babysitting."

She shrugged. "He can prove he doesn't need it, but I'm not holding my breath."

"I'm not either," said Atticus. "But I'll work on him." He shouldered his rifle to leave. "So wish me luck, Lieutenant."

"You look like a man who doesn't need luck, Mr. Bragg."

"Don't believe it," he said. "I carry extra."

CHAPTER THREE

It was a rough ride down. The planet's atmosphere was thick, and the little transport was buffeted by high level winds and jolted by air pockets. The ship bounced and jerked and shimmied as it fell toward the planet, skating across each boundary layer with a sickening slide followed by a sudden drop. But through it all, the troop compartment squeaked and rattled in a normal way, giving Atticus confidence all was ultimately well.

"I like her," said Walt. He and Atticus sat together, bouncing.

"Who?" said Atticus. "The pilot?"

"Yeah, who else? And I'll tell you what I like about her most. I like that she doesn't knuckle under. She swooped right down and got us. That's not the commonest thing, you know—courage." The gunner posed as dramatically as he might in a drop seat. "The sword is brittle, spear will break its thong! 'Tis courage strikes the best, the temper strong!"

"Nice one," said Atticus. "Is holo-poetry a thing too?"

"Poetry ain't a living, heathen. It's a way of life."

"Well, my way of life isn't—"

An intense flash of white light filled the compartment, accompanied by a strange sound like a gong struck twice. Shouting erupted on the comm circuit and the ship tumbled violently, flinging Atticus against his restraints. He struggled to make sense of what was happening. He could hear a thunderous rush of air escaping the ship and there was now a large ragged hole in the hull at the front of the troop compartment.

Two headless soldiers sat beneath it. Blood poured from their necks to be sucked from the ship. What was strange about that horrible scene wasn't the unfairness of their deaths—that was the ugliness of war—but the fact the hole's edges curved outward: something inside the compartment had left it in a tremendous hurry.

Atticus dragged his head against the roll of the ship to examine the opposite wall. There, high up, near the overhead, a neat circle had been punched in the hull. The edges of this hole were curved inward, and now Atticus understood completely: the ship had been hit by a rail gun round. No question about it. It had come through the hull, tumbled through the bay, and then exited with far less tidiness than it had entered. But the transport was far too small, and moving far too fast, for accurate projectile aiming.

It had been another lucky shot.

It was an accepted truth in the Service that some places had bad mojo. If a place had it, it had it—no matter how tight the ball into which you rolled your shit. No amount of preparation, and no amount of counter-hexing, would break the curse. It was now plain to Atticus this planet was one of those places. He knew he should have seen it right off, and told the General thanks, but no thanks. But he hadn't and here he was again, neck-deep in it.

"Comm check! Comm check!" said Thorkin. His voice stuttered against conflicting g-forces.

Atticus lifted a thumb that gyrated wildly in front of him. "You're five by five, Sergeant," he said.

"Do I have any casualties?" said Thorkin. "Other than the obvious."

There was no response.

"All right, here's how this is going to go," he said. "Everybody get small and tight. Visors down, suit joints pulled in and locked, seat impact gyros on. That's the green button under your right hand. Double-check your weapons and gear are locked into their seat cradles. I don't want any of your shit flying around and greasing me!"

Atticus checked his gear and glanced at Walt, who was pulling down his blast visor, frowning. Atticus recognized that look. It was the old soldier's recognition that the hand of fate was shaking the dice and all you could do was wait for the throw. The ship might land, or it might crash; they might live, or they might die; they might be rescued, or they might be captured and executed. Something would happen, but the grunts were only along for the ride.

Atticus pulled down his own blast visor and it clicked into place. He could feel small taps and jerks against the ship's gyrations, which told him Grippa and the flight computer were working to regain flight control. Maybe they would, but in the meantime Atticus's head beat erratically against his helmet, and he felt nauseous. Others had already vomited into their helmets. That was a terrible predicament, since no one knew how long they would be living in their suits on the surface. Certainly days, maybe weeks.

Atticus closed his eyes. He was thinking about his missed opportunities when the impact came to shove him rudely into unconsciousness.

* * *

When Atticus woke again, he was still in his seat and still restrained. The compartment was quiet now, and the only light came from a tiny window set in the far wall, the two rail gun holes in the hull, and dozens of pancakes blinking their yellow and red emergencies. Hot metal ticked and dust hung in the air around him. The ship was on the ground, somewhere, and it seemed to be in one piece.

Atticus raised his blast visor and lifted his right arm to look at his pancake. Amber alert lights flashed but his vitals were high nominal: he would apparently live. He told the suit to turn on his neck lights and to shut down other, nonessential functions. The power plant could last for months, but right now he had no idea how long he'd be wandering around this planet.

He turned to Walt. The gunner was leaned forward against his restraints and his helmet was down, but only non-critical warnings flashed on his pancake. He would live too.

Atticus released his own restraints and stood, very carefully, pushing against the armrests. Pain flickered around his hips and back. The ship had hit hard. The scrape of boots against the deck told him others were coming around also, but most of the platoon was still out—or dead. In the rear of the compartment, the ramp frame and the surrounding bulkheads were crumpled dramatically, as if the ship had bounced on its stern before coming to rest upright. He could see the bodies of four soldiers there, contorted in the wreckage and most certainly dead.

He reached down to unclip his rifle from its cradle, then moved carefully toward the cockpit, avoiding outstretched feet and legs. Turning the wheel on the hatch, he opened it and looked inside.

A hundred lights and indicators still blinked and stuttered on the ship's consoles, but the chairs were empty. He stepped inside the small space and noticed daylight entering from his left, below the command console. Atticus lowered himself painfully to his knees and found a circular hole in the hull, forward of the command chair. Through it, he could see the planet's rusty red soil two meters below.

It was an emergency hatch. Grippa must have popped it and climbed out.

He jammed himself beneath the console, and pushed his feet and legs through the hatch. The fit was tight but he wormed through, and dropped to the ground below with a scratch of gravel. He reached up to pull his rifle after him, then stepped out from the shadow of the ship.

It had landed, or crashed, in a shallow, bowl-shaped depression about three hundred meters across, likely a crater or a dry lake bed left over from some gentler era when the planet was more than just a place to avoid. Beyond the bowl, tall mountains of jagged red rock rose to meet a tan sky which carried faint ribbons of darker dust. Some of the higher peaks wore traces of white snow. The planet's yellow sun sat now in a saddle between two sharp horns of rock. Whether it was rising or setting, Atticus didn't know.

What bothered him most about what he could see was the rim of the crater: it blocked his view in every direction. That was a problem. Anything could be out there beyond that ridge, and anything was something for which no amount of preparation was sufficient. The unknowns needed to become knowns, quickly. Above all, the first order of business was to get clear of this vulnerable position.

* * *

Grippa appeared now, walking around the front of the ship toward Atticus. She wore an exo-suit, with her name and rank bar embroidered on the outer shell.

"Bragg!" she said. "I'm glad to see you! I looked in the back before I popped the e-hatch, but no one was moving."

"There's KIA by the ramp," said Atticus. "At least four. Walt's okay, but I don't know about the others."

She frowned. "Four by the ramp, damn. We did hit ass-first. I couldn't stop it. The good news is there are no fires and no obvious fuel leaks. The ramp is unusable, and so is the side egress door. That e-hatch is the only way in or out of the ship."

"It'll have to do," said Atticus. "Where are we?"

Grippa turned up her hands. "Who knows? We fluttered all over. I do know you're damn lucky I put us on the ground to be scratching ourselves and wondering what happened. I also know we passed through their comm barrier because sat-nav dropped. So we're certainly behind Repsian lines."

"That doesn't narrow it down much."

"No, it doesn't," she said, "but it's all I've got for now. We got tagged by a lucky ass shot. It's totally ridiculous. Probably some bored bug spit-balling and he hit the million-to-one jackpot. Sirens, flashing lights, the whole works."

"So it seems," said Atticus. "But nice flying, again. You have a charming way of keeping me alive."

"And we only met yesterday," she said. "You're a dangerous man to know, Atticus Bragg."

Before Atticus could respond, a suited figure slid from the emergency hatch and dropped to the ground. It was Rail, who stepped aside to let Thorkin come out behind him. The Sergeant missed his landing and stumbled, cursing.

Rail immediately turned to Grippa. "Where are we, Lieutenant?"

"That's the question of the hour, Captain. In a word, I don't know."

"Why not?'

"The bug comm barrier, sir. We blew through it. The ship can't hear our satellites or the station, and the external sensors the inertial navigation system uses to dead reckon were damaged by the hit. The ship has no idea where it is, sir. Neither do I."

Rail blinked at this, then he gazed around at the crater rim and the mountains beyond. "We need a perimeter," he said. "There could be bugs over that ridge." He turned to Thorkin. "Check the troops. I want a full report on casualties in fifteen minutes. Anyone who can walk, send them out with a tool to start digging."

"Aye, sir."

"A half-hour after that, I want a brief on functioning weapons, ammo stocks, food and water supplies, and effective strength."

"Aye, sir."

"Get on it."

Thorkin climbed back into the ship with a boost from Atticus. The Captain turned back to Grippa. "Can we send a distress call?"

"Yes, sir, we could. But it won't get through the barrier. Someone on this side of it might hear, but I don't know what they could do for us. It wouldn't be more than a one-man patrol, or a small recon team. They're out there, but they may not be listening, or close enough to help."

"Do it anyway," said Rail. "What can you do to get a fix on our position?"

Grippa blew out a breath. "Well, sir, there are maps in the nav computer. I could pull them up, and—well, I don't know, maybe something. Maybe not."

"Do that too," said Rail. He swung to Atticus. "Since you're out here first, Bragg, you can have the first job. Go scout over that ridge, all around." He swung a gloved finger in a circle. "If there's an enemy bunker, outpost, comm installation, or anything, I want to know about it immediately."

"Aye, sir. Sir, we really should—"

"Not interested, Bragg. Go check out that ridge, and take your sidekick with you."

"Aye, sir." Atticus reached up to the hatch to climb back into the ship. This Captain would be a tough nut to crack, but Atticus decided he could be patient.

More soldiers were awake in the troop compartment now, but they milled aimlessly, and Atticus had to shove his way back to Walt. "Are you all right?" he asked the gunner.

"I can't complain," said Walt. "No, actually, I can. This is my third crash landing, and I have a strong feeling I've used up all my chits now. A man can't expect to walk away every time."

"They didn't," said Atticus, gesturing to the soldiers folded into the rear of the ship.

"Poor bastards," said Walt. He shook his head. "Alive, last eve, to idle another day; then dead, this morn, with loves unsaid to say."

"So you do eulogies now?" said Atticus.

Walt nodded. "I'm full service."

"You're full of something. Get your stuff. We're going out to take a look around, me and you. Rail's orders."

"You mean we're taking the first kick in the teeth. Sending the mercs to draw fire never drew a black mark on any young officer's fitness report."

"I did it myself," said Atticus. This was true: in the Service, he had given little thought to the lives of the mercenaries attached to his command, and it was an oversight he now regretted greatly. The same treatment by Rail made Atticus's current straits—and Walt's—more difficult and dangerous than they would be otherwise.

They gathered their kit and pushed through the crowd to the cockpit. The troopers were moving with purpose now: checking their gear and responding to Thorkin's roll and sick calls. It seemed the injuries that hadn't been fatal were trivial: cuts, bruises, and welts. Mostly caused by the ends and edges of their own suits as they gyrated through the atmosphere under crushing g-forces.

Outside the ship, Atticus drew Walt away to screw down everything that might go wrong on their scout. While the gunner worked on his own gear, Atticus carefully examined his plasma rifle, re-seating the plasma pack and firing a test round at a rock. Then he ran a gloved finger over each joint and seal of his suit, and wiggled each hose and fitting, while watching his pancake for a leak alert. But the screen remained pleasingly dark. Atticus turned off his neck lights, and keyed the overland program to optimize his suit for extended walking. Finally, he clipped the rifle tether to his suit, and settled the rifle into his crossed arms.

"Ready to go," he told Walt.

The gunner locked an ammunition belt into the feed tray of his mech-gun, then lifted the weapon to sit level in front of him. The weight of the muzzle was supported by long straps clipped into metal rings on his suit. "Ready, boss!" he said.

"All right, let's move."

Atticus picked a direction at random and led Walt across the bowl. The yellow sun had sunk behind the forks of the mountain, allowing gloom to soften the harsh land. The ground beneath their feet was flat and dusty, and free of vegetation.

At the ridge, their boots slipped on loose scree, making the climb more work than Atticus wanted to do, so he settled into a zig-zag path that carried them slowly upward. Just below the crest, he held up a fist to stop Walt, then lowered himself to crawl the last few meters to the top, feeling slightly foolish. Their ship, screaming down from the sky and slamming into the ground, had announced the platoon's presence to anything with eyes to see, or ears to hear, for dozens of klicks. Still, it was a good habit to keep, and even Walt kept his mouth shut for once.

Putting his eyes over the top of the ridge, Atticus saw a wide, boulder-strewn valley that ran between two tall peaks of red rock. Low shrubs grew along the edges of the valley, each pushing out only a few dark leaves. It was the first plant life he had seen on this barren planet. He examined the valley carefully, but there was no sign any Repsian had ever visited this waste of parched earth, bare red rock, and difficult terrain. He took a sip of water from his reclamation tube and brooded over the planet's evil karma.

Walt crawled up to lay beside him, taking in the view. "Well, look at that!" he said. "Nothing! Nothing at all. Just wonderful. You're not volunteering me for anything else, ever again."

"What else were you gonna do?"

Walt snorted. "Sleep. Drink. Go find that blonde we saw. Not be here."

Atticus grinned, but his eye was caught by a flash of movement. He pointed to a distant spot where the valley gathered into small hillocks, now darkening with shadow. "Look out there," he said. "Fifty meters. Something moved."

Walt's helmet bobbed as he peered into the distance. "I don't see anything."

"It wasn't much," said Atticus, "but I did see something."

He murmured a command to his helmet to magnify his view, but still he saw nothing more. He cycled through infrared and ultraviolet filters, but these revealed only a landscape that glowed with residual infrared in the rapidly fading daylight.

"Nope," said Walt. "I sure don't see anything."

Atticus muttered off the enhancements. "Yeah, I don't either. Let's circle left. Stay on the inside slope."

"Aye, boss."

They stood to work around the bowl, slipping on the loose hillside. Below them, in the distance, more of the platoon had emerged from the ruined ship. Their neck lights were on. Someone tall walked among them, pointing. It was surely Thorkin, directing the construction of Rail's perimeter.

"They're digging a damn trench down there," said Walt. "Are we staying?"

"That looks like the plan. I agree it's a bad one."

"No, I mean me and you, At. Are we staying?"

Atticus had considered this already and rejected it. He wasn't the type to run when things got tough, and the Captain needed all the help he could get. "We have a job to do, Walt," he said. "This doesn't change that."

"You and I both know we'll have to bug out eventually."

"I know that, and we'll have to convince him. Our problem here is pretty simple. The main constraint is food. We have a limited supply, which gives us little time to wait for search and rescue. Under ordinary circumstances we might wait anyway, but we're out of comms, which makes us hard to find. So it's an easy decision—or it should be. We look for our own way out."

"Maybe that Sergeant will agree," said Walt. "What do you think our chances are, At? Our no-bullshit chances, if we bug out."

"Who knows?" said Atticus. "The typical shit sandwich—the plain one with no frills, but still shit—has comms or a decent position fix to work with. We have neither of those things."

"So we got the special," said Walt.

Atticus nodded. "Served with a pickle."

They trudged for another hour around the crumbling rim, circling the ship below. Twice more, Atticus thought he saw a flicker of movement in the dusky twilight, but no amount of staring or fiddling with his optics produced the cause. He was certain it wasn't his imagination, which didn't run in that direction; but each time the little twitch of motion was too doubtful, and too far away, to justify crossing the valley to look. It was probably a small animal, or whatever passed for ordinary insects on this planet.

After making a complete circuit of the ridge, they slipped down the scree and walked back to the ship. In their absence, a defensive belt had taken shape around the wreck. Fighting holes, connected by shallow trenches, had been dug and fortified with parapets of piled stone. Flood lights stood ready to illuminate anything that might attack in the night. The platoon could give a good account of itself now, but it appeared there was no one around to test the issue.

Atticus found Rail standing beneath the hatch with Thorkin and Grippa. Craddock, the platoon's medic, dropped from the ship as Atticus approached.

Rail gestured impatiently. "Report, Bragg."

"Sir, the ground beyond this ridge looks more or less like it does here," said Atticus. He gestured to the bowl. "But rockier, with big boulders. Fallen from above, I guess. Broad valleys lead away in that direction, and that direction." He pointed.

"Thank you for the geography lesson, Bragg," said Rail, "but what about enemy activity?"

"Nothing, sir. No bugs, no structures, no roads or tracks. Nothing at all. We're in the boonies, sir." Atticus considered mentioning the movement, but that seemed a small thing now, and he didn't care to be sent into the darkness of a strange planet to investigate. It had been a long day.

"Very well," said Rail. He turned to the medic. "What's our status, Craddock?"

"Eight KIA, sir. All in the back by the ramp. They're a sad mash back there. As for the rest, I don't have much to do. Cuts, bruises, one possible concussion. Everyone not dead seems fit to fight."

"What about med supplies?"

"We have the standard drop ship med-kit, plus what I brought. I can handle anything, sir, short of catastrophe or a cold."

"So we have thirty-eight fit to fight?" said Rail.

"Yes, sir. Plus these two." Craddock gestured to Atticus and Walt.

"Thank you," said Rail. He turned to Grippa. "Lieutenant Warren?"

Grippa gathered herself. "We have no non-local comms at all, sir. The gear seems okay, but we're locked down tight behind the bugs' barrier. Nothing in, nothing out."

"So no hope at all?"

She shook her head. "None, sir. Short of the barrier coming down."

Rail frowned. "I'll take a look at the unit. What about a position fix?"

"A little better there, sir. We have no satellite link-up, but I did mine the nav computer for whatever telemetry data it had. There wasn't much, but I think we're in a mountain range a hundred to a hundred and fifty klicks behind the last known fighting in the central highlands."

"You think?" said Rail.

Grippa spread her hands. "It's dead reckoning, sir. Worse, actually, since the telemetry data is basically garbage. I do want to try to match up what we can see around us to a map, and maybe I can get a better fix. But that'll take some time."

That's time we don't have, thought Atticus, glancing at the Sergeant, who had shifted his feet. *Thorkin knows it too.*

"Find us, Lieutenant," said Rail. He turned to Thorkin. "Sergeant?"

"The good news first, sir," said Thorkin. "Water and O2 are not a problem. The synthesizer took minor damage that's being repaired as we speak. Every troop has a functioning light weapon with at least three extra plasma packs, plus the standard personal issue of grenades. The flamethrowers were in the back with Second Squad, but three units survived in functioning condition. We have enough firepower to defend ourselves, sir."

"And the bad news?"

"Food, sir. We're only provisioned for a quick move to a secure area. We have enough for one week with rationing, starting now. Tighten our belts more, and we can go a bit longer. But that puts us to a choice, sir. Do we—"

"Correction, Sergeant," said Rail. "It puts *me* to a choice."

Thorkin dipped his head in agreement. "Of course, sir. The question—for you—is do we stay here and hope for search and rescue to find us before we starve, or do we make a run for it while we still have chow to march on? Sir, in my opinion, this position isn't—"

"We will remain with the ship," said Rail, cutting off the Sergeant with a wave of his hand.

Thorkin's nostrils flared at that. "Sir, we are overlooked—"

"We will remain here," said Rail, "and wait for search and rescue to find us. It's possible the station can extrapolate our general position from our last known trajectory."

"That's highly unlikely!" blurted Grippa. "Sir, we fluttered all over—"

"Silence!" barked Rail. "I didn't ask for a debate." He glared at Grippa, then Thorkin. "I've made my decision, and I expect each of you to fall in behind it! Is that understood?"

"Understood, sir," said Thorkin tightly. He gave Atticus a look that was a plea for help, but Atticus ignored it: ganging up on Rail now would do more harm than good.

"Understood, sir," said Grippa. She crossed her arms.

Rail tugged at his suit and glanced around the small group quickly. "Blundering into the wilderness will only make the search and rescue effort more difficult," he said. "This ship is our fortress, and I do not intend to leave it until I know where we are going. That might be never. In the meantime, we have to think about our defense. Sergeant Thorkin, I want listening posts established on that ridge at all four points of the compass, and I want a fully entrenched perimeter around the ship by noon tomorrow, whenever that may come." He looked around the group. "Anything else?"

There was an uncomfortable silence, then Grippa spoke up. "One more thing, sir. The ship has a heavy caliber cannon, and plenty of ammo for it. It's still inside its housing and not damaged, as far as I can tell. Someone handier than me could yank it off the hard-point and use it. Maybe mount it on a carriage or something. There's a welding unit in the repair bay." She paused. "Just a thought, sir."

Rail raised an eyebrow. "Thorkin?"

"It can't hurt, sir—if we can get it off the ship. I'll put Wilkins on it."

"Very well. Carry out your orders."

Thorkin spun on his heel to stalk toward the trench line, and Grippa climbed back into the ship, leaving Atticus and Rail standing together.

"He's right, sir," said Atticus. "Food is the problem. And this is the worse tactical position I can imagine. We need to move."

Rail responded coldly: "Doctrine states we dig in and wait to be pulled out, Bragg. You know that as well as I do."

"Yes, sir, but only if we have comms or a position fix. We're off the grid, sir, in bad country. We should start walking—"

Rail waved a hand at him. "Report to your squad leader, Mercenary Bragg."

"Sir, the General ordered—"

"I don't care what the General ordered! I have command here! This is my decision, and mine alone. Surely you, of all people, can understand that."

Atticus nodded. "Yes, sir. I do."

"Then report to your squad leader."

"Aye, sir."

Atticus walked away. The Captain was dead wrong: it was foolish to sit here eating their food and hoping for a miracle. In a week, a bad situation would be desperate. But the Captain was also right: he commanded this platoon, and it was his decision. Atticus had been in charge himself once, and he understood well the loneliness and heavy responsibility of command in a doubtful situation. But Rail was scared and he was letting his fear rule him, which was more dangerous than anything that might lie beyond that ridge. The Captain needed help now more than ever, and he was the only one who didn't know it.

Atticus took turns with Walt digging a fighting hole with a small shovel. The ground was baked hard by the planet's two suns and it was full of stones. But they dug deep, carefully piling the spoil to form a low wall facing the ridge. The sky was fully dark now, and a dome of white stars had emerged to watch them work.

"All this fancy tech," said a voice in Atticus's ear, "but still we need grunts digging holes."

Atticus looked up. Thorkin gazed down at him from the edge of the hole. "Yes," said Atticus. "And we always will. Only blood takes ground."

"Indeed, it does," said Thorkin, "and only blood holds it. Take five, Bragg, and come give me your professional opinion about something."

"I'm glad someone wants it," said Atticus. He accepted Thorkin's hand up and followed the platoon sergeant through the darkness to the far side of the ship. There, a soldier was working under the glare of flood lights to weld together two pieces of metal. A naval cannon lay on the ground nearby, trailing color-coded wires.

"This bastard's heavy," said Thorkin, standing over the gun, "but we pulled it off. Wilkins is making a mount for it, but I don't know whether to tell him to put wheels on it or not. You've been here, Bragg. What's to shoot at, if we do bug out."

Atticus understood the Sergeant's dilemma. The cannon would be awkward to pull through the mountains, if it came to that, but a heavy gun was a heavy gun.

"All I saw yesterday were bugs and assault carriers," he said. "This thing would do for both. But what I really see it for, Sergeant, is triple-A. We're more likely to see a sweep-ship than troops, this far back."

Thorkin grunted. "True. All right, we'll set her up with wheels. God help us if we have to drag it far. And it'll have a kick on it like chuck-fruit whiskey."

"It will," said Atticus. "Where's the Captain?"

Thorkin made an ugly noise. "In the cockpit. He's been in there for two hours now."

"Don't complain," said Atticus. "My top sergeant always said the best place for an officer was well out of the way."

Thorkin laughed. "He wasn't wrong, but I do wish you were leading this bunch, Bragg, instead of that boy. I'm not choking on confidence right now."

"I don't have a magic wand, Sergeant."

"It's not magic I'm looking for, Major." Thorkin held Atticus's eye a moment, then he turned to supervise the cart-making.

Atticus went back to the hole, aware their last exchange was the real reason the platoon sergeant had pulled him away. He dropped into the hole next to Walt, who had stopped digging and now lay at the bottom of the hole.

"You know, Walter," said Atticus, "maybe I did get ahead of myself when I dealt you into this thing. It sure seemed like a grease run at the time."

"It ain't Walter, but they always seem like cake at the beginning. Happens every time. But I'm a free man. I could've bucked you off and disappeared if I'd wanted to." He sat up with a grunt to make room for Atticus. "Besides, it seems you need minding, my friend."

"Punch me in the face before I drink that much again," said Atticus. "Firewater stirs demons that ought to sleep."

"I hear you," said Walt. He raised their shovel to the sky boldly. "One glass a smile, then three a laugh, four glee! The man is six, but eight the man he'd be!"

"Good one," said Atticus, clapping. "Are you writing these down?"

"I thought you were."

They dug for another hour before quitting. Rail came out of the ship once, briefly, for a perfunctory inspection of the platoon's dispositions. Thorkin had spaced his troops around the perimeter with instructions to report anything, no matter how small; and Atticus watched over the lip of the hole as Rail stalked around the trench line with the Sergeant, receiving a report.

The Captain's brusque, impatient manner was betrayed by his neck lights, which flashed brand jerked awkwardly in the darkness, never resting on one spot for more than a moment. In his place, Atticus would have offered a word or two of encouragement to the troops, but Rail made no effort to inspire hope or confidence in the soldiers under his command. Perhaps he thought that was

Thorkin's job. Whatever the reason, Rail soon disappeared into the ship, leaving an uneasy mood behind.

A few minutes later, Grippa appeared at the hole, looking anxious. Atticus climbed out.

"You're a mess," she said.

"I'll comb my hair later. What's the word?"

"Well, if you've been wondering where your Captain has been all day," said Grippa, "he's been crowding me in my cockpit, trying to get comms to work. But it's a lost cause. Honestly, I think he's scared."

"Bingo," said Atticus. "That's not unreasonable, but keep him in there with you. He's only in Thorkin's way out here. Have you found us?"

"There's good news and bad news," she said. "Which do you want first?"

"The bad news first—always."

She crossed her arms. "We're definitely a hundred klicks behind the lines, give or take."

"So you found us?"

"Yes, I think so, after taking sightings and burning out my eyes studying maps."

"Nice work," he said. "What did the Captain say?"

She lowered her voice, needlessly. "I haven't told him. Because the good news is the straight line between here and the front is open. Or at least it was an hour before we dropped, when the last round of data was uploaded to the nav computer."

Atticus laughed. "So we got our quiet sector after all?"

"Yes, we did. And we can get out from here—I think. If we go now." She cocked an eyebrow at him. "Maybe under someone who knows what he's doing."

"Jesus," said Atticus. "Take a number and wait over there."

"What?"

He waved his hand. "Nothing."

"Atticus, our chances are pretty crappy just sitting here. I think you know that."

"I'm aware of that, but I'm not running this outfit."

"You should be," she said. "What would you think about going for it ourselves? You, me, and Walt."

Atticus shook his head. "No, we're on the team. And these troops don't deserve to get left with nothing to lean on but a bright-green officer. Go give him your news."

"All right, but we're not done with this conversation."

"I didn't think so."

CHAPTER FOUR

tticus was on watch when the light came up again. He was sitting on the edge of the hole, his rifle laid across his thighs. The high peaks surrounding the ship appeared first, limned in yellow, then the light crept down their steep red slopes. Last to emerge from the gloom was the trench line to either side of him, where the dark forms of the men and women of the platoon slept uneasily on their weapons.

Walt slept as well, his forehead resting against the dome of his helmet. His face looked careworn, even in sleep. Atticus felt a stab of guilt for forcing the gunner to come along with him. It had seemed a fine idea at the time, even magnanimous, but no man should presume to know the fortunes of war.

Atticus decided to stretch his legs by walking the trench line. He slung his rifle on his shoulder and stood to look around. On a section of the ridge beyond the ship, he could see two sets of neck lights, bobbing and swinging in the half-light. That was odd. There was a listening post up there, but they shouldn't be standing out in the open. Unless something was wrong.

Atticus walked around the ship and hopped the trench to jog across the bowl and trudge up the sliding hillside. The lights turned out to be Thorkin and the medic, Craddock. They were standing over a small hole in which two soldiers crouched. It was the listening post. The soldiers stared up at their visitors with slack faces and vacant eyes.

"What's up?" said Atticus, keying to a private channel with Thorkin and the medic.

"You tell me," said Thorkin. "These two missed their last sit rep, and now here they sit like two toads in a hole, dazed or something. The doc can't find anything wrong with them, and their flapjacks are green all across."

Atticus swung his lights to the medic, who offered nothing but a shrug. He looked down at the men. "What do they say happened?"

"Nothing," said Thorkin. "They don't know what the fuss is about. But look at'em. They aren't right."

It was true: the men stared absently, unspeaking.

"Drunk?" said Atticus.

"No," said Craddock. "First thing I checked."

Atticus keyed off private and crouched to speak to the nearest soldier. "Tell me what happened, son."

The man looked puzzled and shook his head. "Nothing happened, sir. Why are all of you here? We ain't done nothing wrong."

The other one stirred long enough to shake his head in agreement, then both lapsed into distraction, as if passing time at a station waiting for a shuttle to arrive.

"All right, boys," said Thorkin, motioning to them. "Up and out! Craddock, get these two down to the ship and give'em a good going over. This might be nothing but nerves, but it doesn't feel right."

"Will do, Sergeant."

When they had left, Thorkin turned to Atticus. "Any thoughts?"

Atticus crouched to peer into the hole. There was nothing in it but rocks, and two desiccated fec-pellets ejected by the soldiers' suits. In the dirt around the hole, he saw only boot tracks and shovel marks.

"I don't see an external threat," he said. "No tracks, and obviously they didn't see anything themselves. But let's keep an open mind. Check their suit parameters. Maybe it's environmental."

"He will," said Thorkin. "But there better not be any more of these. Down two more is cutting close to the bone."

Back at the hole, Atticus told Walt about the soldiers.

"What do you think?" said the gunner.

"I really have no idea," said Atticus.

He didn't. He didn't even have a good theory for it. Soldiers sometimes broke under adversity, and that sometimes manifested itself in strange ways, but Atticus found that explanation unlikely: the platoon had been here less than a day, and these were veteran troops. Maybe their exo-suits had malfunctioned, giving them the wrong gas mix, but both suits at the same time? Atticus found that even more unlikely. He hoped Craddock would get to the bottom of it.

Rail's voice cut into his thoughts: "Bragg to the ship. ASAP."

Great. Atticus stood. "I've been summoned to the presence," he told Walt, tapping his earpiece.

Walt rolled his eyes. "We're in for another shit job, aren't we?"

"That would be a good bet," said Atticus.

He picked up his rifle and climbed from the hole to walk to the hatch. Grippa was waiting for him above. She smiled and extended a hand to help him up. In the dim of the cockpit, Rail sat slumped in the nav-chair. His arms were draped over the rests, as if he sat a throne. His suit was clean.

"Bragg," he said.

"Sir?"

"I have a job for you. The Lieutenant tells me she knows where we are."

"Good to hear, sir."

"So I need a scout. That's you."

"Yes, sir."

"Bearing 165 is our way out, if we go, but I'm not saying we will. I still firmly believe we should sit tight, and wait to be pulled out. I'm sure the Lieutenant here agrees with me."

Grippa made a strangled noise, but Rail continued. "Fifteen klicks, no more. I want a full report of what you see, and when you see it. I want to know about any enemy activity, or evidence thereof, terrain difficulty, and other obstacles. You might want to keep a log."

"Yes, sir," Atticus said. *Patronizing son of a bitch,* he thought. *I was doing this kind of thing when your governess was chasing your tiny ass around the playroom.*

Rail turned his chair to face the nav pedestal, dismissing Atticus. "Leave immediately," he said. "And take Sancho Panza with you."

"Aye, sir."

As Atticus lowered himself from the hatch, he tipped a farewell nod to Grippa. She gave him a wide-eyed stare in return, as if to say Rail was making her crazy. Atticus sympathized, but only so much. She hadn't been ordered to walk fifteen klicks into bandit country with a talkative poet.

"Saddle up," said Atticus, dropping in the hole. "We're moving out, me and you."

"Hooray!" said Walt. "We're finally blowing this amateur hour?"

"No, just a scout. Fifteen klicks that way." Atticus pointed.

"I see. So His Holiness thinks that's the way out."

"Grippa thinks so. Not that Rail has any notion to leave. We're just the dangle to draw out whatever might be hiding."

"Mercs to the fore—charming."

Atticus clipped six grenades to his web belt and filled his small mesh bag with enough food tubes for a three-day march. He expected to be back long before then, but one never knew, especially on this planet. He test-fired his rifle and checked the plasma charge: enough for a major battle. A spare pack would be dead weight.

"Ready," said Walt. He had climbed from the hole and now struck a heroic pose, facing the mountains. "The road ahead! I'm stepping forth, to where?" He shrugged theatrically. "To what may be, and what may be-n't—and there!"

Atticus smiled. "Someone decided I needed culture, and sent you."

"They were right."

Atticus informed Thorkin of their departure before leading Walt across the bowl to climb the crumbling ridge again. From the top, he could see their course would take them down one of the wide valleys strewn with boulders. The valley ran straight for about three klicks before turning to disappear behind a shoulder of the left-hand mountain. The day was bright and the yellow sun cast sharp, dark shadows.

"Well, there's the road," said Walt. "but will it make all the difference?"

"Not unless the Captain changes his mind," said Atticus.

Walt sighed. "Just when I was having hope for you." He waved a hand. "Fine, lead on, Natty."

They walked down the far slope of the ridge onto the valley floor. Snow melt from high above had carved deep channels into the mountainsides above them. When these channels reached the flat ground of the valley floor, they pushed across to converge on a dry stream bed that wound away into the distance. It all gave the valley a corrugated look, and made the going harder than Atticus had anticipated from the ridge. But in a little more than half an hour, they had reached the leftward curve of the valley to find it was only a dogleg, beyond which the valley resumed its push along their intended heading.

"There's some luck," said Walt. "So far, so good."

"Lies!" muttered Atticus. "Nothing about this planet is easy."

They walked on, and Atticus surveyed the heights on either side, but nothing moved on them. Scraps of vegetation appeared now and again, hugging the slopes, perhaps in wan hope of being watered by snow melt. Atticus wondered if the entire planet was like this, or he'd contrived to find the worst parts.

"Look at that opening," said Walt, after a time. Atticus turned to find the gunner pointing up and to the right. "There. See? It might be a cave."

Atticus did see it: a thick slash of black shadow, twenty meters above the valley floor, next to a tall rock that had weathered from the mountainside. He trained his rifle on the opening as they passed beneath it. The scree below seemed compacted, even groomed, as if something traveled in and out regularly.

"I think we won't disturb whatever might be in there," Atticus said. "It's not a military threat."

"My thoughts exactly," said Walt.

They moved on, and soon the planet's small blue sun rose for the first time to join its yellow brother. Together the suns cast a green, unreal hue over the landscape that made Atticus anxious. Three hours and eight klicks into their journey, they stopped to rest, sitting on the ground and cracking food tubes to shove into the nutrition ports by their mouths.

"Faster-than-light travel hasn't solved everything," said Walt, after an experimental suck on his tube. "There's still bad pop music, and this—whatever this is. I want a steak and a beer."

"I think that's what mine is supposed to be," said Atticus. "That, or fish."

"We could keep on going, you know—if this really is the way out. We could push through and bring back the cavalry. We'd be heroes!"

"We'd be court-martialed," said Atticus. "Once in a lifetime is enough."

"Yeah, that was—"

"Yes, I know," said Atticus. "It was a shame. It was, but it's also ancient history. There's no sense picking at the carcass."

"Sorry, boss. I did watch the holo coverage of the trial, you know. Well, for the most part. I didn't stay on every day like some people did."

Atticus was sorry to hear that, but maybe there was no such thing as a clean break from the past. "Then tell me this, Walter. Did I keep my honor?"

"Why ever would you ask that?"

Atticus shrugged. "It doesn't feel like it. People seem to think I'd hop a carrier for anywhere."

Walt laughed. "Actually, we should do that, you know. Beats

the hell out of this shit. As far as honor goes, my friend, I'll put it this way. Those stuffed shirts, with all that ribbon and gold braid, didn't lay a hand on you."

"You think so?"

"Hell, yeah!" said Walt. "All that pontification about higher duty and the good of the service, that was just big wind blowing nobody any good. Those lives you saved, At—those were real."

"A lot more died."

"We ain't gods, At. We deal with what's in front of our snouts as best we know how, and just muddle through."

"I guess so."

"Some muddle worse than others," said Walt. "I don't think much of that Captain."

"Give him a chance," said Atticus. "Things aren't critical yet, and we have time to convince him to leave before they are."

"And if we can't?"

Atticus stood to leave. "One problem at a time."

An hour after lunch, the long valley ended and they passed over a narrow, rocky saddle lying between two mountainsides. A hanging glacier perched dramatically over the left slope, and it released a steady stream of water that bounced down a succession of little white falls into a tangle of boulders. It was the first water Atticus had seen on this world. He walked toward it.

"Stop, At!" said Walt.

Atticus halted in mid-stride, looking back at Walt.

The gunner was pointing at the fall. "Something moved up there," he said. "Not the water."

Atticus looked to where he pointed, but saw nothing.

"Look to the right of that triangular rock," Walt said.

Atticus saw it then: a large animal with long, rust-red fur closely mimicking the rock of the mountainside. Atticus muttered for magnification and his helmet zoomed in to show an odd-looking creature standing on two hind legs. It had knees not unlike a human's, but its feet were prehensile and they gripped the rocky slope. Two thin arms, or forelegs, reached out from its chest to touch the steep slope, perhaps to keep the creature balanced. It had a long head and a beard of red fur that concealed its mouth as it browsed on vegetation growing by the fall. Either the thing hadn't noticed them, or it didn't care.

"There's another!" said Walt, pointing again. "And another! They're all over the slope!"

Atticus's eyes had adapted now, and he could see a dozen of the red creatures browsing around the fall, some small enough to be juveniles. "Speaking of steak," he murmured.

Walt laughed. "Dare we?"

The history of humans eating exo-meat was spotty. For every new delicacy that emerged, there was an equal and opposite story of fatal shock and homicidal madness.

"No," said Atticus. "I'm not looking for a bellyache today, but let's take five here." He looked at his pancake. "We've come thirteen klicks."

They propped their weapons on a boulder, and sat to rest and watch the creatures. Atticus drank from his reclamation tube, and murmured again for zoom. Studying several individuals, he decided their eyes were located on the sides of their heads, well hidden by fur; and they had long ears that swiveled constantly as they ate. They were wary of something, yet seemed undisturbed by the two mercenaries far below.

"Ugly things," said Walt.

"They're thinking the same about us," said Atticus.

"About you, maybe. Hey, do you think an older, literary type with nice hair and a big gun would have a chance with Grippa?"

Atticus laughed. "You're not that old."

"Older than you."

"Not by much, but don't kid yourself about that hair."

Walt squawked. "Well, friend! Let me tell you about that haircut of yours! It's not—"

Atticus raised a hand to cut him off. The furry herbivores were now bounding across the slope rapidly, swinging from hold to hold. "Something's spooked them," he said.

"Maybe us," said Walt, but he bent to pick up his mech-gun.

"Not likely. We've been sitting here for half an hour. Let's see what shows up."

"To eat us instead?" said Walt. "I'm against that."

Atticus didn't respond, but eased down from the boulder to pick up his rifle. The red creatures had disappeared around a shoulder of the mountain, leaving the little waterfall to clatter on. It filled the narrow saddle with white noise. Atticus scanned the sky and the barren land beyond the saddle, but he had no idea what he was looking for.

"Goddamn!" said Walt. "Look at that!"

Atticus followed the gunner's finger. High on the mountainside, to the right of the fall, an enormous beast moved across the steep slope, displaying an unlikely grace. Like the Repsians, it was insectile, but its body plan was fundamentally different. It was low to the ground and long, at least five meters from nose to tail, and it seemed to undulate across the slope beneath closely-fitted plates of chitinous armor that rippled and threw off green glints of reflected sunlight. Atticus called for magnification and saw the creature's head thrust from a gap in a tall armor plate, and its muzzle was long and pointed, like a dog's. Massive canines dropped from its upper jaw. Hints of feet moved beneath the shining carapace, gripping the rock and pulling the creature across the steep slope. The thing was clearly carnivorous, and it was clearly on the hunt.

"Damn!" said Walt. "That's a whole bunch more ugly, right there."

"Don't move," said Atticus.

"Nope, not moving, boss."

The creature stopped by the fall to push out a long, thin tongue, which it worked delicately over a section of rock, tracking the red-haired creatures. Retrieving the tongue, it drank from the fall before crossing to move briskly over the mountainside, following the herd. Atticus was glad to see it go.

"Tho' nature," said Walt. "Red in tooth and claw!"

"Tennyson," said Atticus.

"I'm astonished," said Walt.

"I was educated once, you know."

Walt bowed to him. "I had imagined your youth misspent."

"I didn't say it wasn't," said Atticus. "Let's move on."

Watching their back-trail carefully, they walked down the far side of the saddle, where they found another valley paralleling the one they had just traveled. It was also dry, flat, and rocky. Atticus wondered if there was any loveliness to be found on this planet.

"Let's turn back," he said. "Down this valley. Maybe the walking will be easier there."

"Suits me," said Walt. He gestured for Atticus to march on. "Our report to Captain Rail will be short," he said. "We found more of the same, Your Captain Holiness Sir! It's turtles all the way down, don't you know!"

"Eh?" said Atticus.

"Forget it."

Some hours later, they found an animal carcass at the bottom of a steep incline. It had rolled down from above to lay forlornly on the red desolation of the valley floor. It was obvious the animal had been dead for a long time: its body was sunken and rotting, and the skin beneath its red, matted hair was dry and tattered. It seemed strangely undisturbed.

"One of those beasts from the fall," said Walt.

Atticus poked at the carcass with the toe of his boot, watching it come apart. "Yes, but why haven't scavengers been at it? Or one of those armored beasts. There's not a lot to eat out here, and this was a buffet—or it was at one time."

"Look here," said Walt. "A hole." He reached down to move a hank of red fur aside, revealing a ragged tear in the animal's skin. The edges flared out like an exit wound and the skin was curled back tightly, dried by the heat of two suns.

Atticus pondered the hole. "Shot?"

"Maybe," said Walt. He pushed at the corpse with his boot. Pieces of it fell off. "Here's another hole, just like that one. And another. They're all exit wounds. I don't see an entrance wound anywhere."

"So not shot," said Atticus. "Maybe something came out?"

"So it would seem," said Walt, "and in messy fashion. I'd say it's what killed our boy here. Poor bastard."

Atticus looked up at the heights, but saw nothing but rock. He eyed the corpse again. "Maybe a parasite?"

Walt frowned at his gloves and bent to scrub them on the red dirt. "You had to say that, didn't you? If I wake up with two-foot worms popping out of my chest, give me a plasma breakfast. You can have my stuff."

Atticus passed his rifle to Walt and pulled a knife from his web belt. "It might explain why the corpse wasn't scavenged. We should get a tissue sample."

"Good Lord," said Walt. "Whatever for?"

"It's a threat," said Atticus. "Maybe Craddock can make something of it."

"Fine, but you're not sleeping in the hole tonight."

"That's a blessing," said Atticus. "You kick."

He squatted to cut a rough circle around one of the exit wounds, then grabbed a handful of the long red hair and yanked. A plug of rotten flesh came free, and he held it up.

"Is this where you do a war dance?" said Walt.

Atticus grinned at him. "Not this time." He gathered the food tubes from his mesh bag, handed them to Walt, then stuffed the hank of hairy flesh into the bag, drawing it closed.

Walt was silent.

Atticus sheathed the knife and took his rifle back. "No couplet for this?" he said.

Walt shook his head. "There's no eternal truth to be found in that. You're just a gross bastard."

They left the corpse and moved on, plodding through the second valley toward the ship. The unvarying terrain steadily eroded Atticus's vigilance, and he found his thoughts had turned to Grippa. She seemed to have no loyalty to the platoon, or to the common soldiers with whom Atticus still strongly identified. She had been ready to ditch them on that first day in favor of bugging out with Atticus and Walt. It seemed likely to him Grippa was just rash and impulsive. If so, it was married to skill and competence, and that combination had saved Atticus's life two days ago. It made her interesting to him, but Atticus knew he no longer had anything to offer anyone, certainly not the daughter of a general. At one time he had been an up-and-comer, even marked for greatness by some, but now he slept on station floors and got stiffed by one-armed diplomats.

Clouded in thought, Atticus didn't see the beast attack Walt. But he heard it: a heavy impact behind him, followed by Walt's shout in his ear and the frantic scrabble of hard claws on parched dirt.

Atticus turned to see Walt on the ground, rolling away from the huge armored beast they'd seen at the waterfall—or another one like it. The creature had leaped from a tall rock that Atticus had passed under moments before, but it had landed poorly and struggled to find its feet, allowing Walt to escape.

When it was up again, the beast shook itself like a dog. Its overlapping armor segments rippled and flashed in the blue sunlight. This close, the creature seemed gargantuan and unstoppable.

Atticus raised his rifle and fired at it. A blue bolt flashed from the muzzle and bounced from the creature's carapace to strike the mountainside, blasting a smoking hole in a boulder.

Oh, that's not good, thought Atticus. *Not good at all.* He felt a trill of fear.

But the creature ignored him, turning its long, predatory head to Walt, who was still on the ground struggling under the weight of the mech-gun. It hung at an odd angle, denying him leverage to stand.

Atticus sighted more carefully, aiming for a seam in the creature's carapace, but again the blue bolt bounced off—this time narrowly missing Walt.

"Whoa there, hoss!" he shouted.

"It bounced off!" said Atticus. "Get up!"

"What a good idea! Why didn't I think of that?"

Cursing, Walt managed to roll himself into a sitting position with his legs splayed in front of him. The creature stalked toward him, hissing. He pulled the mech-gun across his lap and fired a burst, but the angle was poor and a line of red tracers zipped over the animal's back to scatter from the tall rock. Walt lowered the barrel and fired again. This time the heavy rounds clattered off the creature's hard shell, leaving no mark.

"Holy shit!" said Atticus. "Why does this son of a bitch need armor like that?"

"Kill it now please!" said Walt. "Science later!"

Atticus moved in closer, trying to put a bolt through a gap in the beast's armor plating. But its sinuous motions made accurate aim impossible, and the deflected bolts posed a danger to both of them. Walt put a hand on the ground and pushed himself up, trying to stand, but the beast darted at him and he was forced to drop and roll away again. But the weight of his mech-gun, firmly clipped to his suit, worked against him, and the beast was on top of him in a moment. He flailed at it.

"Goddammit! Get it off!"

Atticus pulled his knife as a final hopeless hope, but then an idea came to him—a crazy one. He put the knife away and untied the mesh bag from his web belt.

Walt saw. "What the hell are you doing?" he said. "Kill this thing!"

The creature opened its long jaws and clamped its teeth around Walt's forearm. He screamed and thrashed on the ground beneath the beast. The thing shook its head violently, trying to wrest the arm free, but the gunner's exo-suit did its primary job of holding his parts together.

Atticus stepped toward them and thrust the mesh bag, with its rotten contents, into the creature's face.

The effect was immediate. The beast opened its jaws to utter a yelp, then skittered back.

"You don't like that, do you?" Atticus snarled. He advanced on the thing, brandishing the bag. It kept a respectful distance, growling and clicking its teeth in a quick chatter. "Walt, get up! I don't know how long this will work!"

"Doing my best, boss! I'm like a bug on its back with this god-damn gun!"

Atticus forced the angry creature back farther still as Walt recovered his dignity in a cloud of swearing. Soon he stood next to Atticus, his left arm hanging limply from its shoulder.

"It's numb," he said, "but I think it's okay. Now I know how the hare feels in the jaws of the wolf!"

"Good to know," said Atticus. "Now what?" He shook the mesh bag, hoping a little extra jiggle would make the beast turn and run, but it roared back at him in hunger and frustration.

"I don't know," said Walt. "You tell me. You've been the genius so far."

"It's your turn now. How can we hurt this thing?"

"I do know a few scandalously bad poems," said Walt.

"With tits?" said Atticus.

"You're disgusting. Actually, yes. One of them."

"Later. I guess it's a standoff then. Let's keep moving."

So they marched on, in step, slowly, backward, in the direction of the ship. The beast followed, keeping a distance of five meters and maintaining a threatening growl. The ship was still eight klicks away, and Atticus calculated it would take five to six hours to get there walking backward, hoping not to be ripped apart.

"This is cozy," said Walt. "Is this the part where we confess our greatest regrets in life, and utter steely resolves to be better men if we're lucky enough to live?"

"You can," said Atticus, "but I expect he'll give up soon. There's easier prey to be had out here than two skinny strangers with tough skin waving the Bag of Badness."

"There's no bad time for self-reflection," said Walt.

"I'm reflecting on giving you the bag and running," said Atticus.

Walt sniffed. "Fine, I'll start."

But before he could open his mouth again, the beast gave a frustrated grunt and turned to bound up the mountainside, disappearing into the rocks.

"You were saying?" said Atticus, tying the mesh bag to his web belt again.

"Never you mind," said Walt. "But I do have a new and profound respect for that scalp. So much respect, in fact, that you may walk fifty meters ahead of me."

The gunner did lag farther than Atticus would have liked, but the remainder of their return to the ship was uneventful. They passed along the valley for six more klicks before striking left into the mountains to look for the first valley and its straight road home.

Atticus groped blindly for a route over the mountains, and

they were forced to traverse two steep and difficult slopes, and walk along an exposed, knife-edge ridge with long drops to either side. Finally, not long after Atticus had turned off Walt's complaining, the first valley opened below them and they descended to retrace their earlier steps. They passed the dark opening in the mountainside, moving quickly and quietly, but once again nothing emerged to disturb them.

The scene around the ship was unchanged. Soldiers sat in the trench, waiting, and Thorkin stalked among them, trying to keep the platoon alert against no obvious threat.

"Well?" he said to Atticus.

"No bugs," said Atticus. "At least not the smart kind." He told the Sergeant about the armored beasts.

"Jesus," said Thorkin, "this planet doesn't stop, does it? I'll pass the word. Come give your report to the Captain."

They followed Thorkin into the ship, where Rail treated them brusquely, as if they were late. "Report," he said.

"We went out nearly fifteen klicks, sir," said Atticus. "No sign of bugs—no patrols, no roads, no structures." He described for the Captain the terrain, the cave, the red-haired animals, the strange carcass, and the fight with the beast. "Plasma and slugs did nothing to it, sir."

"Did you aim at it?" said Rail.

Walt opened his mouth to respond, but Atticus overrode him. "Yes, sir. Those armor plates are impenetrable to light weapons. Sir, we should give thought to why that thing needs such an absurd level of protection."

"Does it matter, Bragg?"

"It does, sir. That was one hell of a beast, but it was definitely not at the top of the food chain."

"This isn't a science expedition, Bragg," said Rail. "That was an adequate report. Dismissed."

"Yes, sir."

Rail turned to Thorkin, who had been listening. "Are you satisfied now, Sergeant? There are creatures out there impervious to our weapons—or so we're told. We will continue to sit tight and wait to be pulled out."

Thorkin said nothing. It was clear they had been arguing the point prior to Atticus's arrival.

"Sir," said Atticus. "The way is clear of Repsians."

"I thought I'd dismissed you, Bragg. All we know is the way is clear for fifteen klicks. The Lieutenant here says we're a hundred klicks out. Leaving was risky yesterday, and now you're telling me it's even more risky today. We'll stay put. You are dismissed. Leave."

Atticus and Thorkin exchanged glances, but neither said anything more, and Atticus followed Walt out of the ship.

"Well, shit," he said.

"Indeed," said Walt. "Let's go eat."

"Not yet. One more stop."

Craddock held the bag with the rotten tissue sample away from himself, between a thumb and forefinger. "This is a mess," he said.

"Treat it nice," said Walt. "It saved our lives."

The medic opened his mouth to ask, but Atticus waved him off. "Long story. But I want you to look for a parasite, or something else that might be a threat."

Craddock raised an eyebrow and held the bag out farther. "Okay, I guess I can run some tests for you, if you really want. Speaking of tests, I've gone over the two boys from the listening post. Well, mostly—the Captain won't let me remove their suits for fear of contagion. That's not the worst idea, but it has prevented me from doing several of the deeper diagnostics. I did what I could, at any rate."

"And?"

"Nothing. Their temps are up, but nothing concerning. Their brains and other bio are normal."

"So they're better?" said Atticus.

"No!" said Craddock. "That's the thing. They're worse now. They're staring idiots. I can't figure it. They've just checked out, and I don't know why."

"Any other cases?"

The medic shook his head. "Nope. One more thing, probably nothing. Their suit pressure was down when I brought them in—both of them." He shrugged. "That's all I've got, and I haven't the faintest idea how that could be significant. Just coincidence, probably."

Atticus nodded. "Let me know about that sample."

"Right. I was hoping you had forgotten about that."

The ship's cannon, mounted on a metal cart, now stood behind their hole, its barrel pointing to the waste beyond the trench. Grippa was waiting for them there.

"They return," she said.

"They do," said Atticus, "with dogs barking." He sat on the ground beside the hole and put his feet up on a rock, gesturing for Grippa to sit. Walt passed him a food tube. The paste tasted like fish, but that didn't mean it was.

"What's the word?" he said.

"It's been quiet here," said Grippa. "Boring even."

Walt snorted, speckling the inside of his helmet with something. Craddock had examined his arm and pronounced it only well-bruised. The medic had refused the gunner's plea for 'the good stuff.'

"Rail's still holding court in the cockpit," said Grippa, edging away from Walt. "Shouldn't he be out here inspecting something—the trench, soldiers, weapons, something? Or maybe just standing tall and looking thoughtfully into the distance with a jutting chin? He doesn't inspire much confidence."

"He wasn't meant to," said Atticus. "We were headed for a quiet spot, by your father's design. No experience necessary."

"He's obsessed with the comm-link," she said. "He won't stop fiddling with it. And what the hell does he know about electronics anyway? Don't those people study things like art and dance, or looking important?"

"He's scared," said Atticus. "He doesn't really know what to do, for all his false confidence. So he's channeling his fear into the comfort of a single-minded purpose, as misguided as it is."

"You psychoanalyze now?" said Grippa.

"I'm a smart guy."

"I can tell," she said. "By your choice of profession, and your obvious success in it."

Walt brayed a laugh, but Atticus only shrugged. "Someone has to be the bad example for the kids," he said. "What about you? How are you holding up?"

"Honestly, I'm scared shitless too. I'm a pilot, not a grunt, Atticus. Being on the surface makes me feel—I don't know, trapped."

"Welcome to ground warfare," said Atticus "It'll always be with us. Wasn't your father a suit-monkey?"

"He was. All over—the Astral Belt, Pictor Tert, the Fornax Action. He was always somewhere else. I think that's why he keeps me close now."

"Oh?"

"Yeah. Every time he's reassigned, I get new posting orders from Cent Command, and there he is."

"I see," said Atticus. "It's good to be the king."

She frowned. "Right about now, he's tearing out what's left of his hair."

"Maybe that's what the good Captain is banking on."

"I guess so," said Grippa. "But facts are facts, you know. We're off the map. Do you have any kids yourself?"

"Yes," said Atticus.

She waited for more, but Atticus yanked the food tube from his nutrition port and dropped it to the dirt. Screw this planet.

Grippa stood and brushed off her suit. "Right. Well, I better go see if your Captain has broken my nav-puter." She walked away toward the ship.

"Nice one, bucko," said Walt.

"What? I do have kids. Well, one."

"I don't see how that happened."

"Itchy trigger finger," said Atticus.

"Is that what they call it now? Jesus, my arm hurts."

An hour after sunset a half-moon rose, bright and close in the sky, to cast a pale light on the red horns of rock that watched over the ship. Walt was asleep, slumped against the wall of the hole. Atticus fished another food tube from his mesh bag and shoved it into the nutrition port by his chin. He sucked on it dubiously. He hadn't looked at the label, but thought it might be grown-steak, ironically reduced by Imperial provisioners back to the paste from which it had first emerged.

A moon shadow fell over Walt's helmet and Atticus looked up to see Thorkin squatted at the edge of the hole, a dark gap in the white stars. "You need anything?" the Sergeant asked.

"Three fingers of Kentucky's best," said Atticus.

"I hear you. I'm a scotch man myself."

"Snob."

The Sergeant laughed. "I'll rouse you when it's your watch, Bragg. You're after me. Keep your eyes skinned. This little castle of ours is bad news. We should be up on that ridge, or gone."

"I don't disagree," said Atticus. "But the man has spoken, and we obey."

"Yes, we do," said Thorkin, "but this ship is nothing but a shitty place to die. Speaking of, you were at Sardis, weren't you? The System War?"

"I had that displeasure."

"As did I," said Thorkin. "On Sardis Minor. I was a wet-eared sergeant then, with a boot lieutenant. A bad combo. He was scared shitless, just like this one here." The Sergeant nodded his helmet toward the ship. "Well, that green lieutenant on Sardis got it lodged in his damn-fool head that if he could get a shot up track-carrier moving again, the heavens would open and the finger of Almighty God would emerge to squash all his pressing problems. The details of which I'll spare you."

Thorkin's helmet moved against the sky as he surveyed the trench line around him. "It's funny what the mind does, Major, when a man's faced with taking a bite from the sandwich. Some square up for it, some don't. There's no telling, but that boy didn't. He worried on that dead track like a dog on a bone while shit stormed around us. I cut my teeth that day, and got my first rocker for it. But a lot of good soldiers died before I thought to grab the tiller. Anyhow, long story short, Major, I'm seeing that same shit going down here. The Lieutenant says our comms are flat negative, but the Captain's in there twiddling dead knobs while we sit out here eating our chow and thumbing our nuts. These grunts deserve better—a whole lot better."

"Where are you going with this, Sergeant?"

"I ain't going anywhere with it—not yet. I'm just telling you. I've seen this before, and I won't be late to poke my head up this time around. But I ain't the only horse waiting at the gate, if you take my point."

"I do take your point, Sergeant. But we're still a long way from that."

"Maybe we are, but maybe we aren't. I'm not the only one to think like I do. But I thought we'd take a moment, you and me, to understand each other."

"All right," said Atticus. "Noted."

Thorkin said nothing more, but stood to move away down the trench line. Atticus watched him go. *Goddamn that Captain, and goddamn that Sergeant more for trying to get his hooks into me.*

CHAPTER FIVE

"It's the same thing," said Craddock.

He and Atticus were in the troop compartment of the ship, looking at the afflicted, who were seated together against one wall. There were five of them now: three more had appeared after the last period of darkness.

Craddock ticked off their symptoms with his fingers: "Reduced awareness, glassy stare, denial, a mild affect. No physical symptoms at all except a slightly elevated temperature. It doesn't fit anything I know of."

"Where were the new ones found?" said Atticus.

"In the trench. In close proximity to each other."

"No contact with the other two?"

"No," said Craddock.

"What about suit pressure?" said Atticus. "You mentioned that before."

"Yeah, it was down for these three too, slightly. But it's too close to normal pressure loss across an op to be obviously related." Craddock shrugged. "Maybe just a coincidence."

"Maybe," said Atticus, "but I wouldn't assume anything at this point. Keep at it."

"That's the plan," said Craddock. "One more thing. The first two are complaining of itching."

"Itching?"

"Yes, but not external." The medic tapped his chest. "Here. Inside. Blevins got a little hysterical, so I gave him something for it."

"We need to keep a lid on this," said Atticus. "The others outside are getting jumpy."

"I understand," said Craddock. "I'll keep them quiet, and in here."

Atticus studied the five soldiers. Something had gotten to them, no question about it. But what? And how? And why? "Did you turn up anything in that tissue sample?" he said.

"I did take a look at it," said Craddock, "with the small microscope in the med closet."

"And?"

"Well, it's not clear. It does look like something pushed out from inside the animal. It wasn't too big. Five to seven centimeters wide, I'd imagine. It certainly did a lot of damage. Fatal, obviously."

"So it was some kind of parasite?" said Atticus. That had been his suspicion, and the implications for the five afflicted had been hovering, unacknowledged, in the back of his mind. The possibilities were too horrifying to think much about without solid evidence.

"Well, maybe a parasite," said Craddock. "But maybe not. Parasites tend not to kill their hosts, at least not quickly. There's no evolutionary advantage to it. But, guessing, I'd say incubation was a better term."

Atticus's eyes turned to the five soldiers, who were now

staring placidly at the forward bulkhead. "Incubation?" he said. "As in—hatching?"

"Something like that. Again, I'm speculating. I'm just a medic."

The wheel on the cockpit hatch turned, and the door opened. Rail stepped over the coaming into the troop compartment. "Bragg," he said. "I have no idea what you might be doing in this ship, but I want to talk to you."

"Yes, sir."

"Privately."

Craddock excused himself, and Rail switched Atticus to a private channel. "Has Sergeant Thorkin been talking to you?" he said.

Atticus decided to play stupid. "About what?"

"You know exactly what I'm talking about, Bragg. He's been running his mouth to the troopers. I have a good idea what he's saying to them, but I want to hear it from you. Exactly."

Stupid wasn't going to work: Rail had too much information. Atticus didn't feel any particular loyalty to Thorkin, but this was dangerous territory for the Sergeant. Plotting to subvert lawful command was punishable by death. Not later, after a trial, but now, in the field. For all his obvious competence, Thorkin was acting the fool.

"Before I answer that question, sir," said Atticus, "are you sure you want to ask it?"

Rail's eyes narrowed. "Maybe that answers it well enough. I can't trust Thorkin now," he said, "and that might leave me having to trust you."

"You could do worse," said Atticus.

"Could I? You're a vagabond, Bragg. A fallen man, and apparently penniless." Rail dropped his eyes to Atticus's suit. "A man of my station shouldn't have anything to do with you. I resent it."

Atticus held his tongue. He had wormed into position at last, and he didn't intend to give Rail a reason to push him back out. But he was enraged by the Captain's arrogance: if this hadn't been about survival, but only money, Atticus would have called the man out of the ship to answer for his words.

"But I will admit to you," said Rail, "that I need advice. I don't like it, but I do."

"In that case, sir. I recommend—"

Rail held up a hand to stop him. "We're not leaving, Bragg. I promise you that you will not do any better than Thorkin did on that subject."

"Not what I was going to say, sir. I recommend you leave Sergeant Thorkin where he is. Breaking apart the platoon's command structure is not a good idea right now. We're in a bad spot, and every edge counts."

Rail looked dubious. "Then what should I do with him?"

"Nothing, sir. He's doing more than a competent job as your platoon sergeant, as far as I can tell. I'll try to keep him tamped down."

"Fine, you do that," said Rail. "Thank you, Bragg. You can clear out now. I haven't elevated you to the high counsels yet. Report to your circle of dirt."

"Aye, sir."

Atticus left the ship with his head buzzing: things had taken a sudden sharp turn in the last five minutes. He felt uneasy about being co-opted by the Captain, since it seemed to Atticus he might be forced to choose a side opposite Walt and Grippa. But he was pleased he'd contrived to protect the impetuous platoon sergeant from the man's own understandable, but potentially disastrous, determination not to repeat a mistake of the past. Now Atticus would have to sit on Thorkin, or things would continue to fall apart.

The rest of the day passed without incident. Thorkin kept the platoon busy piling rocks in front of their holes, and scraping dirt from the trench walls until they met the bottom at crisp right angles. Like any good NCO, he appreciated the need to keep the soldiers occupied, despite their grumbling. Thorkin was still doing his job well, for all his own unrest.

For a time, both suns stood in the sky, making Atticus queasy and unbalanced on top of everything else. He sat in the hole with Walt, idling. He had told the gunner about Thorkin's overtures, and his own new-found, if precarious, status with the Captain.

Walt had taken the news philosophically: "That boy in there is scared, and he has no good idea what to do, but you're right, he doesn't deserve a mutiny. That ill-wind would blow nobody any good."

Hearing this, Atticus decided he could trust the gunner with nearly anything, and this realization gave him an unexpected measure of happiness in the midst of what was otherwise a raging mess. It had been a long time since he had a friend he could trust.

"I'm glad to hear you say that," he said. "That damn platoon sergeant has turned into a loose cannon. Who would have thought it?"

"Not I," said Walt. "He looks like he would salute and jump out an airlock without a suit, if ordered."

"Those are the worse kind," said Atticus. "They're black and white thinkers, who put up a good front but have trouble adapting to the unexpected. They need a strong officer."

"And scorn a weak one," said Walt.

"Exactly."

"So he's after you."

"Yes," said Atticus. "Or he might take over the platoon himself, but I think that's unlikely. He wants someone else to take the fall for it and I'm the perfect candidate, ready to hand. I have nothing to lose, right? I'm already disgraced." Atticus crumbled a clod of soil in his hand. "Jesus, this goddamn job gets worse all the time."

"They all tend downhill," said Walt. "I'm sure we haven't hit bottom yet."

"That's really cheering, Walter. Thanks."

"I'm here to help!" said the gunner. He leaned over to slap Atticus's bad shoulder. "C'mon, let's eat."

"If you call it that."

They broke tubes and sipped reclaimed water as the suns set behind the red mountains. The blue one went first, in a small mercy.

"Do me a favor?" said Atticus.

"I thought this was one."

"Another one. Go hunker down on the far side of the ship tonight."

"And leave our palatial hole in the ground?" said Walt. "Why?"

"I want you over there keeping an eye on Thorkin. The way he's been gnawing at the bit, I want to know if he's still stirring the pot elsewhere."

"Oh God!" said Walt. "You're right, there's no way I can sleep in that snarl of metaphors." He slung his mech-gun from the hole and followed it, stalking away without speaking another word, his ammunition belts clicking gently.

Atticus chuckled. He liked the gunner, for all the man's odd dreams and quirky manner. The mercenary profession was dominated by plodding meatheads and trigger-happy psychopaths. That made Atticus himself stand out. The job ferrying the diplomat had fallen into his lap precisely because he wasn't a meathead or a psychopath. And he could drive. He growled at the memory and shifted against the bottom of the hole, looking for something close enough to comfort that he could sleep.

He was awakened by the scrape of boots. Two dark figures, silhouetted briefly against the night sky, passed the lip of the hole, running toward the ship. Atticus grabbed his rifle and climbed out to follow. These could only be the soldiers from the listening post in front of him, bugging out. Something had happened out there, and it wasn't good.

He found them talking to Thorkin under the hatch. Atticus tapped his helmet and the Sergeant keyed him in.

"—sounded like tapping on the ground," said one of the soldiers, breathless. "We couldn't figure it. Then it got louder, and closer. All across our front. Then—"

"Why didn't you report this?" demanded Thorkin.

"It happened so fast, Sergeant! When I flipped my lights on, there they were!" The soldier jabbed both arms forward. "Right there!"

The other nodded agreement. "Yeah, three or four meters out. They were coming right at us!"

Thorkin flailed his arms in confusion. "What? What was coming right at you?"

"These things, I dunno, like crabs. But there were hundreds of them. They were coming right at us!"

"You mentioned that," said Thorkin. "So you ran from crabs?"

"No! God, Sergeant, they were—"

"Hit the floods," said Atticus. Something was coming, and they needed to see it before it got to the perimeter, whatever it was.

"Yeah," said Thorkin. He took three steps toward a bank of batteries and flipped a toggle switch. The ground in front of the trench for thirty meters lit up, as if the planet's two suns had chosen that very moment to shine only upon their little ship. Atticus blinked and shaded his eyes.

"Sweet Jesus!" said Thorkin.

"That's them!" said the first soldier.

In the bowl, beyond the trench, the rocky ground seethed with small pale creatures, thirty to forty centimeters tall. Their gait was crab-like, but they walked more upright, like a praying mantis, with two small arms that waved. But the soldiers had been wrong about one thing: there weren't hundreds of them. There were thousands, jostling and climbing over one another like insects, the whole boiling toward the ship like the rising surge of a broken wave.

"We don't have enough firepower for this," said Atticus. He keyed for Walt. "You got incoming on your side?"

"Incoming?" replied Walt. "Negative. What's with the lights? What's going on over there?"

"Good question. Wake up everyone and sit tight on alert. Tell me if you see anything."

"Aye. What—"

Atticus cut him off and turned to Thorkin. "We should get everyone in the ship! We can't stop this. There's far too many of them."

"Negative, Bragg," said Thorkin. He looked away, and his voice came up on c-channel. "Everyone, eyes wide! We have incoming from 186. Report incoming on other bearings. Captain Rail to the cannon please! ASAP! Flamethrowers, assemble to me!" The Sergeant turned back to Atticus. "We'll fry the bastards as they come in."

A figure dropped from the hatch and stepped into the glare of the floods. It was Rail. He stared at the oncoming wave. It was twenty meters from the trench and Atticus could see individuals more clearly now: they were segmented like insects, but walked on legs that crooked up like a spider's. The horde made no move to avoid the trench but came on steadily, as if to storm it. Two dozen rifles and flamethrowers waited. The soldiers in the trench shuffled nervously, glancing back. A few edged toward the rear wall, drawing others with them.

"Sir!" said Atticus. "Recommend we get everyone in the ship! There's no sense fighting those things—assuming they're hostile."

Thorkin grabbed the back of Atticus's suit and shoved him away. "Mind your place, Bragg!"

Atticus stumbled three steps and caught himself before falling into the trench.

Thorkin addressed Rail again: "Sir, the flame units are here. We can hold them off. We dug this damn trench, now let's use it!"

Rail swung his helmet around to look at Thorkin. The Sergeant's neck lights shone back at him, illuminating suspicion and resistance on the Captain's face. Rail was clearly wondering about the Sergeant's motives. The break between the platoon's leadership was open now and bleeding, perhaps fatally.

"Negative, Sergeant," said Rail. "Get the platoon in the ship!"

"Sir! We can—"

"Get the platoon in the ship!" shouted Rail. Fear gave his voice a ragged edge.

But it was too late: critical seconds had passed, and the leading edge of the pale carpet of creatures was now less than three meters from the edge of the trench. They had eyes, black and cold, and a round mouth that seemed to work in anticipation. The soldiers in the trench lifted their weapons.

"Burn'em!" shouted Thorkin, and four brilliant jets of orange napalm crossed over the heads of soldiers in the trench to play on the oncoming horde. Dozens of the creatures caught fire and died, keening in agony.

But it wasn't enough. The first creature to reach the trench gathered itself on the edge, and leaped. It landed on a soldier's chest, clinging to her suit with short claws. She screamed, pushing at it, but the thing held fast. It opened a round mouth and thrust out a lance-like proboscis that punched through the tough fabric of the woman's suit and into her chest. The creature paused for a moment then, perfectly still, then retracted the proboscis and leaped away. Almost immediately, the woman's hands fell to her sides and her helmet sagged. She dropped to her knees, then fell over to curl into herself on the ground.

"That's it!" said Atticus. The soldier was now afflicted. He was certain of it. It all fit together now: the nighttime occurrences, the absence of large tracks, the erasure of puncture marks by the self-sealing suit function. There would even be a loss of pressure long enough for Craddock to detect it an hour or more later. Exo-suits were no protection against this attack, and it was imperative everyone get into the ship.

Now.

"Captain!" shouted Atticus, but a chaotic babble had risen on c-channel. Two more insects leaped and clung to soldiers, opening their mouths to puncture their victims' suits. Then another jumped. And another. Each choosing a different victim, who was then ignored by the others. The creatures were falling into the trench by the dozen now.

"Get out!" shouted Atticus over the tumult, waving his arms. "Up and out! Up and out! Let's go!" He reached down to help a soldier scramble out before turning his neck lights on Rail's face. "Captain! We have to get into the ship! Call a retreat, or we're all gonna be like those soldiers in the ship!"

Rail licked his lips and stared back at Atticus, wide-eyed. "Yes, yes. You're right, Bragg." But the man only wandered away in the direction of the ship, overwhelmed by events.

Atticus turned back to the fighting, but it was already a catastrophe. There were hundreds of creatures in the trench now, with thousands more coming behind. Plasma lanced in every direction, threatening everyone, and those with flamethrowers used them indiscriminately, flailing fiery napalm to keep the creatures from leaping.

A fully intact exo-suit would protect its wearer from a direct hit with napalm. But the unlucky ones who were punched by the creatures lost their suit integrity for the ten to twenty seconds needed for the self-healing function to work. That was all the time they needed to die. Burning jellied petroleum found its way into the suits of several and they fled across the perimeter, screaming and burning, before stumbling to roll on the ground, clawing at their suits. But they were doomed: when the self-sealing function finished its work, the burning agony was trapped inside. There was nothing anyone else could do.

Near Atticus, a soldier dropped her rifle to struggle against a clinging creature. He took two steps toward her and reached to pull the thing from her before it could drive its proboscis home. He pried it free, but the creature wiggled in his hands with astonishing power, shrieking and thrashing its head, trying get its mouth around to puncture his own suit. He threw the thing into the trench to burn with the others.

Walt appeared beside him, carrying a plasma rifle he must have scavenged from the dead.

"We need to get everyone into the ship!" shouted Atticus. "Lay down some fire! Keep those bugs back!"

"Aye, boss!" said Walt. He turned to put down a curtain of plasma in the direction of the trench.

Atticus looked back to the ship. Rail stood below the e-hatch, helping a soldier into the ship. He had still made no call for retreat. Suddenly, an orange jet of napalm played over Atticus's leg. He looked down to see a creature explode and fall away in fiery pieces. He raised a thumb of thanks to his unknown savior before grabbing a newly afflicted by the arm and dragging him toward the ship. "C'mon!"

But Rail shook his head at their approach. "No, Bragg! We'll save only those who can fight!" He shoved the confused soldier away.

"We don't leave wounded behind, Captain!" shouted Atticus. "Call retreat to the ship, sir! So we can organize this. Otherwise, we're all going down!

Rail ignored him, passing his plasma rifle to someone in the ship.

There was a heavy tap on Atticus's shoulder and he flinched away, punching at his suit, but it was Thorkin.

"Leave him!" said the Sergeant.

"Goddammit, Thorkin, that man needs to lead this platoon!"

"Leave him! He's locked up! We need to form a tight perimeter to get everyone on board!"

Atticus nodded agreement, and together they turned back to the fighting. The remaining soldiers had already pulled themselves into a knot by instinct, and they held back the rising tide of creatures with a profligate expenditure of plasma and napalm. Atticus made a quick survey of the trench line: the attack was coming from one direction, and he knew that was the only thing keeping this together. If the creatures had assaulted the ship from all sides, it would be over by now.

He keyed e-channel. It was less crowded. Comm discipline had been the first thing to go.

"Listen up!" he said. "Fall back one at a time when I tap you! Repeat, one at a time! If everyone bolts, everyone goes down!"

He tapped the nearest shoulder, a blonde with a thin face and a frightened frown. She flinched at his touch before flashing him a tired smile. She lifted her arms to the hatch and hands reached down to help her up.

The Captain had already gone in.

Atticus tapped another soldier, taking the man's place in the knot. But the creatures were wary now, and they held back. Their numbers had been reduced dramatically by the defenders' fire, and the tide of insects no longer marched inexorably forward. Instead they milled in the glare of the floodlights, less sure of themselves, trampling the remains of their dead compatriots. The soldiers whose suits had been punctured now lay in pools of open ground, carefully avoided by the swirling mass of creatures. The newly afflicted seemed asleep, only moving an arm or leg from time to time.

Atticus tapped another shoulder then raised his rifle to scorch a line of five insects creeping forward. He worked fast now, tapping every few seconds while the swarm seemed uncertain. Soon the knot of soldiers behind the trench was down to four. The creatures edged closer now, seeming to find more will.

"You, and you, go!" said Atticus, pushing two of the four. They bolted for the hatch, leaving Atticus and one other. He tugged at the man's arm to draw him toward the ship and they stepped backward together, firing, until the hatch was above them. The creatures moved strongly again as resistance fell to nearly nothing.

"Up you go!" said Atticus.

"Thank you, sir!" said the man.

Atticus fired a wide volley to discourage the nearest insects and waited five seconds. Now it was his turn. "Covering fire!" he shouted.

Three muzzles poked from the hatch to fire at the approaching creatures. Atticus slung his rifle and reached up to grab the lip of the hatch, but he found the barrel of a fourth rifle aimed directly at him.

He looked along its length into Rail's eyes.

They stared at each other for a long moment before the Captain pulled back his rifle to offer a hand. But the message hadn't been subtle: the Captain would enforce his demand for Atticus's loyalty by whatever means necessary. Atticus wondered whether the greatest danger to the platoon now wasn't these creatures, but its own leadership.

As the hatch door closed behind him, one of the insects jumped up to clang against its underside. A long needle-like proboscis thrust through the gap, searching across the deck, but the heavy door fell to snap off the organ with a crack. The ugly, dead thing rolled across the deck, scattering the crowd in the cockpit.

Atticus scrambled to his feet and pushed into the troop compartment, where Craddock stood over the five original afflicted and another who had somehow gotten into the ship during the fight. They were all tightly belted into their seats now. The medic wasn't taking any chances.

"Well, now we know what happened to them," said Craddock, glancing at Atticus. "The self-sealing function fooled me, for sure—with help from the Captain since he wouldn't let me remove their suits. That kept me from discovering their puncture wounds. He still won't let me do it."

"What about the first two?" said Atticus, nodding to them. "Same status?"

"Yeah, still perfectly stable. Physically healthy even. Good vitals. But they're just gone. Mentally, you know, as if—"

"As if something wanted their bodies without interference."

"Exactly."

Atticus looked down the row of afflicted. They appeared bored, looking at nothing. One stared at her fingers, moving them slowly, as if they were new and fascinating. He thought about the blown-out carcass in the valley. These soldiers needed a med base as soon as they could get there.

Suddenly, there was a stricken wail on the circuit: "Goddammit, get this thing off me! I killed Richards! I burned him! I fucking burned him!"

Atticus looked around the troop bay. Near the far wall, a tall soldier was frantically stripping off a flamethrower unit and throwing the pieces at the deck. He jerked and shuffled his feet in agitation. Others moved to stand around him, reaching out.

"Quiet on the comm channels!" said Rail from the cockpit. "Stow that talk!"

The man drew his helmet back and slammed it into a bulkhead. "I saw him burn! I saw it! Oh God, I saw it!"

Rail barged through the cockpit hatch. "Thorkin, silence that man! It's not good for morale! Listen up, people, we were surprised and it was a tough fight. But we recovered, pulled it together, and gave'em hell."

"Some of us did anyway," said a voice.

Rail jerked his helmet around, searching the compartment. "Who said that?"

But the others only stared at him, frozen. There was silence on the channels. Atticus frowned: the comment had been the first murmur of discontent from the ranks, no doubt sowed by Thorkin's own discontent. There was no telling how much damage the Sergeant had done, or would do.

"I don't want to hear that kind of talk again!" said the Captain. "Or you will all suffer for it! Sergeant Thorkin?"

"Sir."

"The platoon will remain in the ship for the rest of this dark period. Those things may be gone by morning."

"Aye, sir, but what about Manzak and the others out there?"

"No one leaves this ship as long as those things are out there. No one."

"But, sir—"

Rail whirled on Thorkin, pointing. "I gave an order, Sergeant, and I expect you to carry it out without comment or argument! Do I make myself clear?"

Thorkin let a moment of dead air last longer than was proper before responding. "Clear, sir."

"Good. No one leaves the ship. Have the troops clean their weapons, recharge, and get some sleep. We may have to fight our way out tomorrow."

"Aye, sir."

Rail had brought the platoon sergeant down a notch in front of whomever might be in sympathy with him; but after this fiasco, Thorkin would re-double his efforts to topple the Captain. And Atticus hadn't forgotten the shove at the trench, when he had stepped on Thorkin's toes. The Sergeant would be incensed when he realized Atticus had risen to fill the void the platoon sergeant left behind. Perhaps Thorkin would see it as a betrayal. Atticus wondered what Grippa would think about it.

Ten minutes later, Grippa came through the cockpit hatch. She caught Atticus's eye and beckoned him to follow her. He rose from his seat and she led him through an adjacent hatch into a crew ready room. She swung the hatch door shut behind them.

The space was tiny. There was a small writing desk that folded down from a bulkhead, a chair bolted to the deck, and two hideaway bunks. The bottom bunk was pulled out and covered with tousled blankets. She had been sleeping in here. A set of pink pajamas were draped over the back of the chair.

"Nice place," he said.

She picked up the pajamas and stuffed them into a locker beneath the bunk.

"Don't straighten up just for me," he said. "I'm just jealous you have a place to lay your head. I've been sleeping on floors. Not even the nice ones."

Grippa sat on the bunk and crossed her arms. "What if those things don't leave, Atticus?"

He leaned on the hatch. "Then we sit in here and stare at each other until we're found and pulled out. Hopefully, we'll be alive when that happens. But that's the easy question. The harder question is what if those things do leave. Then we have a choice to make—or Rail does—and it doesn't look like he's going to make the right one."

She picked at a blanket. "They won't find us, you know. Not in time. The comm gear won't get a signal past that barrier no matter how much he tinkers with it. Only dumb luck will find us."

"Well, that's iced it," said Atticus. "There's no luck on this planet. Not the good kind."

"So what's the answer?"

"The Captain needs to be led in the direction of his duty," said Atticus. "He's off course."

"You'd need luck for that too," she said. "He's a stubborn one. What's that Sergeant's temperature?"

"Near boiling," said Atticus, "but he's looking for someone else to pull the trigger on the Captain. I'm Candidate One in his eyes, since I'm damaged goods already."

"He's not wrong that you're qualified for the job."

"But I'm not in charge. Your father sent me here to support Rail. I intend to do that."

"You're stubborn too," she said. "Can't Craddock remove the Captain? As medic."

"He can sideline Rail legally, but the circumstances are extremely limited, since Craddock's not an officer. He'd need an ironclad reason with flashing lights and glitter. He doesn't have that, and I don't intend to help him get it."

There was a knock on the hatch and they exchanged guilty glances. Atticus pushed the door open carefully, but it was only Walt. The gunner ducked into the space uninvited to look around.

"Why wasn't I invited to this pajama party?" he said.

Atticus laughed, closing the hatch. "If only you knew, Walter. What's the word?"

"Good news. The light's starting to come up and those things are leaving in a hurry."

"What about the troopers out there?" said Grippa.

"They're still there. Seems once you get stung, that's it. You're left alone."

"To become a zombie," she said.

Walt held out his bitten arm. "At least they don't try to eat you alive."

"Are they going back the way they came?" said Atticus. "In the direction of that long valley?"

"Appears so," said Walt. "You're thinking about that cave, aren't you, At?"

"Yeah. What do you think?"

"I'm gonna say no," said Walt, "because I don't want to go in there."

"What cave?" said Grippa.

Atticus told her.

"So we crashed beside a nest of those things?" she said.

"Or a hive," said Walt.

She waved him off. "Whatever. So what's happened here? The first ones were stung by scouts, and now an army shows up to get the rest of us?"

"Looks that way," said Atticus.

She pointed a finger at him. "There's your lever for Rail! We can't stay here. We're on their front lawn and they'll be back. We're trapped in here!"

"Not completely," said Atticus. "We haven't seen them in daylight. Everyone's been stung at night."

"How unpoetical," said Walt. "Besieged by tiny vampires."

They ignored him. "Atticus!" said Grippa. "Come to your senses! We need to get out of here!" She twirled a finger in a circle, encompassing the three of them. "Us. Let's go. Now. I don't want to sit in here and rot with Rail, or get stung."

Atticus was tempted by her offer more than he thought he might be. She was lovely, and could fly a ship like nobody else, and her impulsiveness drew him to her. But no, he couldn't run away with her. He'd already decided there was at least one solid reason to stay: Rail needed his help, and without it the platoon would suffer. The troops didn't deserve that, plus Atticus didn't leave people behind. That never seemed to factor into his reputation.

He shook his head. "No, I can't do that. Rail needs me. The platoon needs me."

She frowned. "Thorkin's read you all wrong, hasn't he?"

He nodded. "Most people seem to."

"I'll try not to do that. So what now, Major Bragg?"

"I don't know," he said. He blew out a breath and rubbed his face. "I do know I could use a drink."

"In that case," she said, "luck hasn't left you entirely." She bent to flip open a locker door and pulled out a green bottle. She passed it to him.

Atticus turned the bottle in his hand to look at the label. "You can't afford premium hooch like this on a lieutenant's pay!"

"It's good to be the king's daughter."

Atticus grinned and pulled out the old-style cork. Maybe things would start looking up after all.

When the yellow sun was fully up, the creatures were gone. Atticus bent to peer out from a tiny armored window in the troop compartment. He could see the barrel of the cannon and part of the trench beyond it. The ground was black with plasma scorch, charred insects, and charred insect parts. He leaned to shift his view and found a soldier sitting on the ground amid the ruin. The man had his knees pulled up, with his arms locked around them. Like the cannon, he stared into the waste, seeming not to care he sat alone on a barren and hostile planet.

"Rail's called a meeting in the cockpit," said Walt, who had drawn up next to Atticus. "Not that you're invited."

"Thanks."

The gunner swung his helmet back and forth to take in the view from the window. "Look at that poor bastard out there. You'd think nothing was wrong."

"I suppose that's the grace of it," said Atticus. "They have no idea."

"None of us do. We're all waiting for the hammer to fall from somewhere."

"You're a ray of sunshine this morning, Walter," said Atticus, turning away from the window. "I'm off to crash the party in the cockpit."

"You do that, and it ain't Walter."

Atticus moved across the compartment and ducked through the cockpit hatch to find Rail, Thorkin, Craddock, Grippa, and the three squad leaders jammed into the small space. There was only room for him to lean awkwardly against the hatchway behind

Craddock. Grippa smiled at him and nodded, perhaps as some kind of message, then keyed him into their conversation. Atticus put the pink pajamas firmly out of his mind.

"I know some of you disagree with my decision," said Rail, ignoring Atticus's entry. "Maybe all of you do." He looked around, but no one spoke or moved. "But command is a difficult burden."

Shit! thought Atticus, *just in time for a speech.* He settled against the hatch.

"A commander has to weigh many variables," continued Rail, "many factors, before coming to a decision. And he must gather as much information as he can, and make a decision based on what he knows, which may constitute an incomplete picture of the overall situation."

That's straight from Chapter 2, section 3, of A Field Manual for Infantry Officers. I know the crusty bastard who wrote that. I wonder where he is now.

"Here's the information I have," said Rail. He ticked the items on his fingers. "We have no comms. We don't know where we are. No one else knows where we are. We have less than a week of food. And we're down nineteen from the crash, and those things, whatever they are." That was five things so he brought up another hand. "Finally, we've been told there are creatures in the mountains impervious to our weapons." He glanced at Atticus. "So the question is, where are we safest in this situation?"

Nope, wrong question, Atticus thought. *The art of infantry command lies in managing risk, not avoiding it. That's Chapter 4, section 2, of the Manual. And it's precisely what separates the adults from the boys like Rail who are playing with plasma.*

"This ship is our fortress," said Rail. "It protects us. So we will remain here, in our fortress, to be located by search and rescue. There are too many unknowns to be blundering into the mountains. Also, we will ration our food further, starting now, to stretch it several more days." When he stopped speaking, the others looked away, avoiding his eye. Rail didn't seem to notice. "Bragg," he said.

"Sir?"

"I'm glad you're here. I have a job for you."

Shit.

"I want you to backtrack that horde and find where they came from. I'm guessing they live underground, or in a cave. Didn't you see a cave on your scout?"

"We did, sir," said Atticus. "That possibility has occurred to me."

"Go check it out. I want you to seal the entrance, if that's where these things are coming from."

"Seal it, sir?"

"Yes," said Rail. "We don't have anything but grenades, but they should do. Take whatever you think you need. We can stop another attack, right now."

Damn, Atticus thought. Rail was already working to preempt his argument for leaving. "Sir—"

"No argument, Bragg. My mind is settled. Go find those bugs."

"Aye, sir," said Atticus. He wasn't happy about the assignment, but maybe it would turn into nothing. Or maybe he could turn it into nothing. There were options here.

Rail turned to Thorkin. "Sergeant, get everyone out of the ship and reestablish the perimeter defense. Craddock, collect the newly afflicted and store them in the bay with the others. The Lieutenant and I will continue to work on comms in here. Bragg, get moving."

There was a chorus of "aye, sirs," and Atticus swung down from the hatch to find Walt.

Thorkin caught up with him halfway to the hole. The man's face was set and grim.

"Bragg," he said, "this raggedy-ass plan of his will get even more of my soldiers killed, and maybe you too. That son of a bitch is stalling, and one of two things will happen. Either those crawlies will come back, maybe during the day, or the real bugs will roll over that ridge and find us bottled up in a ruined ship with a single, tiny exit. Both of those things are bad."

Atticus turned on him. "I'm doing what I can, Sergeant."

"It's not good enough," said Thorkin. "Right now, our biggest problem isn't bugs in a cave, but the Captain sitting in there making time with that pilot. I call that dereliction of duty. What about you, Major?" He stressed the title. "What would you call it?"

"Look, I know where you're going with this, Sergeant, but I could be summarily executed for attempting to usurp command. No questions asked and no one would shed a tear. I'm just a merc."

Thorkin looked at him, considering, then nodded. "All right, Bragg. Have it your way. But I need to know whether I can count on you when the time comes."

"You're getting way ahead of yourself, Thorkin. This thing's not critical yet. Not even close."

But Thorkin's eyes didn't waver. "Can I count on you, Major? Can we count on you?"

So it seemed Thorkin had allies in the ranks, hidden for now. Atticus had suspected that, but it was good to know. "Listen," he said. "I understand you've had some bad experiences, Sergeant. We all have. Hell has nothing on war. But I won't be pushed around. Not by you, not by anybody. You do what you think you have to do, and I'll do what I have to do. But don't try to box me in, and don't count me on your team. The answer is no. I won't do your dirty work for you, or help you do it."

Thorkin's nostrils flared. "Sorry, Major, I must've mistaken you for someone else."

"You must have."

The Sergeant pointed a finger at him. "One more thing, Bragg. A fair warning. I won't sacrifice anyone to pull your ass out of that cave. If you stir up a hornet's nest in there, we'll hop inside and lock the doors." He jerked a thumb at the ship.

Atticus nodded. "Understood."

Thorkin turned on his heel and strutted away with as much nonchalance as his suit would allow.

Atticus growled and keyed Walt. "Thorkin's been at me again. Everyone thinks they know me, but they're wrong."

There was a pause, then Walt spoke: "The me to you defies the I of me; it hems and shades, until not I you see."

"Thanks. Just what I needed."

"I'm delighted," said Walt.

"You won't be delighted about our new job," said Atticus.

"*Our* job?" said Walt. "I told you, you're not volunteering me for anything else. Period. End of story."

"We'll need a flamethrower."

"I'm definitely out now," said Walt. "No good has ever come of those words."

"Rail is sending us to block up that cave," said Atticus, "assuming that's where the bugs are coming from."

Walt made a disgusted noise. "It's a witless idea. Any animal that lives underground has more than one exit. It's science."

"Well, maybe that cave is *our* exit, if you know what I mean. The one we get visited from. And the other exit is klicks away."

"Good Lord!" said Walt. "There's a hundred ways this could go wrong."

"Great!" said Atticus. "I knew you'd be in. Pack your stuff."

CHAPTER SIX

They did take a flamethrower. The mechanism of it was simple: it was a long, triggered nozzle attached by a hose to a napalm cannister that clipped to Atticus's web gear, below an extra load-out of grenades. An O2 can was slung under the nozzle to feed the jelly stream on low oxygen planets like this one. Atticus clipped two extra napalm cannisters to his back. The leader of Second Squad, a thin-faced man with a scar across his nose, insisted on spares when Atticus asked to borrow the unit.

"It's always better to take more than you need," the man said. "That thing's no better than a club if you run dry. But don't ask me to go, if that's what you're thinking. I ain't volunteering."

Atticus smiled at him. "I wouldn't think of it."

Walt made an ugly noise.

"All right," said Atticus. "We're good to go. Thanks for the jelly!"

The squad leader flipped him a salute. "Good luck, Major."

Tracking the insects proved to be laughably easy. Their passage had stirred the ground in a wide swath that led across the bowl, over the sliding ridge, and down the wide valley. Atticus and Walt followed this track two klicks straight to the cave on the mountainside, where it narrowed and funneled into the entrance, answering that question.

"All right!" said Walt. "Go blow the thing and let's get the hell out of here."

Atticus shook his head. "No. That's solid rock there. Grenades won't crack it. We need a place where the cave narrows, with loose rock to collapse. I'm going in."

"In? You said nothing at all about going in. I'm quite sure of that, or I would have declined forcefully."

"I thought it was obvious."

"Obviously foolhardy," said Walt. "How have you lived this long?"

"Fine. I'll do it all myself." Atticus tested the flamethrower on a large rock, making a dark scorch mark and a dense cloud of black smoke that rolled into the tan sky. *Whoops!* He wouldn't be doing that again unless forced to: it was a beacon for any Repsian that might be passing through.

Walt grumbled something as Atticus moved toward the cave entrance and put his helmet around the edge to look inside. The light of the yellow sun allowed him to see only ten meters into a narrow vestibule before darkness took hold. The floor of the entrance was flat and compacted, and free of large debris. A chaos of tiny tracks led into the darkness.

He took three careful steps inside, casting his shadow across the floor. He murmured for his neck lights and they pushed the darkness back further to reveal a tunnel that widened as it drove into the mountainside. *Damn.* Not what he wanted to see. He needed a narrow, crumbling squeeze.

Atticus paused to give thought to bagging this little adventure and retreating to the ship. The insects were definitely in here, and now he was in here with them, this thing seemed excessively stupid, orders or no orders. He decided he would go in only a short distance to look for something quick and easy. If it wasn't there, he would report no success to Rail.

"You okay?" said Walt.

"Peachy. Going in."

"Terrific. Maybe you should drop breadcrumbs."

"No," said Atticus, stepping deeper into the cave. "It was string."

"Eh?"

"You know. Theseus. The minotaur. String."

"I'm impressed," said Walt. "Who gave you a Classical education?"

"I did," said Atticus. "I wasn't always this cross-grained and cynical."

"I'll sit here and try to imagine that."

Aiming the nozzle of the flamethrower at the darkness ahead, Atticus moved past the vestibule into the throat of the cave. The walls around him were smooth gray stone, perhaps granite. It would be far too strong for grenades to collapse.

Just beyond the last reach of natural light, the tunnel curved to the left, disappearing into deeper darkness. He shifted the flamethrower nozzle to his right hand and poked it around the bend into firing position, then he followed it, sweeping his lights quickly around the corner. But nothing waited for him in that darkness.

He stepped on, slowly, carefully. Looking and listening. What he needed to find was a wiggle hole, or a narrow crack—something to concentrate the shock of explosion. But the passage steadfastly refused to narrow. His heart was pounding and this was looking more and more like a no-go. He took a step backward.

"We got a problem out here, boss," said Walt.

Atticus stopped. "What?"

"One of those armored things is prowling around on the mountainside above me."

Shit! "Has it seen you?"

"It's not charging down to eat me," said Walt, "so I would say no, not yet."

"Come to the cave entrance," said Atticus. "It's clear."

"Right," said Walt. "I knew I'd end up in there somehow."

Atticus tried to remember where the yellow sun had been when he'd entered the cave, but he had no grasp on the comings and goings of the damn thing. The amount of daylight remaining was an unknown variable, together with the wanderings of the armored beast.

"I'm in," said Walt, "and I don't like it. How far back are you?"

"Thirty meters. Around a corner."

"What's it like?"

"Come and see," said Atticus. "Kinda boring really, if you forget about the life-sucking vampires. I thought caves had stalactites and shit."

Thirty seconds later, Walt was standing beside Atticus, looking around. "There's no surface water here to make stalactites," he said. "Also you need limestone for that, and this ain't it."

"Thank you, Geology Jim," said Atticus. "Shall we crack a tube while waiting for the beast to depart?"

"I guess."

Atticus dug into his mesh bag. "You want ham and eggs, or chow mein?"

"Seriously, At? You didn't burn that bag?"

"Hell no! This is my lucky—" Atticus froze with his hand in the bag, listening. Then the noise came again: hard nails scraping over dry, gritty ground, followed by the click of something smooth and hard bumping against stone.

The beast was in the cave.

"Of course!" said Walt, throwing up his hands. "Everybody loves a cave!"

"Look who's cynical now," said Atticus. "Let's discuss options."

"Options?" said Walt. "You mean there's more than one? I guess we haven't tried the flamethrower."

Atticus shook his head. "I'm dubious, and that's a last hope I'd rather not explode. Not quite yet anyway."

The scraping and clicking were louder now, and Atticus turned to aim his neck lights deeper into the cave. It was more of the same as far as he could see. "Follow me," he said.

"I have been," said Walt. "Look where it's gotten me."

They moved deeper into the mountain, their neck lights glaring a harsh white on the gray rock. For a time the tunnel remained taller than their helmets, sometimes far taller, and it was wide enough they could walk side by side with a few centimeters between them. And the smooth walls amplified their small sounds: footfalls, the scrape of heavy fabric against stone, and the gentle clicking of Walt's ammo belts.

"I suppose I don't have to say," said the gunner, after a long silence, "that it's likely we're just pushing our graves deeper into the mountain."

"Yet you said it anyway."

"Yes, I did. Everyone needs someone speaking truth into his ear."

"I could use about six more of your truth-speakers," said Atticus, "armed with plasma cannons and demo-packs. But we don't have that, so I don't see any choice but to push on. If it discovers we're here, things are likely to get desperate and dicey. That's bad in a cave. It's bad anywhere. But as it is, we can do some looking and thinking as we go. Maybe something will turn up."

Walt didn't reply, and they went on, passing through vaulted rooms and meandering corridors of stone. Soon they were wading through broad, shallow pools of clear water that reflected their neck lights. It was the first standing water Atticus had seen, and he suspected the insects would be near it. He held up a hand and they stopped to listen. For a few moments, Atticus heard nothing but his own pulse, then a soft splash echoed in the darkness behind them, followed by a small grunt and the sound of water being lapped up.

"He thirsts," said Walt.

"Damn. Let's move."

They walked on, passing through a rough tunnel that widened, then widened again, and finally emptied into a large chamber.

"Holy Jesus!" said Walt.

Atticus froze. The insects were here, gathered thickly on the floor to the limit of his neck lights. There were thousands of them, maybe tens of thousands, and the nearest was only meters from where he stood. Atticus's heart hammered in his ears, but there was no reaction to their sudden appearance in the chamber. That enormous army stood stone still, and the only sound was a nearly subliminal rustling, like a thousand papery shells rubbing together lightly.

Atticus stood for thirty seconds, unmoving, before edging carefully toward the nearest creature. It continued to ignore his presence. "I think they're sleeping," he said. "Or dormant. Maybe because it's still daylight outside."

"Let's torch the place," said Walt, who stood in the tunnel still. "Much better than your grenade plan."

"There's far too many," said Atticus. "If we wake them before we're done—or if we run out of jelly—we'll be overwhelmed. It only takes one, you know."

Walt muttered something under his breath.

"Yes, I know, Walt, we're between the Devil and the deep blue sea here."

"And the Devil approaches," said the gunner.

Driving home his point, a questioning grunt echoed from the tunnel behind them. The beast was close.

"All we can do is move on," said Atticus.

"Fine. You go first."

There was little room to walk between the sleeping creatures, and in many places there was none. But after initially taking exquisite pains, they discovered that merely brushing the insects' rough, leathery skin wouldn't stir them from their somnolence. This increased their speed and soon they moved steadily across the floor of the chamber toward the far wall, easing the little creatures aside with shushings and gentle nudges.

"How well do you think that beast sees?" said Walt.

"Eh? I don't know. Why?"

"We're lit up like Rec City, At."

"Good point," said Atticus. "Yeah, turn'em off."

Atticus told his suit to kill his neck lights. Walt did the same, and the resulting darkness was complete. The subtle undercurrent of rustling seemed louder now, and more threatening. Atticus was wondering how things could possibly get worse when something brushed across his leg.

"Walt?" he said.

"Yeah. Dark, isn't it?"

"No, I felt something move. When do the suns set? Both of them."

"No idea," said Walt.

Just then, the armored beast entered the chamber from the tunnel. Atticus could hear it clearly: snuffling and scratching the dirty rock of the chamber floor with its claws. In their rush to stay ahead of the creature, it hadn't occurred to Atticus to wonder why this beast might want to venture into the lair of something so absurdly dangerous. But the question occurred to him now, and it was answered immediately by the sound of snapping bones and loud chewing. He almost laughed.

"You're kidding me!" said Walt.

"It's dinner time," said Atticus. "Imagine having to put on armor to eat."

"I feel that way about food tubes," said Walt. "So what now, boss? It's tucked in for a feast."

"Well," said Atticus, "an esteemed exo-biologist once told me it was science that every burrow has a back door." He felt a soft touch on his leg again, almost a caress, and he jerked away. "So let's go find it. Quickly. I'm getting more movement here."

"Me too," said Walt. "Okay, let's try the far wall, opposite the tunnel entrance. I mean, this has to be the main chamber, right? Here, take my hand."

Something whacked Atticus's chest from the darkness, knocking him back a step. It was Walt's arm. "Whoa there!" said Atticus.

"Come on, At! Take it! I'm getting nervous!"

Atticus reached out to catch Walt's arm as it swung to find him again. The gunner clasped his hand and pulled him forward anxiously; and they moved across the chamber, brushing aside insects with their boots. Atticus wondered how the things knew the outside world was growing dark, and when full darkness would come. Maybe it had already.

Atticus was listening to the beast gorge itself when his faceplate struck rock.

"Goddammit! Warn me!"

"Sorry," said Walt. "Okay, here's the plan. I'll go right. You go left. Don't lose contact with the wall."

"Right."

"No," said Walt. "You go left."

Atticus did go left, shuffling forward gingerly and trailing his gloved fingertips over the cave wall. Occasionally, his hand fell into a hollow space in the rock that seemed like an opening until it wasn't. This search for another exit wasn't a bad idea, but it was slow. They had no idea when ten thousand stinging insects would wake at once to take an interest in their visitors.

"Nothing yet?" said Walt.

"Nope."

"Bugger."

The sound of feeding was louder now, and Atticus decided his section of the wall had curved around to approach the mouth of the tunnel. "Turning back now," he said. "I'm getting too close to the beast."

"Okay. Reach higher this time."

Good idea. Atticus reached up to explore the wall above his head as he retraced his steps. In the end, they might have to turn on their lights and make a dash for the tunnel. Surely one of them would get past the beast. Atticus resolved it would be Walt, who really should be sitting on a barstool at the station, not backstopping Atticus's bid to escape abject poverty.

His fingertips closed over a lip of rock. Atticus stretched to reach deeper, expecting to meet hard stone, but nothing stopped his fingertips. "I might have something here," he said.

"Really? Nothing over here. I'll come your way."

The beast uttered a high-pitched roar. It sounded like annoyance, or distress.

"Hurry," said Atticus.

"I'm high-stepping it, boss. What do you have?"

"Something. Maybe a hole. Here, above my head."

A minute later Walt was perched on Atticus's shoulders, poking his head into the wall.

"Promising!" said the gunner. "I'm going in."

His boots pushed off and Atticus was left standing alone with ten thousand insects, and an agitated beast that was now snorting and stamping its feet. Dinner must be stirring on its plate.

"We might have a winner," said Walt, "but it's a tight fit. You'll have to suck in your gut."

Something dragged across Atticus's leg, making a dry, leathery sound. Something else probed gently at his boot. "Hey, Walt!" he said. "Come give me a lift up! The cast of thousands is stirring."

"Coming, boss."

It seemed to Atticus an hour before a finger finally tapped his helmet. He passed up the mech-gun and his rifle, and reached to grab Walt's outstretched hands.

Something grabbed his calf.

No!

Atticus kicked the leg frantically and swept a hand down, knocking away an insect. Another touched him gently. He spun away from it and put his back to the wall to bring up the flame-thrower nozzle. He pulled the trigger, aiming at the floor around his feet.

Napalm sprayed into the cave, illuminating the vast horde with a harsh orange light. They seemed awake now, but only swayed in place and stretched, like sleepers awakened in the deep of night. Those nearest Atticus burst into bright flame and burned like torches, illuminating the high ceiling of the chamber. He could see the armored beast retreating toward the tunnel. It stopped to look back and uttered a grunt of surprise when it saw Atticus, then turned to gallop into the tunnel and out of sight.

Walt knocked on Atticus's helmet. "Quit screwing around, At! Give me your hands!"

Atticus methodically scorched the floor around him before hooking the nozzle to his web belt and taking Walt's hands. The gunner's eyes and faceplate reflected the fiery orange light below, as if they were escaping the hottest depths of Hell. Atticus grinned. *Practice for later, when even the Devil can't keep his thumb on me.*

Walt scowled at him. "You're enjoying this, aren't you? Jesus, I'm dropping you like a bad sandwich when this is over."

Atticus laughed despite everything, and he lifted a boot to find a toehold in the rock. Soon he stood on the ledge next to Walt, looking down at the inferno blazing in the chamber below.

"You know," said Walt, "you really are a crazy bastard." He punched Atticus's bad shoulder. "But you managed to redeem yourself by finding this hole. Maybe. Pray this thing runs to the surface."

"I'm not the praying type," said Atticus.

Walt raised his hands to the ceiling of the chamber. "Hear us! Hear us! they wail, the undistressed! But we distressed, we fools, think we the blessed!"

"Bravo!" said Atticus. "Best one yet. Now lights on. You go first. I'll cover our backs."

Walt's neck lights came on to reveal a low opening at the back of the ledge. The gunner dropped to his knees and crawled into it. Waiting to follow, Atticus surveyed the dimming inferno below. His eye was caught by a dark presence, deeper in the chamber. The dying fires hinted at its shape, tall and spreading, and it loomed over the tiny insects beneath it; but its features were obscured by the darkness beyond the fires. Atticus wouldn't linger to see what it might be.

"They're all moving now," he told Walt, "and a whole bunch are coming this way."

"Then move your ass, Bragg!" said Walt. "I ain't waiting for you!"

Atticus knelt to enter the tunnel on his hands and knees. It was tight, but passable. The nozzle and the extra cannisters clinked against the rock walls. There would be no turning around to use the flamethrower. Their salvation now lay in speed.

Atticus crawled behind Walt, hearing only his own harsh breathing. The tunnel here wasn't much wider than he was, and he pushed himself along with his elbows and toes. If this passage narrowed, he and Walt would plug it until the end of time. Mission accomplished, in a way.

After twenty minutes of struggle, Atticus saw the soles of Walt's boots. They were sliding frantically against damp rock as the gunner wormed through a narrow choke. Atticus reached up to push, shoving him through.

"Thanks," said Walt. "That was awful. One more beer and I'd have been the cork in this tunnel."

Atticus crawled forward to examine the choke. His lights showed the tunnel widened considerably beyond it. "This might do," he said.

"Might do what?"

Atticus unhooked the napalm cannisters and pushed them through the narrow gap, then pulled himself after. The space beyond was wide enough he could turn around on his belly. He could hear the scratch of claws and the sigh of skin on rock, amplified by the close space.

It was now or never.

He stripped the grenades from his web belt and laid all but one in the narrowest point of the choke, then he placed the two spare napalm cannisters next to the grenades. The rock here was less granite-like, but it was probably still too hard for grenades alone to crack. The potential energy locked in the pressurized napalm cannisters might make the difference. He tinkered with the placement of the grenades, then unhooked the primary cannister from his web belt and placed it in the hole together with the nozzle. In for a penny, in for a pound.

He held the last grenade in his hand and pushed himself back away from the squeeze. "How's it looking ahead, Walt?"

"So far, so good, boss. What are you doing?"

Atticus didn't answer. The rustle of skin and the tick of claws from the tunnel beyond the choke was louder now. The lead insects couldn't be more than ten meters away. He backed off farther and thumbed the primer on the grenade, fusing it long, then rolled the grenade into the gap to lie next to the others.

He turned quickly and scrambled through the tiny passage after Walt. "Fire in the hole!"

"What?" said Walt.

"Grenades and jelly, coming up!"

Walt moaned. "Oh, shit no!"

"Haul ass, brother, or clear the road!"

The essential unwisdom of triggering a large explosion in a cramped, collapsible space was not lost on Atticus: he knew stupid when he saw it. But sometimes you had to jump in head-first anyway, hoping for the best. This was one of those times.

It turned out even better than he expected. The little passage tremored for a few seconds, and bits of the ceiling fell on his helmet, giving Atticus a bad moment, but after a strong pressure wave fluttered his suit, it was over. He stopped to listen. Debris crashed from the ceiling from time to time in the distance, but Atticus could no longer hear the steady tick of small feet. Satisfied, he crawled on, following Walt, who only remarked on his pleasure that Atticus hadn't been blown up his ass.

They crawled for another half-hour before the ceiling lifted enough they could shift to their hands and knees. Then it lifted again and they could walk, at which point Atticus's thoughts turned to the legacy of this misadventure. They had come to the cave to block the exit near the ship, but they had succeeded only in making it perhaps the creatures' only outlet to the world above. Captain Rail wouldn't be happy about that. But maybe he didn't need to know.

Atticus cleared his throat. "Ah, Walt?"

"Yes, I can keep this under my hat."

"You're a good man," said Atticus.

"And you're an unreasonably dangerous man to know," said Walt.

"I've heard that. I think it makes me interesting."

"Interesting like the tube farts," said Walt. "But one good thing did come from this reckless stunt."

"Do tell."

"Something really must be done with 'grenades and jelly.' What do you think, At? A bar? A heavy weapons boutique?"

Atticus laughed and keyed his pancake. "Bragg to Thorkin."

"About time, Bragg. Where are you?"

"Good question. We're coming out another exit and need a fix."

"Stand by," said Thorkin.

Atticus was relieved the man didn't ask any questions. He and Walt walked from the cave to find a darkening sky as the Sergeant homed on their suit signals.

"Jesus," said Thorkin, "you're five klicks away. Steer 238."

"Understood, 238."

"Hustle, Bragg. We're getting into the ship and zipping up."

They arrived at the ship with full dark, and with Atticus looking forward to sleeping off the adrenaline. When he put his head through the emergency hatch, he found Rail standing in the cockpit with his arms folded, waiting. Sergeant Thorkin stood behind him. Walt, who had gone up first, stood against the far wall with his head down, like a naughty schoolboy.

Rail raised an eyebrow. "Well, Bragg? Did you close it?"

Walt raised his head to look a question at Atticus. But now, facing Rail, Atticus decided there was no hiding the truth. He would have to accept the embarrassment of failure, and take whatever lumps might be coming to him. So he gave Rail a full account of the expedition, leaving out nothing.

When he was done, Rail regarded him for a long moment before saying, "This turned out rather conveniently for you, didn't it, Bragg?"

"Sir?"

Rail sneered at him. "You've been agitating to leave the ship since the beginning, and now a threat I sent you to eliminate still remains. I don't think your heart was in this mission, Bragg. In fact, I think you sabotaged it. That was an incredible story, and I'm not convinced this fabulous impervious beast exists either." Rail turned to Thorkin. "Are you in this too, Sergeant? I can easily believe it."

Thorkin showed his open hands to Rail. "Sir, I didn't—"

"Silence! I am well aware of your efforts to undermine my authority with the ranks. You have attempted to belittle and check me from the moment we met, and now I am surrounded by failure, sabotage, and rebellion in a crisis! It was your job to prevent that, Sergeant, but it was you who lit and fanned the flames!"

"Sir, I only—"

"Do not interrupt me, Sergeant! I'm not finished! And stand at attention!"

Thorkin clapped his mouth shut and drew himself up, staring at the bulkhead.

"Bragg convinced me to leave you in your position," continued Rail, "but now I wonder if that was a good idea. Maybe it was a mercy you didn't deserve."

Thorkin shot a glance full of suspicion at Atticus. "Permission to speak freely, sir," he said to Rail.

"Denied."

"Sir, it is foolishness not to leave—"

"I said, denied!"

Thorkin bit off his words. His face flushed to a deep, burning red.

"You are dismissed, Sergeant," said Rail. He pointed a finger at Walt. "You too."

Thorkin turned to walk stiffly from the cockpit, ducking through the hatch into the troop bay. Walt followed without a word. When they were gone, Rail collapsed into the nav-puter seat and ran his eye over the console. "You failed me, Bragg," he said.

"Not intentionally, sir."

"Perhaps. Everyone seems to have their agenda here, don't they? Thorkin wants to depose me, apparently in favor of you. Lieutenant Warren wants to leave and go somewhere, but she can't get a good fix on where we are, or where anything else is. And you, Bragg—you want to keep me alive, I presume. To collect your swill-money. Isn't that what the disgraced do? Sit at bars and soak themselves, maundering about better days?"

This hit far too close to home, and Atticus flushed. "I wouldn't call myself disgraced, sir." He had, but he wouldn't take that from anyone else.

Rail continued as if Atticus hadn't spoken. "I'll tell you what *my* agenda is, Bragg. I have no intention of dying on this roach-world. None whatsoever. And my future does not include a uniform or an exo-suit, except for show. I am a ruler, not a soldier, as I'm certain the General has told you. Since I want to stay alive, and you want to keep me alive, I suggest we work together to accomplish that."

"What are you suggesting, sir?"

"I want you to do the job General Warren sent you to do."

Atticus digested this. Rail was asking for help, finally. Thorkin had failed him, for reasons that could be laid in part at the Captain's own door, and Rail now had nowhere else to turn. He was in far over his head. Atticus didn't see fear on the man's face, but he knew it was there. Atticus himself felt it.

"How far does this go?" he said.

"As far as I want it to go," said Rail. He swung the chair around and pretended to adjust a dial on the console. "But I don't want to hear anything about leaving, Bragg." Ah, there was the fear—right there.

"Then I'm not sure there's anything I can do for you, sir," said Atticus.

Rail swung back around, angry. "I can't get loyalty from anyone in this platoon, can I?"

"Sir, it's not a question—"

"Yes, it is! My father commands the loyalty of those around him! Ministers, generals, men of wealth and power. But I can't get the loyalty of a used-up sergeant and a homeless mercenary!" Rail pounded the console before putting his forehead in his hand.

Seeing this, Atticus felt something shift inside him. This was a frightened boy, thrown into the fire. Rail's behavior, his arrogance and insecurity, had made that difficult to see. He was fixated on staying with the ship because leaving meant exerting the kind of leadership he was not capable of, and he knew it.

"Sir," said Atticus, "I won't fight you on leaving, but I promise you if we do leave, I will help you get us through."

Rail raised his head to eye Atticus with suspicion. Atticus knew it galled the man to rely on those he believed to be far beneath him, but it galled Atticus equally to be viewed as a lesser man. Their match wasn't well made, but maybe it would keep them alive.

"I may accept that offer," said Rail. "But if I do, and we get out of this mess, not a word will be spoken of it."

"I wouldn't think of it, sir."

"I wonder. You're dismissed, Bragg."

Atticus left the cockpit and found a seat next to Walt in the troop compartment. He had made a commitment to Rail and he intended to honor it. Perhaps they would all benefit in the end. With an ember of hope in his heart, Atticus fell into a deep sleep, and dreamed he was lost in a maze of tunnels unable to call out for help.

Loud pounding on the hull woke him. Rail and Thorkin were talking on c-channel.

"I don't know what it is, sir!" said the Sergeant. "All I can see out the cockpit windows are those little things swarming around. They aren't doing much of anything."

The insects had returned to the ship with darkness. This was no surprise to Atticus: last night had been fruitful for them, despite their losses.

"Go look again!" said Rail. "Find out what's doing that!"

The pounding continued. It seemed to be centered on a section of hull above the back of the troop compartment, where the ramp and the soldiers near it had been mangled. Something outside was trying to destroy the ship, or get inside. Something large, it seemed.

"Could it be the Repsians?" said Grippa. She had come into the troop compartment from her ready room.

"Doubtful, ma'am," said Thorkin. "The bugs wouldn't try to punch in the hull like that. They'd just shoot us up with heavy stuff. The ship's skin ain't that thick."

"I'm aware of that, Sergeant," said Grippa. "This is a troop transport, not a combat ship. It's not designed to take a physical beating."

There was an immense bang and the ceiling near the ramp buckled sharply, as if struck by a hammer. Whatever this thing was, it was tremendously strong, and the insects outside didn't seem to be bothering it. Atticus picked up his rifle and went to stand beneath the dent: it was slightly conical, as if something pointed had made it.

"Walt, get your gun," he said.

"Aye, boss."

"What do you recommend, Bragg?" said Rail, on a private channel. The question surprised and pleased Atticus.

"Well, sir, we don't have anything to reinforce the hull, so all I know to do right now is blast the thing in the face—if it has a face—the moment it comes through. Maybe that will shock it into leaving."

BANG! The ceiling dented further, and now a rip appeared in the metal at the point of the indentation.

"What about those insects?" said Rail. "They'll come in."

"Yes, sir, they will. Get the burners into position, and order everyone else into the other compartments. And make sure everyone's zipped up tight in their suits. It's gonna be a mess in here in about one minute."

Rail gave the order, and most of the platoon moved through the hatchways to jam themselves into the cockpit and Grippa's ready room. The hatches were swung closed to be dogged on the far side, leaving Atticus, Walt, Rail, and three troopers with flamethrowers in the troop bay. Rail had ordered Thorkin into the cockpit.

BANG! The rip widened and now Atticus could see movement beyond it. What the hell was this thing?

"Walt," he said, "when that tear gets big enough, jam your weapon in there and give it hell."

"Aye, boss." The gunner moved to stand beneath the dent. "Even the mercs send the mercs to the front," he grumbled.

BANG! The dent grew deeper and the rip grew longer and wider. And for a moment Atticus saw what looked like the end of a long white pole. It pulled back, then reappeared, slamming through the dent to fully puncture the hull. The end of the pole was sharp—and organic.

Atticus's mind went back to the cave: to that looming presence on the far side of the chamber, beyond the fires. Walt had been right: it *was* a hive. And here was the queen, come to take her revenge for the fiery destruction Atticus had done to her brood.

The pole pulled back again and Atticus shouted, "Let her rip, Walt!"

The gunner lifted his mech-gun to jam the muzzle into the tear and held the trigger. The weapon roared in the confined space and shell casings rained on the deck, bouncing and tinkling. Outside, there was a high-pitched scream and the pole rammed through the hole, opening it wider and flattening Walt against the deck. As he fell, the gun fired a dozen rounds into the compartment. They missed Rail by inches before punching through the hull of the little ship. The Captain shouted something before dropping to lay on the deck.

The pole pulled back and three tiny insects tumbled into the compartment through the tear. Two landed on Walt. He shouted and flailed his arms frantically to knock them away. "Get'em off! Get'em off!"

Three bright orange lines of napalm lit the compartment like daylight, converging on Walt. All three insects were caught in the fire and they exploded, their internal fluids instantly boiled into rapidly expanding steam. More insects fell to replace them, and they too died in the orange fire. But there were far more outside than could be killed with the platoon's limited stores of napalm, and the troop bay was now fatally compromised.

Atticus reached down to haul Rail to his feet. "We can't stay here, sir!" he said. "That hole's too big, and there's nothing we can do about it now!"

Rail nodded. He crossed the compartment to bang on the cockpit hatch. "Open up!"

Atticus caught his arm. "Not that way, sir! Not all of us at once"

The Captain looked at him with savage, fearful eyes, and he pulled his arm from Atticus's hold. "You presume too much, Bragg!" He turned back to resume pounding on the hatch door, but it didn't open. Atticus was glad someone on the other side had some sense.

Atticus turned back to the others. Walt had regained his feet and he was now backed against the bulkhead near the cockpit hatch. His mech-gun hung silent in front of him: it was nearly useless against tiny single targets. He needed to get out first. No, second—after Rail. The Captain was a hindrance.

In the back of the compartment, the flamethrowers were burning everything that came through the ceiling, but insects fell in by the dozen now, and the soldiers were close to being overwhelmed. Orange light and the high keen of dying creatures filled the compartment.

"Grippa, you there?" said Atticus.

"I'm here. What's going on back there?"

"Never mind for now. Open up for the Captain first then Walt, then shut it while we get things under control for the rest of us to get out. There's too many insects in here to keep the door open for more than a second or two."

"Understood. Tell me when it's clear. Hurry."

Atticus stood between the door and the inferno in the rear of the compartment, his rifle tucked into his shoulder. He scanned the deck near the hatch for insects that had managed to avoid fiery death.

"Okay, clear, Grippa! Two seconds max! Captain Rail! Walt! Go!"

The hatch door groaned open behind Atticus. He swung his rifle to shoot a burning bug that lurched awkwardly from the holocaust. Two seconds later, the hatch shut with a clang. Atticus wondered if that was the sound of his tomb door.

"We're in, At!" said Walt. "I don't like it, but we're in."

"Copy," said Atticus. He was relieved the gunner hadn't argued. "Flamethrowers on me!"

The three soldiers began backing toward Atticus, scorching everything in a wide arc as they came. The paint on the deck and drop seats had been incinerated, filling the compartment with smoke; and the bare metal beneath now glowed a sullen red. Insects rained through the rip in the hull, landing on the ashes of those that had gone before.

"Here's the plan," said Atticus. He pointed to one of the soldiers. "You go first. Give me that flamethrower." The woman unhooked her last cannister and left it with him before moving to the hatch. "Grippa!" he shouted. "Open up! Two seconds!"

The soldier slipped through the hatchway, then the door banged shut behind her just as a horde of insects surged forward from the back of the compartment. Atticus set his back against the bulkhead near the hatch door and played a stream of napalm over them. Heat rippled the air. He felt it through the protection of his suit and wondered how any of the insects were living through this Hell.

Suddenly, Atticus's stream sputtered twice, then it died. He shook the nozzle, then the cannister, but the system produced nothing more. A few seconds later, another stream died and the soldier dropped the nozzle to run for the door. He pounded on it, screaming for it to open. An insect coiled itself and leaped for Atticus. He ducked low and it landed on the panicked man.

Shit!

Atticus moved to help but the man spun away, scrabbling over his suit with his gloves, trying to dislodge the creature. He stumbled away toward the inferno and out of reach. Atticus moved to grab the other one, who still sprayed the floor.

"Grippa!" he shouted. "Open for two seconds!" He would fling the man bodily through the open doorway.

The hatch door groaned open again. At that same moment, an insect leaped for the last man and clung to his shoulder. He screamed and flailed, throwing fire everywhere until his flamethrower unit sputtered and ran dry also. Now there was nothing to stop the creatures and there were hundreds of them in the compartment now.

"Come to the hatch!" shouted Atticus.

He surged toward the man, reaching, but then something caught his suit from behind. It dragged him backward. His helmet bounced from the hatch frame as he was pulled through into the cockpit.

"No!" he shouted. *I don't leave people behind!*

But the hatch slammed shut and the wheel spun, running the dogs into its frame. It wouldn't be opened again.

CHAPTER SEVEN

Until dawn, they heard the tapping and scraping of insects exploring the ruin of the troop compartment. Before leaving, the great beast had punched two more holes in the ship, but mercifully neither penetrated the crowded cockpit or the ready room. Whatever that thing was, Atticus remained certain it had come from the cave, seeking vengeance for the hundreds, maybe thousands, of deaths he had caused in the great chamber. Two courageous soldiers had paid the price for that destruction, not Atticus, and in his grief he had lashed out at Walt, who had yanked him from the final inferno in the compartment. But in the end Atticus conceded the man wasn't wrong: rushing after the second soldier would have only resulted in three more afflicted, instead of two.

But that didn't make it hurt any less.

When the yellow sun was fully risen, Rail sent the platoon back outside to man the trench. Thorkin immediately put the troopers to work improving their fighting positions. But it was clear to everyone this was only make-work, to divert their minds from the night's events. The ship was fatally compromised, and now it was only a question of when they would leave, not whether. Craddock gently collected the two newly afflicted from the troop compartment, and he gathered them all in the shade of the ship to wait for the inevitable. There were eleven now, far too many.

Rail called a command meeting for 0700 in the cockpit. The small group that waited for him there was subdued. The three squad leaders clustered in one corner, quiet, and Thorkin stared at the deck, fidgeting his fingers over his rifle. He refused to meet anyone's eye. Even Grippa seemed edgy. She gave Atticus a tight smile when he entered, but didn't offer to chat.

Precisely on time, Rail climbed through the e-hatch to join them. "There's a new plan," he said without preamble. "We will be leaving the ship. It can no longer protect us. Our course will be 165, which Lieutenant Grippa believes to be the correct bearing to friendly forces." He turned to Thorkin. "Sergeant, what's the status of our expendables?"

Thorkin pulled his head up but didn't meet the Captain's eye. "Four spare plasma packs for every trooper fit to fight, sir—taking everything from the afflicted—and twelve hundred rounds for the cannon. But we can't carry that much. With everyone humping a few rounds, and loading down the afflicted, we can manage about half of that, I think. Six hundred rounds, give or take—if we bring the cannon, of course. As for food, we lost some in the troop compartment. We have enough remaining for three days, barring the unforeseen."

"Three days?" said Rail.

"Yes, sir. A bit more with rationing, of course, but that's a hard thing to ask traveling through rough country on foot. Also, I strongly recommend we package up the floods and batteries to travel, since those things seem to come at night. The afflicted can hump the floods."

"So they're pack mules now?" said Grippa.

Thorkin smiled tightly. "That's the life of a grunt, Lieutenant. They'd be loaded down for travel even if they were still Alpha-1."

"I agree on the floods," said Rail. "Let's talk about the cannon."

"The cart's been reinforced for travel," said Thorkin, "but it'll take four troops to haul it, more on inclines. The cannon itself is nominal. Wilkins welded on hand grips and a stock. It's nice work. The real question is—"

"—is the cannon worth the trouble?" finished Rail.

Thorkin nodded. "Yes, sir. But the Major's right—"

"Don't call him that."

"Aye, sir. Bragg is right that the cannon is the only thing we have to take down aircraft. It also might have the muzzle velocity to stop those armored things he saw."

"Which no one else has seen," said Rail.

Atticus held his tongue. He liked his new status with the Captain, but it didn't seem to come with any perks. On the other hand, he doubted Rail ever offered respect to anyone he considered his inferior. Atticus would have considered that a character flaw, but the nobility played by their own rules.

Thorkin pushed on. "Sir, I recommend we do take the cannon. If it gets to be too much, we can ditch it."

"Very well," said Rail. "Get it ready to leave. What's our effective strength?"

"Twenty-four fit to fight, sir, including yourself and the mercenaries, plus the Lieutenant."

"Thank you, Sergeant. Craddock?"

The medic licked his lips. "There are eleven afflicted now, sir. They can and will do simple tasks such as carrying or digging, but their higher mental functions are deteriorating rapidly. I can't tell you where it will stop—it may not. The first two are the most far gone, as you might imagine. They both complain of internal itching and strange sensations, which I've treated with sedatives and histamine blockers." The medic stopped there, wearing a strained look on his face. Like the others, he seemed unwilling to voice the now-obvious conclusion. "I suppose the good news, sir, is we don't have to carry them out like wounded."

"Yes," said Rail absently, seeming not to notice the medic's distress. He looked around at the little group in the cockpit. "I think we all have an idea what's to come for those soldiers. Thank you, Craddock. Keep me informed."

"Aye, sir," said Craddock.

Rail turned to Grippa. "Lieutenant Warren?"

"No change in comms status, sir. No non-local comms at all, and no sat-nav. I still believe 165 is the way out."

"Very well," said Rail. "All right, Thorkin, get everyone out and button up the ship. We will leave at 0930 sharp, to get as much distance from the ship as we can before nightfall—whenever the hell that is. There will be three sections for the march—lead, middle, and rear. Thorkin has the troop assignments. The cannon will be in the middle, with myself and the afflicted. Craddock, you will shepherd them. Thorkin will have the rear element. Bragg, you will begin by walking point under Corporal Retze, who will have command of the lead element. Your sidekick is assigned to flank security."

Mercs to the fore. No surprise there.

"If we're attacked," continued Rail, "the lead and rear sections will collapse immediately on the cannon to form a perimeter around it. Flank security will not come in before assessing the force against us. Stay together, and in contact. No one is to get split off from the rest of the platoon. Understood?"

There was a murmur of assent.

"Saddle up," said Rail. "I want the platoon moving at 0930 sharp. Dismissed."

Atticus followed Walt out of the hatch. Rail had finally done what was necessary, but eleven soldiers had paid a high price to make that happen. Atticus resolved to be more forceful with the young Captain, even if it meant some broken crockery.

The platoon spent the next hour preparing to leave. For Atticus and Walt, that meant testing their weapons, checking the valves and seals of their suits, and visiting Craddock under the hatch to draw their ration of food tubes. Rail had charged the medic with distributing what little remained.

"Take some lasagna and beef roast," said Craddock, offering each of them a handful of tubes, "since you're the first ones here. They go fast."

"Thanks," said Atticus. He stowed the tubes in his mesh bag, ignoring Walt's noise of disgust. "Anything more on that sample?"

Craddock shook his head. "No, but I think we all know what happened to that poor animal. The question now is how long before—" He turned up his hands with an anguished look.

Atticus nodded. "Yeah."

"You know, I expected Thorkin—or you—to come to me," said the medic. "About the Captain. I heard the rumors going around."

Atticus raised an eyebrow. "Oh? What would you have said?"

"I would have turned you down flat."

"Not unexpected," said Atticus. "It's not medical."

"Exactly," said Craddock. "Foolishness and incompetence are not medical problems. And who's to say he was wrong anyway?"

"Me," growled Walt.

"That's your opinion," said Craddock, "but I am glad we're leaving. This place is a death trap, and these people need a med base as soon as they can get it."

"They do," said Atticus. "Any change in their status?"

"Negative. Still the same symptoms. Mostly complaints of internal itching and tingling, which is causing generalized anxiety. I've nearly used up my sedatives keeping them calm."

"What's your best guess on how long they have?"

"No idea," said Craddock. "Absolutely none. And, honestly, I don't want to think about it much. There's nothing I can do."

Atticus nodded. "Yeah, this could get real bad, real quick. Thanks for the tubes."

Atticus was standing with Retze and four others, waiting for the word to move, when Grippa approached them, carrying a plasma rifle. She stopped in front of Atticus with the rifle held across her chest. She looked defiant. "I'm with you," she said.

"Says who?"

"Says me."

"You're not a grunt," said Atticus. "You belong in the middle, with the cannon and the Captain."

She arched an eyebrow. "I know for a fact you're not in charge here, Bragg."

Atticus nodded to her rifle. "Have you ever fired one of those at anything?"

She shrugged. "A few things. Sickle-claw raptors, a tangin beast that wouldn't get off my ramp, a clingy ex."

Retze cackled at that and waved her forward. "You'll do, Lieutenant. Don't sweat it, Major. There's nowhere safe on this pleasure cruise."

"Fine," said Atticus. "But she's not walking point with me."

Grippa smirked. "Don't get delusional, Bragg."

The Corporal laughed again and Atticus glared at him.

Rail's voice came up on c-channel: "Retze, get moving. Steer 165 true."

Retze acknowledged and looked at Bragg. "You're up, sir."

"Right."

Atticus checked his rifle a final time and began walking toward the ridge. Now that they were leaving, he felt the visceral pull of the ship. Rail was an ass, but he had been right about one thing: for all its drawbacks the little ship had been a fortress, giving them a sense of security—however false that turned out to be.

Atticus heard Walt sniff as he opened their private channel, then the gunner spoke. "Off to the flank I go," he said, "to be stabbed in the chest or eaten alive. If you bury me shallow, Bragg, I'll haunt you."

Atticus laughed. "With dreary couplets, moaned in the dark of night?"

"No," said Walt. "With lectures on temperance, and the evils of self-enforced poverty."

"Consider me reformed," said Atticus. "Take care of yourself out there, buddy."

"Likewise."

"Sorry about the shit assignment. The General had better pay up. This job sucks."

"They all do," said Walt. "At least you have Grippa up there. You can woo her with dashing war stories. Just remember to work in some mysterious romance, and intrigue."

"Like that double-jointed whore in Rec City?"

"No," said Walt.

"I was intrigued."

Walt clicked off.

Smiling, Atticus stepped onto the crest of the ridge and turned to look back. Grippa, Retze, and the rest of the vanguard still labored up the slope behind him. Fifty meters behind them, the cannon rolled on its cart, pulled by four soldiers hauling with a mix of ropes and chains. Rail strutted in front of them like a victorious Tribune, working hard to look important. Thorkin and the rear section were just now leaving the trench line.

Memories of a dozen other bug outs presented themselves to Atticus. Some had been more desperate than this, some less. Some had ended well, while others had ended in blood and sacrifice. But each had begun like this one did now: with a little swell of hope, and a tiny scrap of a plan.

Atticus led the little column along the wide valley he and Walt had traveled twice already. Here and there, he saw traces of their prior passage: a boot print or a rock knocked from its dirt bed. For the most part the column walked in silence. Even the Captain was quiet, occasionally coming up on c-channel to tell the rear section to close up.

At the cave of misadventure, Atticus walked up the slope to reconnoiter the entrance. It occurred to him that closing the back door might have been serendipitous: the platoon wouldn't camp by it tonight, unaware of its existence. He moved closer to look into the vestibule, murmuring to his helmet for infrared and ultraviolet, but he saw nothing but the cross-hatched prints of many tiny feet.

Back on the valley floor, he keyed c-channel: "There's a cave ahead of you, on the right, with a known nest of the small creatures. Negative contact at the moment. Recommend you pass ASAP."

"Understood," said Rail. "Move along, Bragg."

Atticus put the cave behind him and continued up the valley, scanning the heights for the armored beasts, but there were none to be seen. An hour later, after far too much stopping and starting, the platoon reached the end of the long valley, and passed over the narrow saddle beneath the hanging glacier. This time no red-haired beasts browsed by the little waterfall.

"Pretty," said Grippa. She had come up to stand next to Atticus, near the boulder where he and Walt had rested.

"Yep," said Atticus. "Nothing much beautiful on this planet."

"It is a rock," she said, "but I've seen worse."

"Oh, have you?"

"I've been to a few places, mister! I'm older than I look."

Atticus smiled. "I wouldn't be robbing the cradle? Walt thinks I should be chasing you."

"Oh, does he? What do you think?"

"I think he's a daffy romantic not too much smarter than his own gun," said Atticus. "You're looking at a washed-out field officer who can't seem to make a living pulling contracts. I'm a turnip. Good bourbon is my comfort, not a girlfriend."

"That's a sad story."

"It's all my own," said Atticus.

"I don't think you're that hopeless," she said. "A good woman might turn you into something passable. The bones are there."

Atticus laughed. "Yes, I'm a shambling skeleton of a man. That sounds about right."

"That's not how I meant it, but you are a major project."

"I like straight talk," said Atticus, "but you could've taken something off that."

"And you could scrape yourself off the bottom, Bragg, and float a little."

Atticus looked at her. "I'll come see you when I'm feeling a bit too full of myself."

"You do that," she said. "I'll give you an earful."

Atticus opened his mouth to reply, but Rail's voice interrupted: "The cannon's up, Bragg. Let's move."

"Aye, sir," he said. He took a last look at Grippa before turning to work his way down the far side of the saddle. The slope was steep and crumbling, and full of loose stones that rolled under his boots. Reflecting on his conversation with Grippa, he wondered whether he was right that he didn't have anything to offer anyone, or if he was just being reflexively defensive. He didn't know. It had been a long time since he'd really tried. Maybe Grippa was right: maybe it was time for him to pull himself out of his rut and fly again. Having friends again would help. That had been a long time, too.

The platoon camped shortly before dark on a low hill rising from a flat, rocky valley. Rail ordered the cannon pulled to the top of the hill and fortified; and the rest of the platoon scraped a shallow fighting trench around it, lower on the slope. The flood lights were erected on poles behind the trench. They would remain off unless needed.

When the work was done, Walt and Atticus found a spot in the trench to sit and push food tubes into their nutrition ports.

"Craddock was right," said Atticus. "The best one is lasagna."

"Nope, too salty," said Walt. "The curry's better. But the gas is worse."

"No argument there. So how was your vacation from the rest of us?"

"It was good actually," said Walt. "I didn't see anything that wasn't a rock or one of those scraggly-ass bushes."

"I can say the same," said Atticus. He looked at his pancake. "Nineteen and a half klicks today. Better than I expected."

"Yeah, me too." Walt held up four fingers. "Four more days."

"Maybe three and a half," said Atticus. "If we can keep pushing like this, and get a little luck."

Walt made a noise. "I'm sorry, sir, but that kind of good fortune is not available on this planet. Please try again at another location. We apologize for the inconvenience."

Atticus laughed. "Amen, brother."

There was a garbled shout on e-channel, followed by silence.

"What was that?" said Walt.

Then Thorkin's voice came up. "Who was that? Identify yourself!"

"It's Eckles, Sergeant," said a new voice. It was young and shook with excitement, or fear. "Come quick!"

Thorkin barked for the floods, and night became day in a wide circle around the hill. Atticus blinked until his helmet compensated, then he grabbed his rifle and scrambled from the trench to follow the platoon sergeant. He scanned the flats below the hill over his rifle sights, calling up infrared and ultraviolet views, but there was nothing to see.

He found Thorkin looking down at two soldiers lying on the ground. They were writhing on the red dirt, slapping themselves and scratching fiercely at their suits, trying to reach something through the heavy fabric.

"Sweet Jesus!" said Thorkin. "It's those first two."

It was, and they were screaming silently behind faceplates fogged with hyperventilation. Rail had long ago removed the afflicted from the comm circuit. The nearest, a blond-haired boy, bobbed his head frantically, trying to peer at something down the neck of his suit. A small fountain of blood erupted inside his helmet and ran down the bowl.

"Captain Rail to the afflicted!" shouted Thorkin. "They're hatching, sir! We have to shuck these boys out of their suits!"

Rail's voice came up immediately. "Negative, Sergeant! Do not touch them!"

Something small and insectile skittered across the inside of the blond's helmet. It crossed in front of his face, leaving a trail of blood across the dura-glass. He followed its progress, horrified, then lifted his eyes to Atticus. His mouth was twisted in terror.

Atticus dropped his rifle and pulled the knife from his web belt. But someone caught his shoulder and spun him around. It was Rail.

The Captain shouted into his face over c-channel: "Stand down, Bragg!"

"They're soldiers, Captain! They're dying"

"They're already dead! We can't let those things out!"

"We can't let those boys die!" said Atticus.

Rail's face was savage. "Yes, Bragg, we can."

Atticus wanted to put a fist through the man's faceplate—or better, stab him dead where he stood.

Walt came up to put a hand on Atticus's arm. "He's right, At. You can't do this."

Atticus jerked his arm away. "We can't let them die like this!"

"We can't let those things out," said Walt. "Who knows what they would do? I don't like it any better than you do, At, but put away that sticker."

Atticus took a few deep breaths then he let the knife fall to his side. Maybe Rail was right, just maybe, but that didn't absolve the Captain of the consequences of his decision.

"In that case, sir," said Atticus, grabbing the Captain's suit and spinning him to face the dying soldiers, "you can do these brave men the honor of bearing witness to their courageous sacrifice!"

Rail shoved Atticus away and straightened his suit, muttering something his mic didn't catch. But to his credit, he remained where he was and didn't flinch away. This surprised Atticus: maybe the man would be worth a damn after all.

Someday.

The end came slowly, as the men bled to death in their suits. The little insects—wet, immature versions of the mantises—walked and hopped across their faceplates and moved beneath their suits, searching for a way out. Thorkin knelt to slap at the things, cursing; but the damage had been done, and there was nothing anyone could do now to repair it. Not without removing their suits, and likely not even then.

In time, the men ceased to struggle as their strength ebbed: first one and then the other, until they only stared, their faces white and bloodless. Atticus knelt by the nearest and picked up his gloved hand. Rail didn't object when Atticus keyed the man into e-channel.

"I'm sorry, son," said Atticus. "We couldn't risk it. I wanted to."

The boy's lips trembled. His voice was weak and breathy. "I know, sir." His eyes drifted out of focus. "I'm scared, sir. I can feel myself going. I don't want to go."

Atticus squeezed his hand. "Many brave soldiers have gone before you, son, but none braver."

"Tell my momma—" The boy stopped to blanch in horror as an insect stalked in front of his face. "Tell my momma there was no pain, sir. Please. She couldn't bear it to know."

"I will, son. I promise."

"It hurts, sir. It hurts a lot. I don't want to go. I ain't ready."

This last seemed to take what was left of the boy's waning strength, and he closed his eyes and fell silent. Atticus held his hand until he exhaled a last, sighing breath, fogging his helmet. When it cleared away, the boy stared at the night sky with peaceful blue eyes. Atticus looked over to the other one, but he was gone too: a scowl of denial on his face.

Rail's voice cut across the quiet. "Sergeant Thorkin! I want the other afflicted outside the perimeter! Now! Set a guard!"

The little hill exploded with movement. Dark shadows swung wildly under the glare of the floods as the remaining afflicted were yanked to their feet and pulled down to the flats below the hill. There they were pushed down to sit in a tight circle under the barrels of a dozen rifles, guarded fearfully by soldiers who had yesterday been their friends and comrades-in-arms.

Atticus had seen many deaths in war, and none of them had been easy to stomach, but he knew these two would never leave him. Still kneeling beside the boy, he bent forward over his knees and hung his head until his helmet touched the ground.

Later, when the watch was set and the rest of the platoon slept, Atticus walked past the guards to sit on a small rise a short distance from camp. The planet's lone moon, half-veiled by wispy cloud, hovered over a knife-edge ridge far off in the waste.

But its beauty was an illusion. This planet was nothing but a living hell, and he was tired of it. He was tired of the endless red rock, and the Captain, and his suit, and the expectations and demands of others. He wanted to escape, but the twin oblivions of drink and sleep were denied to him.

A small figure approached him in the moonlight. Grippa climbed the slope and stood over him, her fingers moving on her pancake. "Is this where the insomniacs are gathering?" she said in his ear. Her voice was quiet and tired.

"Pull up a rock," said Atticus. "We'll vote for club president soon."

She sat next to him, hugging her knees to herself. The moon and the brighter stars reflected on her helmet.

"That was hideous," she said.

"Yes, it was. There's no good way to die in war, but some ways are worse than others."

She made a soft sound of agreement. "That was a nice gesture, what you did for that boy."

"It wasn't the first time. They all have last words for their mothers."

"Will you?"

"No," said Atticus, "She's gone."

"And your father?"

He shrugged. He hadn't seen his father since before the court-martial. Maybe he hadn't wanted to give the old man the satisfaction of saying he was right from the beginning, and that Atticus had sold his soul and now drifted without one.

"I might be an orphan in the cosmos by now," he said. "He didn't like my choices in life anyway."

"Nor do I," said Grippa. "You could do better for yourself, Atticus. Taking contracts is a dangerous game."

He laughed. "It's a young man's game is what you mean. You'd be right about that. And you're right I'm no prancing buck anymore. Trust me, I know that better than anyone. But I'm no good for anything else. Not anymore. This is all I know, and it keeps me from drowning in a bottle somewhere."

"I can talk to my father," said Grippa. "He's always working side projects that need good people."

"I don't need rescuing, Grippa." This was probably a lie.

She snorted. "You sure needed rescuing on that pad. What a mess that was!"

Atticus surprised himself with a genuine laugh. "Yes, it was. Every contract seems to end up a mess, one way or another. Thanks for cleaning up that one for me."

"My pleasure."

"Walt likes you, you know," he said. "He told me you have courage."

"He said I have balls is what you mean," she said. "I'll take that from him. He's an odd character, but he means well. He certainly seems to like you."

"Don't hold that against him."

"It is the part that gives me pause," she said.

Atticus laughed again and they sat in silence while he wondered when he'd laughed last when the joke wasn't whiskey.

She shifted against the ground. "What about the other afflicted? I talked to Craddock, but he has no answers."

Atticus blew out a long breath. "I don't either, but it's all timing now, isn't it? The second set was stung the next night, so I guess they have some time yet." He turned up a palm. "Maybe tomorrow, about the same time? If the incubation period is the same. They need a base med facility to have any chance at all. But that's not happening unless we're suddenly found."

"So what do we do for them, Atticus?"

"The same thing we'd do for any soldier—honor their last wishes. Soldiers are willing to die, if they have to, but we don't like leaving unfinished business behind."

"What unfinished business do you have, Atticus Bragg?"

"You cut straight for the bone, don't you?"

"I'm my father's child."

Atticus looked toward the hill holding the diminished platoon. The cannon stood silhouetted against the moonlit sky. "No business," he said. "I'm just a bit of fluff now, blowing here and there on the wind. I like it that way." This was probably a lie too.

"Do you really? What a waste of fine talent."

"There's that bone," said Atticus, "right there."

"You're not a merc, Atticus. Not really. What you are is a leader."

He shook his head. "Not anymore."

"Walt is following you."

"I do seem to have a troubadour now."

She growled. "Fine, be funny. And have it your way. I'm going to sleep." She stood and walked down the little hill.

He stayed, watching the stars turn over the hills, and waited for sleep that never came.

In the morning the mood was somber. Even Walt was subdued. He clipped the mech-gun to his suit in silence, and left the hill to take up the flank with a wave to Atticus over his shoulder. Atticus helped repack the floods before walking down the hill to join Retze and the other soldiers of the vanguard, waiting to leave. He passed Thorkin, who held up a hand to stop him.

"We all know what's about to happen to the rest of them, Bragg," said the Sergeant. "Later on. So if you have any bright ideas, now's the time to spill it."

Atticus shook his head. "No ideas, Sergeant."

"Well, something needs to be done, and the Captain ain't doing it. The rest of those poor bastards have the big-eyes this morning, and there's no telling what they might do. This is bad, Bragg, real bad, and I ain't afraid to say I got nothing."

"I don't either, Sergeant. There are no good answers."

There were some bad answers, however. Putting the soldiers out of their impending misery had crossed Atticus' mind, but he was certain he couldn't pull the trigger. Maybe Rail could, but neither Thorkin, nor the rank and file, would stand for it. Not that way, and certainly not the Captain.

Thorkin looked faintly disappointed now, as if he'd expected Atticus to pull out a rabbit. "So what now, Major?" he said.

"Nothing now. We go on."

"That's a hard one to swallow," said Thorkin.

"Yes, it is," said Atticus. "But you know the score as well as I do, Thorkin. For grunts like me and you, war is a random hammer you can't dodge. You get hit or you don't. Those poor sons of bitches down there got whacked by the hammer."

"We might all get it," said Thorkin, "before this is over."

"We might. But for now, the rest of us are counting on you to help keep things together."

The Sergeant's gaze sharpened. "I don't need to be told my job, Bragg."

"I wouldn't presume," said Atticus. "Now let me do mine." He pushed past Thorkin and strode down the slope to the flat below, where Grippa was waiting with the vanguard.

"What did he want?" she said.

"Answers," said Atticus. "I don't have any."

"People seem to expect a lot of you, Bragg. Were you really all that?"

"I was pretty good once," he said. He waved for Retze and the others to follow him, then walked across the rocky pan to take point. It was true: he had been good once.

"It's still there," she called after him. "That kind of thing doesn't just disappear, you know."

He didn't respond. Maybe she was right, maybe not. But he didn't want to think about it now. All he wanted to do was to put one foot in front of the other, and push on to the end of this mess. If he survived, it might be a good occasion to re-evaluate his choices in life.

The terrain over which they marched that day was ungentle: rough, treacherous, broken by crumbling washes, and tumbled with boulders large and small. Atticus struggled to find a path that the cannon cart could navigate. Around them the heights began to lower, as tall, jagged peaks gave way to rounded mountains, the victims of glaciation sometime in the planet's distant past. But still the platoon saw no sign of Repsians or their works.

"Hold up, Bragg," said Rail, five klicks out from camp. He sounded annoyed.

"Holding, sir," said Atticus. He keyed Thorkin. "What's up?"

"Flanker not reporting in," said the Sergeant. "He's missed two comm checks."

"Is it Walt?"

"No, the other one—Fenrik. The Captain's sending a detail to look. Maybe you should go, Bragg. I have a bad feeling about this. Fenrik is usually steady."

Not the worst idea. Atticus switched back to c-channel. "Bragg here. Permission to accompany the detail, sir."

"Why?" said Rail.

"I can push'em to hurry."

"Fine," said Rail. "You do that. We're already wasting time."

Atticus turned to Retze. "I'm going back for awhile. You should use the time to chow."

The Corporal nodded and Atticus hurried back to the middle section, where the afflicted stood together in a tight group under close guard. They looked worried but remained abstracted, as if they could see danger coming but couldn't muster the focus to avoid it. Nearby, Rail sucked from a food tube as he watched two soldiers working on the cart. He caught Atticus's eye and pointed to a group of four soldiers checking their weapons. "Get back fast," he said. "We're wasting time."

"Aye, sir."

Atticus moved to join the little group. One of them, a corporal, looked up and raised his eyebrows in surprise. "The detail is yours, sir."

Atticus shook his head. "No, son, you're the man here. Lead on."

The Corporal nodded and motioned for the others to follow him. They homed on the scout's suit signal, and within twenty minutes they found what was left of him in an adjacent valley.

The remains lay at the foot of a steep, crumbling cliff that rose several hundred feet to an overhanging lip. Over the eons, rock had fallen from the cliff face to collect in a tall pile at the bottom. It appeared the man had used the pile as cover from something, but it had done him no good: bloody scraps of his exo-suit lay draped over the rocks, as if tossed aside, and the long bones of his arms and legs, ragged with scraps of flesh, were scattered in the crevices. A dark circle of blood lay directly beneath the cliff face, where the man had been consumed.

"Jesus!" said the Corporal. He made a curt gesture to the other soldiers, and they moved to the edge of the rock pile, rifles raised.

Atticus picked up a piece of the scout's suit. Its edges had the long, shiny fringes characteristic of torn dura-fiber. Tremendous force was required to rip an exo-suit. Force so great, in fact, the suits were guaranteed against accidental environmental exposure. Imperial soldiers—Atticus included—felt well-protected even in the harshest elements. But that didn't mean something big enough, or strong enough, couldn't rip a suited man apart.

"Look up there, sir," said the Corporal. Atticus followed his finger, and saw half a dozen plasma scorches on the red rock of the cliff face.

"Panicked," said Atticus.

The Corporal shook his head. "I don't think so, sir. Fenrik was a cold customer, and a good shot. He was shooting at something up there."

They stared at the steep rock wall, and Atticus wondered whether an armored beast could navigate it. That seemed unlikely. He looked around the area, but there were no tracks entering except Fenrik's. The ground around the bloodstain was highly disturbed, however. Wide gouges had been scraped deep into the earth. Atticus could make no sense of it.

"Well," he said. "We found what we came for. Let's get back before the Captain starts calling."

The Corporal bent to pick up the dead man's rifle. "All right, guys, let's move. Eyes up."

Atticus made a last look around as the soldiers filed away, finding no more clues and wondering what new danger had appeared to join the many others already threatening the platoon.

"His suit was in five pieces, sir," said the Corporal. They had returned to the column and he was briefing the Captain. "Like he was dismembered. There wasn't much left of him, sir, mostly the bigger bones."

"So he was consumed?" said Rail.

"It appears so, sir."

"Tracks?"

"No, sir. None we saw."

"Did you look, Corporal?"

"I did, sir," said Atticus. "The attacker came down the cliff and he fired up at it."

"Up?"

"Yes, sir. I have no idea what it might have been."

"I see," said Rail. He drummed his fingertips on his rifle. "Then we should keep moving. Retze, Bragg, get this platoon moving again.”

Atticus walked back to the vanguard. Grippa watched him approach. “Well?” she said.

He told her about the scout and the suit, and for the first time he saw a spark of fear in her eyes. The surge of protectiveness surprised him: it had been long time since he was responsible for anyone but himself.

“Could it be one of those armored things?” she said.

“I don’t think so. That wall was nearly vertical. This was something else.”

She peered around at the mountains. “Wonderful. We’re halfway, right?”

Atticus glanced at his pancake. “We’re at 51.4 klicks. So yes, more or less.”

The Captain’s voice came up: “Move it, Bragg!”

Atticus motioned for the others to follow and stepped off.

“So what’s our plan?” said Grippa. “For when we get to the lines.”

Atticus shrugged. “I don’t know. Rail hasn’t talked to me about that yet.”

“What does Atticus Bragg think would be a good plan?” she said.

Atticus studied the ground ahead of him as he considered the question. There were too many little dips in the terrain here for good sight lines, and it made him nervous.

“Well,” he said, “there’s a pile of us for sure. Probably too many to sneak through any kind of troop concentration. So what I might do, if it was me, is hunker everybody down and send a small party through—maybe three or four—to make contact with

Imperial troops. They could mount a rescue with air assets. That's assuming we don't come out where there's heavy fighting. If we do, we might find ourselves just a small, unimportant problem for the local commander among many far bigger ones."

"That's cheering."

"That's reality," said Atticus. "We need to come out in a nice quiet sector with nothing much happening."

"Great," she said. "So it's a crap shoot, since we don't know anything about where we're going."

Atticus nodded. "Pretty much so."

"How do you live with that kind of uncertainty?" she said. "I mean, you do this kind of thing all the time, right?"

"Good question. I guess the answer is you don't get too attached to things."

"I see," she said. "You're that bit of fluff blowing on the wind."

"That's the one."

"Well, I'm scared to death myself, and I don't like it one bit."

Rail halted the platoon while the yellow sun was still well up in the sky, and they made camp on a rocky plain near a tall cliff that stretched for several klicks. Atticus didn't like it and he studied the cliff face carefully before allowing the platoon to move in and set up. Rail ordered a circle of fighting holes dug and the gun cart placed in the center. The flood lights were rigged on poles around the cart, ready to deny an attacker the cover of darkness. But it wasn't an external threat that occupied the platoon's thoughts now.

When their hole was well dug, Atticus and Walt settled into it to crack food tubes. The space was cramped and they leaned against each other, shoulder to shoulder, their eyes just over the lip of the hole.

Walt pointed to Rail and Thorkin, who stood facing each other beyond the perimeter, near the afflicted. "Those two are going at it," he said.

Atticus had noticed it too, and it was clear Rail was not buying what his platoon sergeant was selling. This continued for several minutes before Thorkin turned on his heel and stalked back toward the perimeter. He saw Atticus in the hole and turned toward it, his mouth muttering something that didn't come over the comm circuit. In that moment, Atticus decided he would give everything he had, and sleep the rest of his life on the sticky floor of the Hole, to have the anonymity of a common soldier.

The Sergeant stalked up to the hole and looked down at them. "Goddammit, Bragg! He won't allow it!"

"He won't allow what?" said Walt. But Atticus knew.

Thorkin ignored Walt and jabbed a finger at the afflicted, who sat in a huddle outside the perimeter. "Those are my soldiers, Bragg! Mine! But he's letting them sit there like sheep, waiting to get torn apart by those—things, whatever the fuck they are. It ain't right, Bragg, and you know it! Venting their suits is the only way to do this proper. Let'em go peaceful!" The man was distraught. He stood over the hole like a thunderhead.

Atticus drew a breath and studied the afflicted and their guards. The guards weren't there to keep their charges safe, but to protect the integrity of their exo-suits. It was cruel, but Atticus understood this perfectly: it was the brutal calculus of command. Rail's first responsibility was to those most likely to survive.

"I hear you, Sergeant," he said. "Loud and clear. But the man's right. Nothing but plasma or a knife will do the job you want, and we can't let those things out. We don't know what they can do, and we don't want to find out."

"No!" said Thorkin. "I won't accept that!" He thrust a finger at Atticus. "You get down there, and you tell that boy how to do right by his troops! Like you did!"

Atticus didn't move. "He's not wrong, Sergeant. Not this time."

Thorkin's finger threatened Atticus. "You owe me one, Bragg! You owe me a big one for stepping on my toes. Now that Captain won't listen to me, and it seems to me you've been bending his wet ear a whole lot lately. That's my job, Bragg, not yours."

"You talked your way out of that job," said Atticus. Thorkin opened his mouth to respond, but Atticus rode over him. "You took yourself off the team, Sergeant. I didn't do that. No, the Captain's not a great leader. We all know that. But he's not wrong about this. Command sucks sometimes, Sergeant. That's just a hard fact of life. I'm damn sorry about those soldiers, I really am, but—"

Thorkin slashed his hand viciously to cut off Atticus. "No! I don't want to hear your goddamn buts, Bragg! Those are good soldiers down there, and they don't deserve to die like that!" He glared at Atticus for a long moment before seeming to falter and run out of steam. He looked away, muttering. "Jesus Christ Almighty, I can't get nothing from nobody anymore. This is a god-damned, no-good, dirty business."

"Yes, it is," said Atticus.

Thorkin snarled at him. "Fuck you, Bragg! Fuck this goddamn planet! And fuck that goddamn Captain!"

"Yeah," said Atticus.

Walt grunted agreement, but Thorkin had already turned on his heel to walk away. The man was right: this was a dirty busi-ness. Dirty and unforgiving, and it killed anyone foolish enough to overstay their welcome.

CHAPTER EIGHT

While the platoon was setting up camp, Rail dispatched a small patrol to scout the area. They returned shortly before dark carrying the corpse of a red-haired beast. Atticus could see its fur was scorched in four places.

"We shot it," said the Corporal who had led the scout. He seemed proud of the thing.

"I can see that," said Rail. He gave the Corporal a dark look. "In a volley, it would seem."

"No, sir, on a mountain. There was a bunch of'em, hanging on the side of it. The ugliest things you ever saw."

"So you decided to shoot one?" said Rail.

"Yes, sir. It seemed—well, it seemed the thing to do, sir."

"Did it?" sneered Rail. "And what did you suppose I would do with its plasma-blasted carcass, once you had hauled it back to camp and thrown it at my feet in triumph?"

The Corporal's confidence dimmed. "Well, sir, I don't—I don't really know. Sir. I—we didn't think about that."

"No, I suppose you didn't. What was your job, Corporal? Out there." Rail waved at the waste beyond the camp.

"Scouting, sir."

"That's correct. Scouting. Did anyone tell you to find dinner too?"

"No, sir."

"Can we eat this?"

"Oh, sir, I wouldn't. It's—"

"Then why is it here?" said Rail. "And why does everyone in this platoon feel the urge to do whatever the hell they please?" The Captain spread his arms and looked around. "Will someone tell me that?"

The Corporal didn't respond. His hands fluttered over his rifle.

"How long have you been a corporal, Corporal?"

"Three months, fourteen days, sir."

"In that time, has it come to your attention that your job—your only job—is to execute orders?"

"Yes, sir."

"Without a will of your own?"

This last seemed to float over the man's head, but he gamely agreed. "Yes, sir."

"Corporal, you will not keep your new-found rank much longer if you continue to defy my orders. In fact, no one in this platoon is listening to my orders, or giving me the respect due my position. I will have respect, and I will have obedience!"

The Corporal agreed to this as well, but things had clearly moved beyond his depth. Atticus keyed his pancake to open a channel to Thorkin. "You need to be here, Sergeant. Right now."

Thorkin responded immediately: "Understood."

"I want your name and service number," said Rail, "and the names and numbers of every member of this hunting party. You will all receive a negative report, and be docked for the plasma expenditure. I want a written tally of exactly how many shots were fired at this thing."

The Corporal was close to breaking down now. "Aye, sir."

Thorkin walked into the group and looked around. "What's the problem, sir?"

Rail turned on him. "Do you truly not see the problem, Sergeant?"

"I see an animal dead from piss-poor shooting, sir."

Rail pointed to the Corporal. "This man has been frolicking in a war zone!" The Corporal's eyes bugged. Atticus thought he might have squeaked.

"They shot an exo, Captain," said Thorkin. "Big deal."

Rail's tone was wild. "It *is* a big deal, Sergeant! Once again, you are attempting to undermine my authority!"

"Negative, sir."

Rail brayed a high, false laugh. Atticus recognized it: the man was close to a breakdown. The pressure of commanding the platoon in an impossible situation was more than the Captain could bear. The dying afflicted had probably been the last straw, and now he was cracking.

"I'm not stupid, Sergeant," said Rail, "despite what you might think. You've been talking behind my back all along, and now it's produced this!" He pointed a long finger at the Corporal and the plasma-scorched beast. "This is a direct affront to my authority!"

"Negative, sir," said Thorkin.

"I'll break you long before you bring me down, Sergeant! I'm the heir to the Sirius System seat in the Imperial House of Lords, not some mineral broker's useless fifth son dropped into a mil-farm. I will not be looked down upon, or undermined, by people like you!"

Thorkin held up his hands. "Sir, I didn't—"

"Yes, you did!" shouted Rail. "And I intend to make you pay for it. This man, too. He flouted my authority by turning his scout into a gun club!"

The Corporal moaned.

Thorkin shook his head. "I will take full responsibility for—"

"No, Sergeant Thorkin, you won't. You are relieved of your duties."

There was a long moment of shocked silence, from which Thorkin was the first to recover. "I'm entitled by law and custom to know the reason, sir."

Rail sneered at him. "As if you didn't know! You are relieved for undermining my authority with seditious talk, eroding military discipline and respect for lawful command, and thereby reducing the platoon's combat effectiveness in a war zone. Is that enough, Sergeant, or do you need more?"

"No, sir."

"Very well. You will join Third Squad as a common trooper. Report to your squad leader."

Thorkin said nothing.

Rail now whirled on the Corporal, who leaned away as if expecting to be struck. "Corporal, take this ugly thing away and dump it outside the perimeter! I will deal with you later."

"Aye, sir."

"Dismissed! All of you."

Atticus was tired of sleeping in a hole in the ground, so he and Walt climbed a short way up the cliff face to pass the night sitting in the open on a rock ledge. It would also let them keep an eye out for anything that might come at the platoon from above. Atticus had decided that whatever ate Fenrik had been flying. Nothing else explained the absence of tracks, or the attack down a sheer cliff face. But Atticus had yet to see a single bird on this planet, and that undermined his theory somewhat. Fenrik's fate remained a puzzle, and it was one Atticus privately hoped not to get an answer to.

"Well, that was a shocker," said Walt, when they had settled on the ledge. "Who's doing Thorkin's job now?"

"No idea," said Atticus. "Maybe nobody. I don't think Rail really knows what a platoon sergeant does, or he wouldn't have zeroed his. But he's stuck with it now. He couldn't bring back Thorkin now if he wanted to."

"Nope," said Walt, "and that's not even our biggest problem." He nodded toward the afflicted. "What about those poor bastards down there? They're just waiting."

"What about them, indeed. I don't have any better answer."

"You know, I could put a couple of slugs into each them from here," said Walt, but he didn't move to lift his mech-gun. "It would be a mercy that droppeth like gentle rain from Heaven."

"Yes, it would," said Atticus. "But also murder it would be."

"A fine distinction here."

"In fairness to Rail," said Atticus, "we're in a fix that would tax the best commander, and he's not the best commander. He's flailing, and starting to break, but his solution is not a bad one, however terrible it might be."

They sat in a long, gloomy silence before Walt spoke again. "We're not getting out of this one, are we, At? At least not with our humanity intact."

"It's looking worse all the time, my friend."

* * *

Atticus was still awake, thinking about the afflicted, when the armored beasts came. They galloped into camp from deep darkness. There were two of them, and he knew immediately they'd been drawn by the scent of the Corporal's red-haired beast. It had been foolish of the Captain to leave the corpse near their camp, allowing news of an easy meal to drift into the waste. Now the great beasts would find more to eat than they ever dreamed possible.

Atticus keyed a general broadcast: "Incoming hostiles! Repeat, incoming hostiles! Everyone up! Somebody hit the floods!"

Somebody did and the lights flared on to reveal the beasts already inside the perimeter and soldiers abandoning their shallow holes. They sprinted across the hard ground with nowhere to go, and the beasts followed. Atticus could see several bodies on the ground already, twisted and broken. Blue bolts of plasma flashed wildly. Below their ledge, a soldier was attacked by both beasts and they tugged his body between them, growling. He screamed, high and shrill, and a fountain of blood erupted as his suit failed with a deep, ripping sound. The beasts had torn him in half.

"Jesus!" said Walt.

Atticus turned away, sickened.

"What's the plan, boss?"

"We have to get down in there," said Atticus, "and see what we can do."

"I was afraid of that," said Walt.

But Atticus didn't know what to do first. The camp was chaos, and the circuit was full of shouts and screaming. Volleys of blue plasma burned across the plain in every direction. Some of it bounced from the beasts' armor to careen wildly across the camp, endangering the soldiers themselves.

Where the hell is Rail? Atticus hadn't heard the Captain say anything on the circuit. He picked up his rifle. Fine, he would start with the basics: establish a base of fire. "I want you up on that cannon, Walt."

"Done," said the gunner. "Get me there."

They slid down the crumbling slope below the ledge. Walt stopped to fire a burst at a beast running past, but the heavy rounds only clattered off its armor. He swore. They pressed on, but the cannon began firing before they reached it. The shots were panicked and several hit the cliff face with a thunderous crackle before spinning wildly into the night.

Thorkin's booming voice now rode over the clutter on the circuit, telling the platoon to hold its positions. But Atticus didn't see any positions—only people running, screaming, and dying. This thing might be beyond effective control already.

Two of the light poles toppled in the melee, sending black shadows flitting across the battlefield. The poles struck the ground with twin crashes to boldly illuminate two tiny patches of red earth. Now half the perimeter lay in darkness. Blue plasma sizzled through it, chewing into the cliff face and making a steady rain of stone fragments.

Thorkin's voice came clear on c-channel now: "Rally on the cannon! Repeat, rally on the cannon!" The Sergeant had asserted authority in Rail's unexplained absence, and cut everyone else from the comm circuit.

The thump of the heavy cannon had stopped and Atticus ran toward it, pulling Walt by the arm. Bodies were underfoot, and parts of bodies. He tripped twice and once kicked a fallen rifle across the ground. Light and shadow flickered around him, and half-seen figures darted between brilliance and darkness. He wondered where Grippa was.

"Sweet Jesus!" said Walt. He pointed to the cannon cart.

A suited figure was draped over it: horrifyingly limp, as if the soldier had been picked up and shaken until every bone was broken. Together, Atticus and Walt dragged the body from the cart and it dropped to the ground like a suit full of sand. Dark figures now gathered around them, heeding Thorkin's call to assemble on the cannon. Walt leaned his mech-gun against the cart and climbed up to put his hands into the cannon's improvised hand-grips.

"Aim between the plates!" said Atticus.

"Don't tell me my business!" growled Walt. The cannon fired a single round, rattling the cart. "Whoa!" he said. "There's a kick in the teeth!"

"For God's sake, don't hit anybody!"

On the comm circuit, Thorkin was working to organize a defense around the cannon, but much of the platoon was sluggish to respond. The soldiers' initial surprise had turned to panic when they found themselves defenseless against the beasts with nowhere to hide.

Above Atticus, Walt fired three rounds from the cannon and grunted in frustration. "I can't see a goddamn thing!"

"Wait one!" said Atticus. He slung the rifle on his shoulder, then ducked under the barrel of the cannon to lift a fallen light pole.

As the pole rose, a cone of white light swung across the battlefield to spotlight a beast charging into a cluster of soldiers. They scattered but one tripped and fell. The beast grabbed a leg with its toothy jaws and shook the soldier like a doll. This was fast becoming a ungovernable massacre.

Atticus waved his arms and pointed to the beast. "Walt, over there! Get that one!"

"On it, boss!"

The barrel of the cannon swung around and the gun barked, but the round bounced from the beast's armor to whirl redly into the distant dark. The creature ignored the insult to trample another soldier who was struggling to rise. He fell back to the ground, dead.

Atticus held the light pole erect with one hand and piled rocks around its base with the other. He ran to the second pole, and pulled it up to illuminate yet more bodies, all of them broken and dismembered. Blue plasma still burned across the battlefield, but the platoon's fire was disorganized and it threatened the soldiers themselves far more than the beasts.

Atticus began to wonder how he could save his own skin, and whoever else he could pull out of this fiasco. Where the hell was Grippa anyway? He pushed aside a distressing vision of the pilot being torn apart by the beasts.

Thorkin's voice rose on c-channel again, uncharacteristically shrill: "They're into the afflicted!"

Atticus's blood went cold. He turned to look. The Sergeant was right: the beasts had charged into the little group of afflicted, roaring to bring down the heavens and thrashing their dog-like heads to bite at anything they could reach. One flung a body across the flats. It spun, throwing out ropes of blood; and just like that there was a new threat.

"Walt," said Atticus, "we need to—"

The cannon fired and the nearest beast staggered. It whipped its head around in confusion.

"I got it!" Walt screamed. "I got the son of a bitch! Right between the plates!"

"Nice shooting," said Atticus. "But it's too late."

"What? Hold on, At, I can get the other one!" The barrel of the cannon swung around.

"No, Walt! The afflicted are compromised!"

"Shit!"

"Yeah, get your ass down here and get your gear. Have you seen Grippa?"

"No," said Walt. He climbed down from the cart. "I could have gotten the other one, you know. Where the hell's Rail?"

"No idea. Doesn't matter now. Get your stuff."

Walt collected his mech-gun and ammunition, and together they ran out of the light of the floods into the night. Thorkin had disappeared from the comm circuit now, and Rail was still MIA, so Atticus keyed e-channel and instructed the survivors to rally two klicks from camp on 165. Then he ran. Shadowy figures moved in the darkness around him and he peered into their helmets with his neck lights, but Grippa was nowhere to be found.

Fifty meters from camp, Atticus looked back to see the surviving beast galloping straight for him. He lifted his rifle to his shoulder.

No, that won't work.

He lowered the rifle and dropped to the ground to play dead. As he lay there, he decided that if he remained limp while the creature shook him, maybe only his long bones would be broken. Those could be fixed later at the station, if the others could get him there—and if he had the credits to pay for it. Captain Rail would have to be alive for that.

But the beast thundered past Atticus without slowing, passing close enough to him that debris thrown up by its feet rattled on his helmet. He turned his head to follow the creature's progress and watched it run past Walt, who had done no more than freeze to stare in horror. Soon the beast's hindquarters had disappeared into the darkness of the valley. Atticus knew this meant one thing, and one thing only.

He stood and broadcast on c-channel: "Move your asses, folks! Those things have hatched! Captain Rail, do you read me?"

At that moment Sergeant Thorkin appeared from the darkness. He looked confused and rudderless in the glare of Atticus's lights. His eyes and mouth were anguished.

Atticus understood immediately: like the Captain, the platoon sergeant was coming undone. His relief by Rail had pushed him off balance, and now the blow to finally knock him down was the destruction of his platoon by forces beyond his control. He had come here to fight Repsians, but instead found himself fighting enemies against which he was powerless, both within the platoon and without. Atticus understood all of this, fully, but there was no time for it. He grabbed the man's suit and shook him. "Sergeant! Pull it together! Your soldiers need you! You have to get them to safety! Those things are hatching!"

This seemed to get through, and the platoon sergeant nodded, but he said nothing to Atticus. Instead, he lifted himself straighter to find his voice and urged the platoon on. But the man would bear watching: something inside him seemed to have broken.

The survivors moved down the valley toward the rally point in ones and twos, their neck lights bobbing in the moonless dark. Some ran, others walked, but they all seemed far too slow. They had abandoned everything in the camp: the afflicted, the wounded, the cannon, the extra stores of food, and the flood lights, which still bathed the dead and dying alike in a harsh white glare. Atticus roved back and forth across the rear, prodding more speed from those too dispirited to push themselves. He kept them facing forward, so only he would see the tiny creatures in the encampment, scampering among the fallen.

At two klicks Rail called for a halt, surprising Atticus.

"Where's he been?" said Walt.

"Good question."

The Captain blinked his neck lights ahead and the survivors drifted toward him. There weren't many but Rail demanded Thorkin call the roll, either forgetting, or ignoring, that he had fired his platoon sergeant. Thorkin raised his pancake and read off the platoon roster. Most of the names were met with a grim silence the Sergeant tried to cut short, but soon their awful losses were evident to all. Three days ago, forty-six soldiers had assembled in Squad Bay 18 to make an easy drop into a quiet sector. Now fourteen remained. Craddock was one of the lost.

To Atticus's great relief, Grippa was not. She responded to her name with a subdued "present" that sent Atticus in search of her. She stood at the edge of the small group, holding a plasma rifle and swaying with exhaustion.

"Are you all right?" he said, looking her over. "I was worried."

"Were you?" she said, then cocked her head. "Is ground fighting always that confusing? I only know what happened right in front of my eyes. Then everyone started running and I just followed."

Atticus nodded. "It's always a mess. Five soldiers will give you five different versions of the same fight. All of them accurate. Darkness makes it worse. So does lack of effective command."

"Yeah, that Captain of yours didn't cover himself in glory, did he? What happened there?"

"That's the question of the hour," said Atticus.

Sergeant Thorkin seemed to be asking that question now, because Rail's voice rose, sharp and cutting, on c-channel: "I do not have to explain myself to you, Sergeant! Or to anyone else here! So take a step back!"

Atticus pushed through the circle of survivors to find the Captain and the Sergeant facing each other. Thorkin, taller by a head, had placed himself far closer to Rail than protocol permitted, and his arms were folded across his chest aggressively.

Rail glared up at him. "I will say it once more, Sergeant. Step back!"

Thorkin didn't move. Atticus understood the calculation driving the platoon sergeant. Rail intended to destroy Thorkin's career to save his own, by putting the blame for this fiasco on his rebellious former sergeant. Now Thorkin was wondering where the loss would be in wresting from Rail command of the platoon, while soldiers remained still to save from the Captain's incompetence.

Atticus moved to stand by Rail's side. "This can't happen, Thorkin," he said. "Not this way."

"Well," said the platoon sergeant, "you've been flushed out now, haven't you, Bragg? Money's more important to you than the lives of the platoon, after all. I'm truly disappointed. I had thought you a better man."

"Everyone thinks they know me," said Atticus, "but they only see what they want to see. I'm no hero, and I'm no rebel, and Lord knows I don't have enough money to worry about having money. But I am a realist and I do want to get out of this alive. I think you do too, Sergeant."

Thorkin said nothing.

"The only way we get off this planet," said Atticus, "is to pull on the rope together. All of us. You're pulling in the wrong direction, Sergeant."

"Some ain't pulling at all, Bragg."

"Maybe they just need a little help, Sergeant."

Thorkin squinted doubtfully at Atticus; but after casting a last, scornful look at Rail, he picked up a boot and took a slow, insolent step backward, away from the Captain. Atticus let out a breath: a final crisis had been averted. But this certainly wasn't finished, not yet, and Atticus doubted Rail knew that. The Captain seemed oblivious to anything not in his own head.

Indeed the Captain's voice rang with renewed confidence: "Thank you, Sergeant. Now, I will explain myself, once and only once, since some here seem to find it important. When the animals charged the camp, I was knocked across the perimeter. I was unconscious for a time. I don't know how long. When I came to, Thorkin, you were calling for a general retreat. So I followed the platoon. I didn't find it necessary at that time to alter your directive, or Bragg's. Once we were clear of camp, however, I resumed active command, which I now have. And I will not be questioned by you, Sergeant Thorkin."

"But, sir—"

"That will do, Sergeant. Now, we don't know if that remaining animal will return, nor do we know if those newly-hatched insects will pursue us, so we will march another five klicks before bivouacking for the night—or whatever remains of it. Follow me."

Rail turned to stride away and the survivors fell in loosely behind him, walking in lonely pools of light. Atticus was the last to step off, assigning himself the rear guard. It was a moonless night, dark and close, but nothing stirred during their march except his own longing to be elsewhere.

An hour later, Rail halted the platoon at an enormous, flat-topped boulder that leaned against a steep mountainside. It seemed a good place to camp, so they climbed the great stone to pass the rest of that ill-starred night above the floor of the plain. Rail ordered a watch set, and Atticus and Walt drew the first shift. Atticus sat with his feet dangling over the edge of the boulder, facing back the way they'd come, his plasma rifle laid across his lap. He could no longer see the glow of the floods in the sky above the ruined camp.

Walt had posted himself on the far side of the rock. "That was terrible," he said. His voice was empty and tired. "Just awful. And you know what the kicker is? We ain't even seen the real bugs yet—the smart ones. I've been to some bad places, At, but this one lords over all of them, head and shoulders."

"Yes, it does," said Atticus. He looked up at the star-lit sky. Somewhere up there in the ether was the invisible comm barrier that kept them trapped here. "The Repsians can have it."

"Goddamn right they can."

"No pithy verse for that?" said Atticus.

"No, I'm tapped. I don't think—"

"Hang on a sec," said Atticus, "I saw something." A flash had caught his eye.

"Saw what?"

"I don't know," said Atticus. "It was a glimmer of something. Back toward the camp." He fixed his eyes on the spot where he'd seen it and called for infrared. Now there was a faint trace of something warm, two hundred meters out. It resolved when he shifted to ultraviolet: the figure of a lone human in an exo-suit. It stood facing the platoon, unmoving and working its pancake. Was it another survivor? Or one of the afflicted?

Atticus keyed c-channel. "Captain, we have a possible afflicted incoming."

"Hail the camp!" a male voice called before Rail could respond.

Atticus brought up his rifle. "We copy, unknown. Identify yourself."

"This is Lima Papa 3. Deep range scout. Permission to come in, sir."

Rail's voice came up now. "We copy, Lima Papa 3. Make the signal."

The figure's neck lights blinked three times rapidly, paused for three seconds, then blinked five times in a slow cadence.

"Signal confirmed," said Rail. "Come in, LP3. Slowly and with your weapon slung."

"Aye, sir."

"I saw the light noise of your firefight," said the scout. He was sitting on the rock now and Thorkin had his neck lights focused on the man's face. He was young, and seemed happy just to be talking to someone. "I went to investigate but then I cut across your tracks. So I turned to follow you. What's going on?"

"You didn't go into that camp?" said Rail.

"No, sir. But I did put my scope on it, from a distance, and I saw all the bodies you left behind. My orders are to avoid contact with anyone and anything, including Imperials, but I decided you might need a hand, sir—orders or no."

"We do, Private. Tell me where we are."

The scout looked surprised by this but he pointed an arm along their original heading. "The fighting is twenty-five klicks that way, sir—or it was last I knew. But isn't that where you came from, sir? Where are the bugs here? I didn't see any."

Rail gestured brusquely to Thorkin, who gave the scout a terse description of the crash, the insects, and their flight from the ship.

The man whistled thoughtfully. "Yeah, I saw a few caves like that, but I didn't see any little insects. Maybe I got lucky. Not much is known about this planet, sir. I know—I studied every holo in the library before dropping in. But I do have one question, sir. I saw a *kravit* dead in your camp. How did you get the damn thing down?"

"A kray-what?" growled Thorkin.

"A *kravit*," said the scout. "Those bastards with all the armor. They're nothing but mean and you can't kill them—or I didn't think you could."

Rail waved a dismissive hand. "I don't know," he said. "Maybe a stray shot." Walt made a strangled noise, but the Captain ignored him. "You're attached to this platoon now, Private. To lead us out."

For a moment the man looked uncertain—he answered to a higher authority than the Captain—but he nodded agreement. "Yes, sir, I can do that."

"Very well," said Rail. "I'm going to sleep. We step off at first light." He moved away.

Thorkin flipped off his neck lights and spoke to Atticus: "I'm sacking out too. I'll relieve you in two hours."

"All right."

The Sergeant lowered himself to lay on the stone and didn't move, instantly asleep. Atticus remembered a time when he could do that, too: before his life went to Hell and left him with far too much to brood over in his idle hours. He keyed a private channel with the scout. "Glad to have you, son," he said. "What's your name?"

"Strabo, sir. Ezekiel Strabo."

"So you're Zeke?"

"No, sir. Hank."

Atticus blinked. "I guess that works too. You're a merc, Hank?"

The man nodded.

"Me too," said Atticus. He offered a hand. "I'm Bragg. Atticus Bragg."

Hank took his hand eagerly. "Are you serious? Fantastic to meet you, sir! I served under you. On Crawford's Planet, right after I joined up."

"No shit?"

"No shit, sir. Delta Company. We were the blocking force in that muddy road cut. Do you remember that, sir? It was a horror show."

"I do remember that," said Atticus, "and it was. When is your scheduled extraction?"

"Not for two weeks, sir."

"Damn."

"Yeah, but no worries, sir," said Hank. "I'll get you out."

"I know you will," said Atticus. "Tell me this, what's the patrolling density behind the bugs' front lines?"

"Low, sir. The bugs don't seem too worried about their rear

areas. There's really no reason to be, sir. This place ain't exactly hospitable."

Atticus laughed. "We noticed."

The scout searched in his web belt. "You got any lasagna, sir?"

"Nope. Ate it all. Sorry."

"Damn, I always eat the good stuff first too."

"How long have you been down here, Hank?"

"Ten days, sir. But I've been on-station for five weeks—doing this and that for the General."

"Warren?"

"Yes, sir. You too?"

"This one," said Atticus. "I got stiffed on the last one down here, out of Central."

"Really?" said Hank. "You, sir, stiffed?"

"Yeah, really," said Atticus. "I'm not popular."

"Says you, sir. But begging your pardon, this one doesn't seem to be going much better."

"No, it's not," said Atticus. He chuckled grimly. He liked this blunt-talking scout. "It was supposed to be an easy one."

Hank growled in disgust. "Aren't they all? What's that Captain like, sir?"

"Doubtful," said Atticus. "A rich noble."

"Doing his time?"

Atticus nodded. "In a bad place."

"Ain't that the truth! Well, at least they got you, Major."

Atticus changed the subject: "I'm glad you showed up, Hank. We're real skinny now. Me, the Captain, Sergeant Thorkin, fourteen grunts, a merc name of Walt, and the ship's pilot, Grippa."

Hank's helmet came up. "Agrippina Warren? The General's daughter?"

Atticus nodded.

Hank whistled. "The General's got to be lighting some big fires up there!"

"Not that we've noticed down here," said Atticus.

Hank edged himself to sit slightly closer. "You do know about her, sir, don't you?"

"No, I don't. What about her?"

The scout double-checked their privacy on his pancake. "Well, sir, by all accounts, she and her daddy don't see eye to eye, if you know what I mean."

"How so?"

"She's a daredevil," said Hank. "It drives the old man bat shit crazy. I guess she's got something to prove. You know what I mean, sir: trying to get herself out of her daddy's shadow and all that kind of thing."

"A daredevil?" said Atticus.

"Yes, sir. She volunteers for all the shit missions. She flew me in, and two other scouts dropped in other sectors. She buzzed a bug triple-A tower, if you can believe that. Nearly hit it. Sure, that was before the fighting started, but she ain't got the best sense, if you ask me."

Atticus thought of Grippa dropping toward the pad with her loading ramp open, and strutting up to him at the vanguard carrying a plasma rifle. He nodded. "Yeah, I can see that."

"Yes, sir, and she's been knocking them down on the station, if you know what I mean. A trail of broken hearts, and all that."

"Oh really?" said Atticus. "Yours included?

The scout laughed. "I wish, sir! Has she gunned for yours yet?"

"I'm safe," said Atticus. "They removed my heart at the court-martial."

Hank made a face. "God, Major, that was a cock up. We were all—"

Atticus raised a hand. "Save it, son, I've heard it before."

"Yes, sir."

"When did you sleep last, Hank?"

The scout looked at his pancake again. "Twenty-one hours ago."

"Get some," said Atticus.

"Aye, sir."

In the morning, Hank pulled out a nav-pad and narrated for Rail, Thorkin, and Atticus his journey to this point. His route had been circuitous, avoiding Repsian patrols, installations, and supply depots, all of which the scout had carefully marked on his scrolling terrain map, along with the hides in which he had passed each night. "We could go back the same way," he said. "It was a quiet sector, for the most part. But it would take four to six days. More like six."

Rail grunted at that. "Thorkin."

"Sir?"

"What's our consumables status?" Again the Captain seemed to have forgotten, perhaps conveniently, that he'd relieved his platoon sergeant.

"It's bad, sir," said Thorkin. "We have a day or two of food, and two strong fights of plasma. That's it."

Rail cast a black look at the Sergeant. "In that case, we can't go his way, can we, Sergeant Thorkin?"

"No, sir, I suppose not."

The Captain turned his attention back to Hank. "Then tell me what's ahead of us here, Private, if we take this straight route."

Rail ran a long finger from the grid section of their present position to a black line the scout had drawn on the map to mark the probable current location of the front.

"I don't know what's there, sir," said Hank. "But if it's like the other areas I saw, there's supply depots and other support facilities in the bug rear. Those aren't well guarded. Forward of those are hard pads for air assets, then what looked like headquarters units and forward supply dumps, and then the front-line troops. I didn't see any major troop formations behind the lines in my sector. The bugs don't seem to have much notion of reserves, sir."

"So all of them are on the line?" said Rail. "Strung out?"

"Sort of, sir. But not strung out even-like, if you know what I mean."

"I don't, Private. Explain."

Hank licked his lips. "Well, sir, from what I've seen, bug tactical SOP is to ball up tight, here and there along the front. Like fists." He held up one of his own. "I suppose that makes some sense. You'd be afraid to move and get a fist in a weak spot. But it also means there's a more than decent chance we'll come out at a thin spot, sir. Or we could come out at a strong point, and then—well." The scout shrugged.

Rail let the silence that followed linger, shifting his eyes quickly in thought. Something bad was coming. Atticus could feel it. The Captain was teetering on the edge of madness and disgrace; and he would grasp at anything, and destroy anyone, to avoid the fall.

"Thorkin," said Rail at last, "what were your primary duties as my platoon sergeant?"

The question caught Thorkin flat-footed and he gave Rail a

suspicious squint before responding hesitantly. "Well, sir, to support command with advice and execution. To maintain the organization of the platoon. To, uh, to conserve—"

"Yes!" shouted Rail, thrusting a finger at Thorkin. "To conserve the platoon's vital stores! And by doing so, maintain its overall combat effectiveness. Am I right, Sergeant?"

"Yes, sir."

"Does this platoon look combat effective to you?"

"Sir, you—"

"Sergeant Thorkin, that retreat from camp was the most disgraceful thing I have ever seen, or heard of." Atticus drew in a breath to speak, but Rail rode over him. "The troops should have been directed to scavenge food, ammunition, and weapons from the casualties before exiting the battlefield. That's standard procedure—a fact of which you are well aware, Sergeant. Instead, you allowed the platoon to become a routed mob, leaving everything of value behind, especially the food."

"But, sir, I wasn't—"

"I'm not finished, Sergeant!" shouted Rail. "I was told—by General Warren, no less—that you were efficient and knew your duty. He was clearly mistaken. My after-action report, and your next fitness report, will reflect your misjudgments, and also your failure to control the troops in active combat while I was temporarily incapacitated. You failed in your primary duties to this platoon, Sergeant. Am I clear?"

Thorkin squeezed his hands into fists. "Yes, sir."

Rail pulled his glare away from the Sergeant. "Good. Now, I have made my decision. Five to six days of travel, retracing this man's route, is no longer an option, due to Sergeant Thorkin's gross negligence with the stores. Therefore we will continue on the direct route to the front." He pointed in the wrong direction until Hank corrected him.

Rail spun away toward the remnants of the platoon, who stood watching this. "All right, listen up! It's been a long tough march to get here, against everything this planet can throw at us, and we've lost a lot of people." He paced in front of them, looking into faceplates. "But now we're close to the finish line, and we will make the last sprint to the front. To freedom and to safety!" He lifted his rifle over his head with one hand and looked around. "What say you, grunts of the Corps ?"

The answering cheer was weak. Atticus knew how they felt: the man was uninspiring.

Rail shook the rifle in anger. "I said, what say you, soldiers of the Corps!"

This time the cheer was louder. A few raised their rifles in reply, but the platoon had been shattered. They were now far beyond the reach of fatuous garrison calls, and everyone knew it but Rail.

The Captain stepped toward a soldier who had stood unmoving throughout. He thrust his faceplate into hers. "That was pathetic, trooper! What's your excuse? Are you with us or not?"

The woman didn't respond.

Atticus's blood went cold. *Oh shit, she's afflicted.* "Sir—"

Rail bumped his helmet against hers. "Wake up, soldier!"

Still there was no reaction.

The Captain yelped and backpedaled across the rocky ground, nearly falling. When he found his balance, he set his rifle at his waist to fire twice. The energy transfer from the plasma blew the woman backward and she collapsed to the ground with a surprised gasp. She writhed on the dusty ground for a few seconds, moaning, before lying still. The chest of her suit was a black hole that flickered with thin flame.

Rail pointed to the body. "Burn her! Burn her now!"

A soldier stepped forward and directed the nozzle of his flame-thrower into the plasma hole. He triggered a jet of bright orange napalm. Atticus turned away as the flames rose, seething, into the woman's helmet.

"Who else?" shouted Rail, waving his rifle. "Who else? Let's find out! Thorkin, line up the platoon!"

The Sergeant didn't argue. "You heard him, people. Line up for inspection." His voice was strained and lacked its usual note of easy authority.

The thirteen remaining troopers scrambled to form a line and Thorkin dressed it hastily before moving to stand at one end. Atticus and the others attached themselves to the other end.

"Ready for inspection, sir," said Thorkin, distantly.

Rail bypassed the Sergeant to stare into the helmet of the first trooper. "State your date of rank, Corporal."

"1641.11, sir."

The Captain studied the man's face for a moment before moving to the next soldier. Hank spoke into Atticus's ear. "What in holy hells was that about, sir? He killed that woman dead!"

"Yes, he did," said Atticus. "I would have too."

Hank gasped. "Sir!"

Atticus gave the scout a terse account of the insects' life cycle as they watched Rail work down the line.

"Jesus!" said Hank. "No one told me that part. I guess that's why the rear area patrols are so light. This goddamn planet defends itself!"

Atticus opened his mouth to agree, but Rail's shrill voice cut him off. "I will repeat, Private! What is your date of enlistment?" Atticus leaned out from the line to see better. The Captain had moved several steps back from the line to level his rifle at a soldier struggling to speak.

"He has a stutter, sir!" said a female voice. "It gets bad when he's frightened!"

"Frightened?" said Rail. "What do you have to be scared of, soldier? Are you afraid I'll discover you're one of them?"

The soldier shook his helmet frantically. Atticus imagined the man's eyes bulging in terror, and his neck muscles working as he struggled to force words past the block.

"Sir, please!" It was the female voice again. A small figure stepped from the line, toward Rail. "You're making it worse, sir!"

Rail snapped the rifle to cover the woman. "Stand back! That's an order!"

The woman raised her hands. "You don't understand, sir! He can't—"

"I understand perfectly!" said Rail. "He can't speak because he's hatching! That's exactly what they looked like when it happened to them! You saw it!" He swung the rifle back to the man, who lifted his hands.

The woman screamed: "No!"

Rail fired.

The range was point-blank. Plasma ripped through the man, blowing out the back of his suit in a spray of blood and shredded fabric. He toppled backward.

The woman fell to her knees.

"Burn him!" said Rail. "Now! Do it!"

But no one moved.

Rail swung the rifle to the soldier with the flamethrower. "Do it, soldier! Or are you one of them too?"

Thorkin stepped out from the line and he lowered his helmet to charge the Captain. Rail brought the rifle around and fired, but the blue bolt flashed past the Sergeant's helmet and disappeared into the distance. Then the crown of Thorkin's helmet knocked the rifle away and carried on to strike the center of the Captain's chest. Rail gasped explosively and both men fell to the ground together. On the circuit everyone shouted at once, as everything seemed finally to fall to pieces.

CHAPTER NINE

As the platoon watched, the two men rolled together on the ground, each struggling to get on top of the other. To Atticus, it was the worst moment yet: the leadership of the platoon was rolling on the ground, fighting like street dogs for supremacy. Thorkin quickly gained an advantage with his greater weight, and now he sat on Rail's chest. He grabbed the Captain's helmet between his hands and beat it against the rocky ground, cursing. Rail's fingers scrabbled over the Sergeant's suit, feeling for a weakness.

Grippa grabbed Atticus's arm. "Stop them! We can't let this happen!"

"It's too late for Thorkin," said Walt. "He's looking at a death sentence now, no matter how this goes."

That was true. Nothing justified attacking an officer, and Thorkin could probably count the rest of his days on his fingers now. But Grippa was right: this couldn't happen. The Sergeant had already created deep fractures in the platoon, and letting this fight run its course risked shattering the unit beyond any redemption. And they would all be complicit if they stood by idly and the fight went badly for Rail, which it almost certainly would. It was time to stop this.

Atticus stepped toward the melee, but several rifle barrels rose to point in his direction. "Let'em be, Bragg," said a voice. "We got nothing against you, but we all know the Captain has this coming."

Atticus turned to identify the speaker. It was the Second Squad leader, the pinch-faced man with a scar across his nose who had given Atticus the extra napalm cannisters. The man's eyes were hard now and unforgiving, but Atticus almost smiled back at him. So here he was: Thorkin's lieutenant in the opposition, neatly identifying himself. He would have to be dealt with, one way or another.

Atticus decided to try the easy way first. "Look, friend," he said, "I don't have any magic dust to throw in the air and wish us back to the station. Sergeant Thorkin doesn't either. If this thing goes down, the only place you'll follow either of us is out a launch tube and straight to Hell."

"The Captain'll kill us," said Scar-nose. "Look how many he's killed already! Sergeant Thorkin needs to finish this, Bragg. We'll all swear it was self-defense, won't we?"

There was a mutter of agreement.

The easy way wasn't going so well yet, but Atticus understood the man's desperation. The platoon was down to nearly nothing, cut off, divided, demoralized, exhausted, and suffering an acute crisis of leadership. All they wanted was a way out, and Rail seemed now an exceptionally poor chance. The poisonous seeds Thorkin had sown over the past days were coming to fruit, and unless the Sergeant could be neutralized, this thing would get settled with plasma.

But as Atticus turned back to the fight, he discovered they had stopped and both men now lay on the ground, breathing hard.

There were no marks on Rail's helmet and it occurred to Atticus they couldn't actually hurt each other, not this way. He gestured to Scar-nose and the others who had lifted their rifles. "Call'em off, Sergeant. This nonsense does none of us any good."

Thorkin rolled to sit on his haunches and survey the stand off. Something seemed to pass between him and Scar-nose then, but the squad leader didn't back down or lower his rifle.

Rail put his hands on the ground and pushed himself up to stand, then moved to pick up his fallen rifle. "You heard him, Sergeant!" he said. "Call off your dogs! You're in enough trouble already."

But Thorkin only looked at Atticus, his face contorted with anger. "Take command of this platoon, Major!"

"Silence!" shouted Rail. "Your life is forfeit under the law, Sergeant! It is my right to execute you on the spot!" He took a step toward Thorkin, lifting his rifle, but Scar-nose and five others moved to stand in front of the Sergeant, blocking his shot. Their rifle barrels weren't pointed directly at the Captain, but the threat was clear.

"Hold up!" barked Atticus. He raised his hands and moved to stand between Rail and Thorkin's defenders. Things had spun well out of control, and the Captain didn't seem to recognize his peril. "Let's talk this out, shall we? Before we start shooting."

"Did you talk it out with that pilot in Rec?" said Scar-nose. "Yeah, we heard about that, Bragg."

Atticus decided then this man was the most dangerous piece on the board: he had revealed himself as a co-conspirator, and now he needed a way out that wasn't a coffin fired from a launch tube. He had nothing to lose and that made him unpredictable.

"It was just a friendly disagreement," said Atticus, smiling.

"But this is serious business. Shoulder your rifle and walk away, son."

"No," said Scar-nose, "I don't think I will."

"Then you'd better think again. There's no way this ends well for any of us, if the Captain dies."

"Dies?" said Rail.

But Scar-nose didn't move. "I also heard you have a financial interest in the Captain here staying above ground," he said, "so I won't be taking my cues from you. You ain't an uninterested party, Major."

"No, I'm not. But I am interested in my own skin, and you should be interested in yours. Here is what I propose and I suggest you take it. You stand down, friend, and stay down. And Captain Rail forgets about this little incident, since it doesn't reflect well on him." He gave Rail a pointed look. "Then we all pull together to get our asses out of this mess. Right now, we're all busy pulling in different directions, and it's not working out too well for us, is it?" Atticus looked around at the others. "What do you say? Fair?"

There was a long moment of stillness, then Atticus saw several tentative nods among the soldiers standing behind Scar-nose. Good. Unlike the squad leader, the only thing they wanted was to get back to the station alive. Atticus decided the way was clear now, with or without Scar-nose.

"Captain Rail?" he said. "What say you?"

"Why should I agree to this, Bragg?" said Rail. "These soldiers are criminals! They should be shot, not pardoned!"

"They've been pushed to the limit," said Atticus. "Partly by circumstances, but partly by ineffective leadership. That will come out at the court-martial, Captain."

"The court-martial?" said Rail.

"Yes, more than half your platoon has been lost in a non-combat situation. There will be inquiries."

Rail hesitated. He had a political future to think about. This was probably the only thing he thought about most of the time, and he surely knew the stink of cowardice had risen around him. "Very well," he said. "I'm willing to forget this, but I want absolute silence. Nothing negative will be said about my performance in the field. Nothing."

"I think we can agree to that," said Atticus. There were nods behind Scar-nose again, and several more from the soldiers who hadn't joined him. This deal seemed to be coming together.

"Not me," said Scar-nose, jerking his rifle to cover Rail. "I don't like it. Nothing's gonna change, and the Captain's gonna get everybody here killed before it's over, including me. The Sergeant's right: we need a change of leadership. Now."

"Is that your final word?" said Atticus.

"That's my final word."

Atticus lifted the barrel of his rifle and fired into Scar-nose's belly. The glaring blue plasma nearly cut the man in half, and his torso toppled awkwardly so the crown of his helmet struck the ground first.

"Jesus!" said Walt.

"No prisoners taken!" said Hank.

"I think we have a deal," said Atticus. "Any questions?"

There were none. That was good. But there remained one final problem to deal with. Atticus turned his rifle on Thorkin, who was still on his knees. "I thought it might come to this between us," he said to the Sergeant, "but I didn't know who would have the high hand when it did. It turns out it's me. So you have a choice to make, Thorkin. Get on the team, or get out." Atticus jerked the muzzle of his rifle toward the red waste that surrounded them. "We'll move on without you, if we have to."

Thorkin stared at Atticus as if he had seen a vision. "I didn't think you had it in you, Bragg," he said. "That one there doesn't have it." The Sergeant gestured to Rail.

"No," said Atticus. "this is between you and me, Sergeant—two old soldiers. Are you in or are you out? Decide."

Thorkin gave Atticus an appraising look, then he stood slowly. "I'm glad someone's finally running this platoon," he said. "I'm in."

Atticus wasn't surprised. For all his competence and bluster, the man needed a strong leader to follow. When there wasn't a strong leader, he looked for one. When he couldn't find one, he came off track. Atticus hoped Rail would see that. Maybe he would, or maybe he wouldn't, but in the meantime the immediate crisis had passed, and there was a new order of things.

Rail cleared his throat. "All right, here's the new word. We'll march toward the front as directly as terrain and enemy presence permits. Bragg, you and that scout are on point. I want to know everything you see, when you see it, and prompt warning of any incoming aircraft. We will seek cover immediately."

He paused for Atticus to nod agreement.

"Very well," said Rail. "You"—he pointed to Walt—"are left flank security, and you"—he pointed to another—"are right. We will proceed at a quick pace. I want eyes up and looking, alternating left and right by the book. This is the last push. We move in five."

Hank edged toward Atticus while they waited. "That was hardcore, sir. But this outfit is toast when we get back, you know. I've seen it before."

Atticus didn't respond, but the scout was right: the platoon had been shattered, and what was left of it would be separated and re-homed elsewhere—if Rail kept his word. If not, then there was big trouble coming. Atticus reseated his plasma pack and test fired his rifle. It was satisfying to watch a rock explode into dust.

Walt approached, with the mech-gun clipped to his suit. "Forget all those things I said before, At. I'm staying on your good side now."

"There isn't one," said Atticus.

"You make a strong case for that."

"The man was a wild card that needed to be put out of play," said Atticus. "This is serious business, Walter, and I intend to survive it."

"I give you the best chance of all of us," said the gunner. He turned to Hank and pushed out a hand. "I don't think we've met, son. I'm Walt, but not Walter."

Hank took his hand. "Hank Strabo. Pleasure."

"Likewise."

Hank eyed the mech-gun curiously. "Wow, that thing's an antique."

Walt drew himself up. "Yes, it is older than you, but most things are."

"Don't get your hackles up, pops. I'm just talking."

"Pops?" grumbled Walt. "Just flesh youth sees, the coat they judge for size! But I, not skin or bone, but me, I fly!"

Hank laughed. "A poet! Did you know that, Major?"

"I'm aware," said Atticus. "And a writer, or wants to be."

"Is that so? I don't read much myself."

"You don't?" said Walt. "Or can't?"

"Ha!" said Hank. "Good one! I got my own hustle, you know."

"Hustle?" said Walt.

"Yeah, I'm gonna be in holos. That's how you get rich."

"Is it?" said Walt.

"Yeah, first you get famous, then you get stinking rich."

"I could stand to be stinking rich," said Atticus. He could move up in the bourbon world.

Hank nodded with enthusiasm. "That's what I'm saying, sir! There ain't no rich poets, am I right? And you got a leg up, Major—on being famous, I mean. Everybody knows you."

"So it would seem," said Atticus.

"Stick with me and we'll make it big."

Walt laughed. "How do you fit that ego into your suit, young man?"

"A little bit at a time, pops—a little bit at a time."

Rail's voice on the comm circuit rode over Walt's reply, ordering the platoon to move.

"All right," said Atticus. "Let's get going. Walt, hobble out to the flank."

The gunner frowned. "Not funny. I don't like that boy much."

They marched through the day under the green light of the mingled suns, seeing nothing but a single Repsian airship that cruised low and far ahead. The chance of being seen was slight, but they hid all the same, scurrying under a shelf of rock, where they slept an hour and wished for more food. The remainder of the day passed as the others had: bright, slow, and fearful.

That night, they camped beneath an enormous, leaning boulder that sheltered them from the night sky and any eyes that might patrol it. Atticus ate his last food tube and settled his mind to go without for a while. He had done it before, and he would do it again. He and Walt drew first watch again and they sat at the edge of the boulder shadow, watching stars roll up from far hills.

"That Hank fellow rubs me the wrong way," said Walt.

"I could tell," said Atticus, "but he knows his business. He led us a straight path today, and he keeps a sharp eye. He's a good troop."

"He ought to have better respect."

Atticus laughed. "Did we, at his age?"

Walt hmphed.

"I know I didn't," said Atticus. "I knew it all, and nobody could tell me anything. Let him have his fire, Walt. We all had it, before we got knocked around a bit."

"Can I knock him around a bit myself?"

"No," said Atticus. "I think we've had enough of that for today."

"Fine. Do you think Rail will keep his word?"

"I do," said Atticus. "He knows he hasn't been effective and it eats at him, no matter what he says. The bottom line is he isn't cut out for command, and it's not really his fault."

"I suppose so," said Walt. "But a lot of people who aren't Rail have paid the price for that."

"War is the biggest waster of lives," said Atticus, "but I do think he'll surprise us before the end."

"Do you? I hope it's a good surprise."

The next morning, they entered the Repsian rear areas, passing vast supply dumps covered with mottled red tarps, enormous tanks of water or fuel, limbered artillery pieces parked with exacting precision, and vehicle pads with service shelters and revetments. It was a vast panoply of war, waiting to be thrown into the fight, and all of it had to be avoided, sometimes by making wide loops that took the platoon far off its base course.

But soon they realized it was all deserted, or seemed to be. The Repsians had built an enormous infrastructure to support their operations, then gone elsewhere, leaving it untended until needed. Atticus supposed the Repsians relied on the unrelenting hostility of their barren planet, and its murderous fauna, to deter sabotage. If so, that wasn't the most unreasonable strategy. Atticus himself would have given long thought to the wisdom of operating a small unit in this waste.

They also encountered roads for the first time. A few had been graded for heavy vehicle traffic, but most were only two ruts cut by long use into the rocky ground. These were the most dangerous, since the ruts were often invisible until underfoot. A single vehicle spotting the platoon and calling for help would end everything.

Twice, they hid from airships passing overhead. These had a curious design Atticus had never seen. A round, horizontal housing extended out from either side of the ship, like an outrigger, and inside each housing a large rotor turned to provide lift. A smaller, vertical rotor rose from the rear of the ship, presumably for control. It was a primitive form of propulsion, but it had the virtue of being noisy: the heavy thump of the big rotors, and the clatter of their housings, gave early warning of the ships' approach.

Atticus was trailing Hank around the shoulder of a low hill when the scout suddenly knelt and lifted a closed fist. "Hold here," he said to Atticus quietly. Then the scout lowered himself to his belly to crawl forward until the curve of the slope took him out of Atticus's sight.

It was noon of the yellow sun, and the light reflecting from the pan below the hill was harsh and bright. Atticus dropped to one knee and brought up his rifle to swing its sights across his forward view, calling for more glare reduction, but there was nothing to see but the endless red waste.

Hank spoke in his ear: "Okay, I see a dump and a pad. Like the one we saw on the left before—the same set-up. The building against the dump is a little bigger though, platoon-size. No windows, one door facing the pad, closed. There's three bug carriers parked close to the building. That's new. Ramps are up, turrets covered, but otherwise they look ready to go. There's one of those rotor airships on the pad. Nothing moving that I can see."

"Anything else?" said Rail, who was listening. "An encampment nearby, or an HQ?"

"Negative, sir. Just this depot. But there's no way that building is empty with those vehicles parked here. They're the first ones we've seen. I'll bet you money there's two dozen bugs behind that door, sleeping off hangovers."

"Understood," said Rail. "Hold where you are."

"Aye, sir."

Atticus sucked warm water from his reclamation tube while they waited. They should take one of the carriers and disable the others—even if there were Repsians in that building. The rotor ship would be the fastest way out, but it was far too risky. They would almost certainly crash it, or get shot down. Plus, he had a grunt's innate distrust of having his feet off the ground. It was usually unhealthy.

Rail arrived with Grippa and two others, and together they crawled to Hank, who had stacked a low wall of rocks to conceal himself while he waited.

"We need one of those carriers," said Atticus. "Think you can drive it, Grip?"

"Are you kidding? I can drive anything."

"All right," said Rail. "Lieutenant, take the three mercs and these two here, and bring me one of those carriers. Disable the others, and that airship."

"Aye, sir," said Grippa.

Rail crawled back to wait with the platoon, and Atticus watched Grippa study the building and the vehicles while chewing her lip. "We're the ground-pounders here," he said to her gently. "Shall I lead?"

She shook her head. "No, I got it. Take Hank and Walt, and set up behind that large storage cube, the gray one next to the red tarp. Watch the door. If anything comes out, blast it. I'll take these other two. There has to be a ramp button, or something, on the hull. Stay where you are until I call you. It'll take some time for me to work out the controls."

Atticus nodded. "Aye, ma'am."

"You have to delay anything that comes through that door until I get the thing spun up."

"Got it."

"Good," she said. "Now go. Be careful."

Atticus rose, motioning for Hank and Walt to follow, and together they ran to the storage container, keeping its bulk between themselves and the door. He set up at a corner and peeked around. The door was still shut. Five meters to his left, Walt lowered the mech-gun's bi-pod and wiggled under the red tarp. Hank had his back to them, standing rear watch. Atticus was pleased both men knew what to do without being told. That was rare.

"In position," he told Grippa.

"Copy. Moving now."

Atticus watched the door, knowing Grippa would be exposed to observation from the building for several seconds. But the door remained shut. He wondered what Repsian hooch was like.

"We're there," said Grippa. "Opening the ramp."

Atticus settled in to watch the building, pondering the wisdom of approaching Imperial lines in a Repsian carrier. They couldn't communicate with friendly forces until they had come out from behind the comm barrier, and that might not happen before friendly fire had started. Maybe they could ditch the carrier short of the front and make a last dash on foot to the finish. That seemed risky too, especially if they were pursued. But this contract had been one scramble to survive after another, so what was one more?

Atticus had been staring at the door for several minutes when he heard a metallic whine, followed by a wheeze, then a thump, then another thump, followed by a steady, rising whoosh.

What the hell is that?

He looked around to see clouds of red dust blowing across the pad from beneath the airship.

Oh shit. "Grippa!"

There was no response.

"The door's open, At," said Walt.

Atticus snapped his head around to see a Repsian step from the open doorway of the building. He would never get used to the alienness of the things: it cantered gracefully from the building on six legs, holding a rifle in two of its four arms. Another followed it.

"Grippa, the door's open," said Atticus. "Two bad guys are out. I hope you know what you're doing." He lifted his rifle to fire at the lead Repsian. The shot missed high and left a glowing trench in the building, but a short burst from Walt's mech-gun cut away three of the creature's legs. It slumped to the ground.

"Nearly ready," said Grippa. "Hold for thirty seconds, Atticus, then retreat up the ramp."

"Understood," said Atticus. He shook his head in frustration. Hank had been right about Grippa, and now she'd made this thing ten times more risky. But there was nothing to do but press on.

Six Repsians were now out of the building, not including the one that lay dying by the door. They had moved into cover behind a gray container on the far side of the supply dump. It would be great if they stayed there.

Atticus sent Hank to watch their left flank, which was exposed to the open maze of the dump. He fired his rifle at the container hiding the bugs, to keep their heads down, but still they leaned out to fire back. An incoming round opened a hole in the container above Atticus, and bits of something hard spilled from it to bounce from his helmet.

Twenty more seconds.

Walt loosed a long burst that left a wandering pattern of holes in the container that hid the Repsians, and something green and organic oozed out wetly to glisten in the strong sunlight. The gunner made a noise of disgust. "I regret that now."

"I got movement in the dump!" shouted Hank. Atticus heard him firing his rifle.

Two more Repsians slipped from the doorway into cover behind the container, and the torrent of fire from them intensified. This was getting dicey. It was time to mix things up. Atticus pulled a grenade from his web belt, thumbed the primer lever, and stepped out to throw. The suit gave him an assist, but the grenade landed short, falling on top of the container with a clang.

"Son of a bitch!"

But the grenade had enough momentum to bounce across the container and drop off the far side. The blast threw an enormous mass of something sticky and yellow against the wall of the building. It had been a piss-poor throw, but in war it was better to be lucky than good.

Ten seconds.

"I've got three over here, boss!" said Hank. "Closing fast!"

"Understood," said Atticus. "Get back here."

"On my way."

The noise of the rotors was a thumping roar now. It was time to leave. "All aboard, Walt!" said Atticus. "Let's go!"

The gunner gave the Repsians two final bursts before wiggling out from under the tarp. In the lull, three more bugs exited the building to dash for cover, followed by a larger one that stepped boldly into the open to look around. It was a meter taller than the others and wore a suit of gray armor, smooth and glistening.

Well now, thought Atticus. *It's Colonel Bug himself.* He raised his rifle and fired, but the plasma deflected from the Repsian's chest plate to blast a smoking hole in the side of the building.

No way.

Hank arrived and tugged Atticus's arm. "Time to move, Major!"

Atticus followed Hank and Walt to the airship. Heavy rounds kicked up dirt around them as they ran. Something struck Atticus's helmet, knocking him sideways. He staggered, tripping over his own boots, but Hank steadied him.

"I think it was just a ricochet, sir!" said the scout.

Atticus staggered up the ramp, disoriented. Hands reached to pull him inside.

"All in!" shouted Walt. "Grippa, go!"

The little airship lifted unsteadily and Atticus stumbled coming off the ramp, but someone caught his web belt and yanked him deeper into the ship. The troop space of the ship was just a large metal box with handholds welded to the walls and hanging from the overhead. The Repsians apparently had no use for seats. Perhaps they didn't sit. Atticus clung to a hold, and they all bounced and swayed as the little ship dipped and skated over the pad, ten meters off the ground. Suddenly, it rotated to expose the open ramp hatch to the building.

"Get down!" Atticus shouted.

Incoming rounds sparked off the ramp and zipped through the compartment to punch holes in the overhead. A dozen thin shafts of light now shone down from above, but Atticus saw no blood on the deck.

"Sorry!" Grippa yelled, and the ship rotated again, swinging the ramp away from the line of fire.

"Is anyone hit?" said Atticus. His head was clearing now.

There was a chorus of negatives.

He moved to the ramp to look for an actuator, then thought better of it: the rest of the platoon, beyond the hill, were close enough that seconds might count in loading them. Atticus looked at the ground below. They were going in the wrong direction.

"Come left, Grippa," he said.

"I'm trying."

"This was foolish, you know," he said. "Have you ever flown a rotor-type like this?"

"Yes," she said tightly.

"Really?"

"Okay, fine, in a simulator." She brought the ship left with an unnerving shudder. "But these controls are shit," she said. "They're far too sensitive for big, course brutes like those Repsians."

Atticus thought of the large Repsian in *kravit* armor. The skill and raw force that was surely needed to mold that impenetrable carapace into a custom suit of armor was unimaginable. It was one hell of an amazing thing, and he wanted a suit of that stuff in the worst way. But there was little honor among mercenaries who didn't know each other: the armor would be stolen from him within a day, probably at gunpoint. Then stolen again within an hour.

"Landing!" announced Grippa and the little ship slammed into the ground. It bounced high and a dense cloud of red dust whirled into the compartment from the open ramp hatch.

Rail was in first, rushing past everyone to get to the cockpit.

"You're welcome!" Walt called after him.

Atticus grabbed a handhold and put his head out the side of the ramp, waving. "Let's go, people! Move it or stay here!" He counted troopers as they ran past him. Everyone but Thorkin gave him a nod or a smile. They were glad to be leaving. He walked down the ramp to double-check his count, but no one had lingered. He didn't see any Repsians either, but they were certainly coming. That Colonel was sure to be a hard-charger.

Atticus stepped back on the ramp and toggled the actuator. "All in, Grippa! Clear to go!"

"Roger, clear to go! Departing."

The airship lifted from the ground and tilted forward to

accelerate across the valley, picking up speed as the ramp pulled shut and locked into place. A ragged cheer went up in the compartment, and Atticus looked around to see exhausted but happy faces. Like him, they were looking forward to a hot shower, hot food, rest, and blowing off a great deal of steam in the Rec Sector. All of that seemed much more real now. Maybe Grippa hadn't been wrong after all.

They'd been flying for less than a minute when the airship climbed sharply. Atticus held tight and watched through a slug hole in the deck as the ground beneath the ship didn't fall away despite the climb. Grippa had nearly driven the thing into a hill, ending everything. He wondered if she was flying in the right direction.

"Hank," said Grippa, "give me a vector from here."

Hank gave Atticus a look before consulting his nav-pad. "Heading 216, ma'am. You're off by 74 degrees left."

"Copy. Off 74 left."

The ship tilted and swung right, and the deck plates vibrated beneath Atticus as Grippa added power. Hank studied his pad. "We're on course now, ma'am, more or less. But now we're off in the hills behind that depot. There's a bunch of high features back here."

"I see them," said Grippa. The rotors complained as she pulled the ship sharply left, then curved back right again, nearly tipping the little craft on its side. The soldiers on the left wall of the bay swung on their holds and swore cheerfully, still in high spirits. Atticus wasn't. He had begun to feel queasy.

"I'm gonna die in a fiery crash after all!" said Walt. He had both hands around a hold, clinging tightly.

"Relax," said Atticus. "She's just getting—"

WHAM!

The ship dropped violently, as if swatted from the sky by a giant hand. Atticus's boots lost contact with the deck and he hung suspended in the bay, falling with the ship.

"I *knew* it!" screamed Walt. "I ain't walking away from this one, At!"

The ship dove. The twin rotors roared in protest, and the troop bay shuddered and rattled ominously. People shouted on the circuit now, their happiness forgotten. Atticus hung in the air still, baffled: whatever had hit the ship had come from above, which ruled out a mountain strike, but he had no idea what it might have been. A shot from a ship above them would have surely penetrated the thin skin of the overhead, but Atticus didn't see a new hole.

The airship's fall was abruptly arrested and the deck now rose to slam into Atticus, and everyone collapsed to the deck in a tangle of arms, legs, and weapons. The ship was climbing smoothly now as if nothing had happened. Atticus picked himself up to look for a better hold.

"Something hit us!" said Grippa. "No idea what! Hold tight!" The ship banked hard right, sending everyone tumbling across the bay again. Atticus heard a whistle of wind and looked back at the ramp, but it was secure in its frame.

"Look!" said Hank. He pointed to a circular hole in the hull, near the overhead. It was about fifteen centimeters across, and it had sharp, ragged edges that curled inward, as if an awl had been punched through the steel.

"The bastards are shooting at us!" said Thorkin.

Atticus didn't think so. The hole was too big for a small-caliber cannon round. It looked more like the rail gun shot that had started all this, but that wasn't possible here.

"There's another one," said a soldier, pointing. A second hole was nearly identical to the first—round and punched inward. Atticus peered around the bay and up at the overhead, but he didn't see an exit hole.

WHAM!

The ship plummeted again. Air whistled through the holes.

"Something's got us!" said Grippa. "Brace for impact!"

Walt clutched his hold tightly. "Clear the road!" he screamed. "I'm bound for glory!"

But the ship decelerated sharply and popped back up, as if checked by a tether reaching its limit. Atticus was thrown to the deck again.

What the hell is going on?

Then the floor fell away again.

"Impact!" shouted Grippa.

Walt gargled.

Atticus lay on the deck and waited for the end. But the impact with the ground was no harder than some combat landings he'd lived through. The deck plates slammed against his back, then settled with a quiver.

Walt crowed into the silence that followed: "I'm charmed! Ha ha ha! Wooo! I may never die!"

"You may be right," said Hank. "You got old age beat already."

Atticus laughed at that, happy to be alive. He was drawing a breath to question Grippa when the far wall of the troop bay buckled inward with a groan of metal. Then two points of something hard and pale punched through the hardened steel like thunderclaps.

What now?

Something screamed over the noise of the dying rotors, high

and feral, then the points moved upward to open two parallel gashes in the hull. Failing metal shrieked and the weird green light of the two suns filled the troop bay. Atticus realized then the two points were claws. Something huge, and absurdly strong, had snatched the little airship from the sky and was now intent on dismantling it, probably expecting to pull out a dozen Repsians for a snack. Atticus wondered how anything could have survived long enough on this fiercely predatory planet to achieve sentience.

The claws pulled away then, leaving long rents in the hull through which Atticus could see distant hills. The cockpit door was pulled open and Rail came through it. He looked at the rents and pointed to Atticus. "Drop the ramp, Bragg. We're getting out!"

"Out?" said Walt. "How is out there better than in here?"

"Do it!" said Rail.

"And go where?" said Atticus.

"I said drop the ramp! That's an order!"

The overhead now buckled with a tremendous bang. Seams opened and more daylight shone into the compartment. Claws scraped on the hull above them and tapped impatiently. Getting out wasn't the worst plan. The hull wouldn't hold this thing back much longer, whatever it was, and Atticus would rather fight in the open than wait in the ship to be eaten. He moved toward the ramp actuator. The thing outside screamed again, and the tip of a claw pushed into the longest of the two gashes in the wall and worked to widen it. Metal curled back, screaming in agony. It was an unbelievable display of strength. Atticus pulled his hand back from the ramp actuator.

On second thought, there was no chance out there. None at all. Zero.

The claw pulled away and a bird-like foot with four sickle talons reached in through the gash to explore the troop bay. There was a rush for the opposite wall, but the foot found a soldier whose escape had been blocked by the others. The long talons closed around the man's waist and he screamed, high and sharp, before the great foot snatched him from the ship through the narrow rent in the hull. A leg fell to the deck with a dead thump, severed by the sharp edge of the hole. Blood poured from it, forming a wide puddle on the deck.

"That was Nickles!" said a panicked voice. "What the hell is that thing?"

"A huge flying beast with teeth and claws," said Rail. "Goddammit, Bragg, drop that ramp!"

A claw streaked red with blood punched through the overhead and peeled it back. Walt pushed the muzzle of his gun up through the opening and fired a burst. The creature roared, and shell casings fell to rattle on the deck plates. Three claws now punched through the overhead, ripping it like plastic.

"I think you just pissed it off," said Atticus.

Rail pushed past him to hit the actuator. The ramp clanked from its frame and whined toward the ground. This surprised Atticus: with the heavy damage to the hull, he'd given the ramp mechanism less than an even chance of operating. Maybe their luck had bottomed out and it would finally start to turn up.

"Repsian troop carrier approaching!" said Grippa. "Two klicks!" Nope, their luck was still trending down. Atticus turned to Rail to suggest raising the ramp again.

"Hold up!" said Grippa. "They're firing at that thing—the dragon—not us!"

Atticus pulled his head up. Now that was interesting. "Grippa! Get out of the viewport!"

"Why?"

"They think we're bugs in here!"

Grippa didn't reply, but a moment later she came through the cockpit door to stand in the troop bay, looking around. "Great Gods, is that a leg?"

Atticus could hear the other carrier's fire now, a deep thumping sound that traveled up his legs from the deck. There were several sharp cracks that might have been cannon hits on the beast. The thing screamed, and the carrier shook violently. The absurd armor on the *kravits* made sense to Atticus now: something that big, that slow, and that full of meat needed massive protection against something like this. It also explained the ruined trooper at the bottom of the cliff. These things were probably territorial and Fenrik had been at the wrong place at the wrong time.

"We need that carrier," said Rail.

He was right, but plenty stood in their way. The ship rocked under the weight of the beast, and the overhead popped and groaned as the thing shifted position. More green light fell into the bay. Looking up through the gashes in the overhead, Atticus could see pale leathery skin with rusty red highlights, and quick movements that might have been huge wings flapping. The incoming fire from the Repsians was loud now, and the creature roared in pain or annoyance. The little ship shuddered as the thing pushed off to fly away.

Atticus stepped to one of the rents in the hull to peer out, avoiding the pool of blood. The narrow opening limited his angle of view, but for a brief moment he saw the flying beast retreat toward a high peak. It was sleek and long-limbed, with a narrow, graceful neck and a wide flat head, and wings like a bat's, spread high and wide. They beat powerfully as the creature climbed. It was grand and terrible, and the most beautiful thing Atticus had seen on this unlovely planet.

He shifted to look out the rent toward the front of the ship. His view in that direction was even more restricted, but he could see one tall Repsian and half of a second, walking toward the ship. They held their weapons loosely, unconcerned now that the beast had fled.

"Incoming bug infantry!" said Atticus. "On foot."

"Assemble on the ramp!" shouted Rail. "Egress formation!"

The platoon, now only a squad, formed two lines on the ramp. Rail walked down the middle. "Left line goes left, right line goes right! They're not ready for us, so strike hard and fast, and it'll be over in a few seconds. On my go!"

Atticus was pleased to see the man take command in a pinch. Maybe he was learning something.

Rail held up an arm and peered cautiously through the angle between the ramp and the hull. A moment later he dropped his arm. "Go! Go! Go!"

It was over quickly. So quickly, in fact, Atticus almost felt sorry for the Repsians. For them, it must have been like arriving at a friend's place, with a deck of cards and a bottle, only to find a starving tiger waiting in the sitting room. The tall, six-legged soldiers put up no more than ten seconds of fight before they lay on the ground, dead or dying.

The platoon followed Rail to the troop carrier at a run. After a careful peek inside to ensure their work was done, they clattered up the ramp into the troop compartment.

"All right!" said Walt. "Let's try this thing again. I feel like a new man!"

Hank peered into the gunner's helmet. "That's not what the wrapper says, pops."

"We're leaving you on this planet, boy."

Atticus found Grippa at the front of the carrier, standing on the end of a narrow, padded bench designed to accommodate a Repsian. She faced a tall podium on which an upright monitor displayed information in an alien script. Parts of the monitor's screen blinked for attention it would never get. In front of the podium, set in the hull, was a wide external viewport overlaid with more alien script.

"These controls are even shittier than the ship's," said Grippa. "If you can believe that."

This was unwelcome news, after their wild ride in the airship. "How so?" he said.

"For starters, this was made for a Repsian to drive, not a human. The steering joystick is over here." She pointed to a fixture on the hull to the left of the viewport. "But the throttle is over there." She pointed to a toggle to the right of the viewport, separated from the joystick by well over two meters. "I'll need help."

"You got it," said Atticus. "Where do you want me?"

"You take the throttle. The button on the left side might be a brake."

"Or it could trigger a distress beacon," said Atticus, "to bring Repsian search and rescue on top of us."

"Mr. Bragg," said Grippa, "the most helpful quality in a pilot is confidence. Show some."

"Maybe, but the pilots I've known lately have been either timid or cocksure."

Grippa sniffed. "I was as surprised as anyone to get knocked from the air by an enormous flying creature. It wasn't me."

"I suppose so," said Atticus, "but the most helpful qualities in a grunt are caution and realism."

"Just step to the throttle," she said, "and think positive thoughts. You'll be fine."

"Yes, ma'am." He moved around the bench to stand by the throttle. Grippa was headstrong, and unreasonably dangerous, but Atticus had decided he liked that about her.

Behind them, Thorkin was counting helmets. Like the ship, the carrier had a troop bay that was simply an open box outfitted with handholds. The remnants of the platoon slumped against its walls, their earlier exuberance now turned to doubt and sullen watchfulness.

Rail stood in the middle of the bay, typing something on his pancake. Atticus imagined it was the Captain's long list of grievances against him and Thorkin, to be aired in excruciating detail when they returned.

"We're ready to move, sir," said Grippa.

"Go," said Rail, not looking up from his pancake.

"Your vector is still 165," said Hank.

"Roger, 165," said Grippa. "Forward velocity please."

"Forward velocity, aye," said Atticus. He pushed the throttle up gently and the carrier jerked backward, throwing Grippa against the viewport. Cries of protest rose on the comm circuit.

"Sorry!" said Atticus. He re-centered the lever and now pulled down carefully. The vehicle moved into a stately crawl forward. He glanced at Grippa, who was laughing. "There," he said. "I tried your confidence thing, but it didn't work for me. I'm going back to my usual stubborn resignation."

"Whatever gets you up in the morning," she said, maneuvering the carrier to avoid the destroyed ship. "Coming to 165. More power, Number One."

"More power, aye." Atticus pulled the throttle down gently and the carrier accelerated to speed briskly across the red, rolling plain. Rail ordered a test fire of the turret gun, and through the viewport Atticus watched heavy slugs throw up tall fountains of dirt and debris. He felt better now: they had speed and firepower, and best of all, they were on the ground again.

CHAPTER TEN

For the next hour the only sound in the carrier was the growl of the engine. Grippa said little, content to drive in silence, and the soldiers in the back used the time to sleep off their adrenaline crashes. Atticus leaned against the hull by the throttle, and closed his own eyes. The illusion of safety in the carrier was strong.

"Installation at two o'clock," said the soldier posted in the gun turret.

Atticus opened his eyes, and moments later it appeared in the viewport: a collection of single-story buildings with no immediately obvious purpose. Rail ordered the soldier down out of view and told Grippa to keep moving.

She glanced at Atticus. "Do you think I should steer away from it?"

"No," he said. "Roll on by, like we're important bugs with places to be."

She nodded, and the carrier passed within a kilometer of the buildings. There was no immediate reaction from them and Atticus let out a held breath. "So far, so good," he said. "But the alert level in this area will be high after we stole that ship. Count on it."

Grippa pointed to the monitor on the podium. "Atticus, look at that."

He did. There was a green box on the screen. The box contained red symbols, and it flashed more rapidly than a human would find comfortable. It hadn't been there a moment before.

"I think it's a comm signal," said Grippa. "Possibly coming from those buildings. Should we speed up now?"

"Yes, we should," said Atticus. He tapped the throttle down another two centimeters and the carrier's engine shifted into higher gear. The vehicle still moved smoothly over the hilly terrain.

Rail stepped into the cockpit area. "What's happening?"

Grippa pointed to the green box. "I think we're not responding to hails, sir. We may be compromised."

Rail stared at the screen. "Very well, Lieutenant, carry on. Inform me of any change." He returned to the troop bay and sent a soldier back into the turret to keep watch.

For the next minute, there was no sound but the engine, then the soldier in the turret spoke: "Bug carrier at five o'clock, sir. Exiting those buildings."

"Direction?" said Rail.

"Bearing on us, sir, and moving at high speed."

"Copy. Give us more speed, Lieutenant."

"Aye, sir, more speed," said Grippa. She glanced at Atticus, who moved the throttle nearly to its stops. The ride became rougher now, as the carrier ramped over every high point and came down hard, jolting its passengers.

"Receiving fire," the soldier reported, and fountains of red earth kicked up near the right front of the carrier. Debris clattered on the hull. Grippa veered away from it.

"That was a warning shot," said Atticus.

"Return fire," said Rail.

Atticus frowned. That wasn't the best idea. If the Repsians pursuing them weren't certain about the situation, they would likely withhold disabling fire until they were, and a battle delayed might never be fought. But the carrier's gun thumped overhead, removing any doubt.

"Maximum speed!" said Rail, pointing to Atticus.

"Aye, sir, maximum speed," said Atticus. He pushed the throttle down to its stops, and the carrier now flung itself over every hump and wrinkle in the terrain. The soldiers in the bay shouted and swore as they were thrown around. Incoming rounds rattled on the hull over the roar of the engine.

"Gunner down!" shouted Thorkin.

Atticus glanced back to the bay to see three soldiers lowering the turret gunner to the deck. He was limp and his suit was soaked with blood.

"You!" said Rail, pointing to a soldier standing near him. "You're next! Get up there!"

The trooper handed his rifle to another and climbed into the turret. The gun began firing again, jerking the carrier. Rounds from the pursuing carrier continued to clang against the hull, but they didn't penetrate. The range was still too great. Even so, Grippa weaved the carrier erratically to throw off the Repsians' aim.

Something near the top of the viewport caught Atticus's eye: in the distance, two specks of something dropped from the sky. They grew larger, very rapidly, and he pointed to them.

"Look at those," he said to Grippa. "Are those ships?"

Grippa said nothing as they watched the specks grow, then their shape became discernible. "Yes!" she shouted. She turned to Atticus and raised her arms in sudden glee. "They're Imperial ships, Atticus! Troop ships!"

Atticus felt a surge of hope. They were close! "Captain," he said for everyone to hear, "we can see two large Imperial drop ships descending to a point maybe five klicks ahead of us."

The comm circuit erupted with joy. The tattered remnants of what had once been a proud platoon shouted wildly and cheered, and Atticus felt their happiness, and he was glad for it. Everyone in the carrier had been beaten down by days of exhaustion, terror, and loss. Now, finally, the finish line was in sight.

"Secure that joy!" shouted Rail over the noise. "We still have bad guys coming up behind us! Lieutenant, I want all the speed you can get from this thing."

"Aye, sir," said Grippa. She looked at Atticus, smiling. He shrugged and gestured to the throttle. It wouldn't move any farther.

"Gunner down!" shouted a voice.

Son of a bitch! Atticus looked back. They were hauling out the second one now. He was cut nearly in half and blood poured from the turret housing to spread across the deck.

"Goddamnit!" said Walt. He pushed forward. "Let me up there! None of you plasma-boys know how to handle a heavy gun!" He stepped over the dead man and climbed into the turret, leaving boot prints in the blood.

Atticus keyed their private channel. "What the hell are you doing, Walter? You'll get killed up there, and you can't hit anything at this speed anyway—no one can."

"Maybe not," said Walt, "but I can give the bastards something to think about!" He disappeared into the turret and the gun began thumping again. Atticus swore and turned back to the viewport.

Their present course would take them over a high saddle that connected two butte-like ridges. Both sides of the saddle were littered with boulders fallen from the heights above.

"Steer straight between those boulder fields," he told Grippa, pointing. "Up and over that saddle."

She nodded. "At this speed we might launch off the other side and fly away."

Atticus chuckled. "Won't that surprise them?"

A solid hit on the hull rocked the carrier on its chassis. Atticus's helmet bounced from the viewport. That was a cannon shot. The bugs must have decided to stop screwing around and switch to the heavy stuff.

"Gunner down!"

Atticus pounded a fist on the viewport. *Goddammit!* He turned to point to the nearest soldier. "You! Get up here and mind this throttle!" She stepped forward immediately, and Atticus rushed back to the troop bay. He looked around for what was left of Walt, but no one in the bay was moving.

"Where is he?" he shouted.

"Blown out, sir," said a soldier standing near the turret housing. "Or fell out. He's not up there anyway."

Shit!

Atticus ran back to the podium. "I'm going after him! Drop the ramp!" He picked up his rifle and turned, but Rail was standing behind him, blocking his way. Atticus stopped. "Captain," he said, "I have to do this."

"I know that," said Rail. "We'll all go, Bragg. Lieutenant, bring us around."

For a moment, Atticus stood uncomprehending. He had fully expected the Captain to order him to remain in the carrier, and he had fully intended to disobey that order, whatever the consequence.

"We have to pull on the rope together," said Rail. "Isn't that what you said?"

Atticus just nodded.

"Then that's what we'll do," said Rail. "Prepare to dismount!"

Still unspeaking, Atticus took his place at the throttle again, and he and Grippa turned the carrier in a wide circle, looking for Walt.

"There he is!" she said, pointing. The gunner lay in a heap on the rocky ground. The Repsian carrier was closing on him.

"Drop the ramp!" said Rail to someone in the back. "Lieutenant, bring us in close. Bragg, you go get him. Work fast. Everyone else, form a perimeter and lay fire on that carrier."

Atticus smiled. Yes, the Captain might be worth something after all. One never knew the demons someone else had to overcome to become the person they ought to be: fear, jealousy, resentment, or the arrogance of a privileged upbringing. Rail finally seemed to be getting on top of his demons, and Atticus decided he would take some of the credit for that, whether he deserved it or not. His own demons ought to take heed.

Atticus pushed forward to stand on the ramp as it dropped, rifle in hand. "When we get to Walt," he said to the troopers around him. "I'll check him out. Your job is to spread out and slow down that bug carrier while I work on him. We don't know what kind of shape he's in."

Helmets nodded around him as the carrier came to a stop.

"Go!" shouted Rail. "Hurry!"

Atticus thundered down the ramp, followed by the platoon. The Repsian carrier shifted its fire to them as they ran toward

Walt. Rounds walked across the red, rocky ground, splashing up debris. Thorkin charged ahead, carrying Walt's mech-gun. Bandoleers of the gunner's ammunition swung from his shoulders. He dropped to the earth ten meters beyond Walt, and lowered the gun's bi-pod to fire on the carrier. Hits sparkled on the vehicle's hull and the head of the Repsian manning its turret gun vaporized in a spray of yellowish fluid.

It was a good start. Not for the bug.

Atticus dropped to his knees beside Walt. The man was unconscious, but Atticus saw no blood and no holes in his exo-suit. Only the kinetic trauma light blinked on the gunner's pancake. Atticus shook his arm.

"Hey, Walter!" he said. "C'mon, buddy, wake up and smell *this* sandwich—it's a beaut!"

The gunner's head rolled in his helmet, but he didn't open his eyes. Atticus glanced up at the incoming carrier. It was far too close, and a new turret gunner was now working to find the range. Atticus keyed to the med function on Walt's pancake and ordered a stim injection. It worked within seconds. The gunner's eyelids fluttered and he frowned.

"Goddamnit!" Walt said. "What heathen stimmed me? Don't do that! That shit is like fire!"

Atticus shook him. "C'mon, buddy! Up and at'em! We got bugs incoming, and they'll do more than stim you."

Walt opened his eyes. "It was you! I should have known. You're a willful bastard, Bragg."

Atticus put his hands under Walt's shoulders and lifted him to his feet, where the gunner swayed precariously. Around them, the platoon still fired on the Repsian carrier, slowing its advance, but soon infantry would dismount from it to press a final assault.

Walt looked around, still unsteady. "Hey, is that my gun?" he said. "That *is* my gun! What's he doing with it? You're a fool to come back for me, Atticus Bragg! A goddamn fool!"

"You're welcome, asshole," said Atticus. He tugged Walt's arm, pulling him toward the carrier. "Everyone up! Fall back to the carrier!"

The carrier had stopped seventy-five meters away, and Repsian soldiers were now emerging from behind it. Thorkin dismembered two in twin gouts of the yellowish fluid.

"Let's go, Sergeant!" shouted Atticus. "The party's over!"

"On my way," said Thorkin.

At the carrier, the others clattered up the ramp ahead of Atticus, who was nursing Walt along. A shot from the Repsians hit the ramp frame near Atticus's helmet and he was knocked backward. Walt fell on top of him.

"I can't catch a break!" said the gunner. "What the hell was that?"

"Very nearly the end of us," said Atticus. "Get off me!"

They untangled themselves and stood to stumble up the ramp just as Thorkin arrived. The Sergeant hit the actuator as he passed, and the ramp lifted beneath Atticus's feet. But the mechanism squealed to a sudden stop less than a meter off the ground, hung on its bent frame. Another heavy round hit the carrier, shaking it violently.

"All aboard, Lieutenant!" said Rail. "Let's move!"

The carrier jerked forward, and Atticus reached out to grab Walt's suit. The man had stumbled backward and nearly fallen from the carrier again.

"Just stuff me into a locker," said Walt. "I'm not doing any good."

Atticus didn't stuff him into a locker, but he did leave the him in the care of a soldier, who promptly sat the gunner on the deck. Atticus moved up to resume his station at the throttle.

"The ramp's trashed," he said to Grippa.

"I saw that," she said. "But the bigger problem is damage to the transmission. We're down about thirty percent from what this thing was doing before."

"Do what you can," said Atticus. "It'll take a little time for the bugs to get mounted up again anyway."

"Negative," said Rail, coming up to stand between them. "Whoever's driving that carrier buttoned up and left his troops behind."

Atticus turned to look through the open ramp hatch. The Captain was right: the Repsian carrier was pursuing already, smelling the kill. "Sir," he said, "I recommend we stay on course for that saddle. We're not far from our lines. Maybe we can limp fast enough to get there."

"I've already ordered it."

Atticus looked at the Captain. "Thank you for that, sir," he said. "Turning around. I haven't known Walt long, but he's grown on me."

Rail switched them to a private channel before speaking. "You remind me of my father, Bragg," he said. "I don't like him much either, but he gets loyalty from his people, and I never understood how. He's an arrogant asshole. But now I see why he gets the loyalty he does. It's something I never paid attention to before, until I saw it in you. He fights for his people, and doesn't let them fall or get left behind. He understands the power of that, and so do you." The Captain looked away. "I didn't understand it, plus I'm a coward at heart, not a soldier."

"That can be worked on, sir. None of us are interested in dying."

"No, Bragg, I won't be in the Service long enough for that, and I don't want to be responsible for any more deaths. All of this wasn't supposed to happen, not like this."

"No," said Atticus, "it was supposed to be easy. But it's never easy, and people can die while you try to find your way through a shit-storm. It took you too long to find your way, Captain."

Rail jerked his head back, stung. His nostrils flared. "I'll take that from you, Bragg, but only once. We're not friends, or equals. Remember your place."

"I'm reminded of it constantly, sir."

The carrier tilted beneath them, and Grippa spoke: "We're moving up the saddle, sir."

Rail turned to the viewport. "Thorkin, where's the pursuit?"

"Half a klick back, sir," said the Sergeant. "It's gaining steadily, but no longer firing."

"Very well. Send up a trooper to slow it."

"Aye, sir."

Soon the main gun was thumping again as the carrier strained to climb the saddle, its engine whining a new and ominous note. Behind them, the ramp rattled and banged in its damaged frame, offering no protection from the pursuing carrier. Atticus sent up a silent prayer, requesting that Imperial forces be just beyond this saddle. He'd seen too much of the random brutality of war to consider himself a religious man, but he liked to hedge his bets.

When the carrier finally came over the top of the saddle, there were no Imperial troops to be seen. Instead, there was a trench that zig-zagged across the bottom of the far slope of the saddle, stretching from one side to the other. The trench barred the way to a broad, undulating plain that carried for several klicks before ending at a tall ridge line. In the trench were Repsian infantry, perhaps thirty or forty of them. They were alert and looking up the saddle, clearly waiting for the carrier to arrive.

Atticus slumped against the hull. "Christ Almighty," he muttered. They had been so close.

Grippa steered the carrier toward the left side of the saddle, where enormous boulders, fallen from the steep heights above, had collected into a treacherous jumble. "Don't give up hope yet!" she said. "We're still moving!"

Something metal ricocheted loudly in the chassis beneath their feet. The carrier lurched forward another ten meters before emitting a rasping growl and skidding to a halt, twenty meters short of the jumble, on the open slope above the trench.

"You were saying?" said Atticus.

"Shut up," she growled. She shoved him aside to work the throttle, but the carrier was dead.

The carrier's turret gun now began firing above them. Atticus hadn't heard Rail order it. He turned to speak to the Captain, but he wasn't in view. In the troop bay, Thorkin was organizing the platoon to leave the carrier.

"Where's the Captain?" said Atticus.

Thorkin jerked a thumb upward. "Putting his ass on the line, if you can believe that. Not sure I do. I think I might have died already."

"I told you he'd surprise us," said Atticus.

"Prepare for egress!" said Rail on the comm circuit, before Thorkin could respond. "On my call, everyone bail out for the rocks! I'll cover you!"

Atticus hit the actuator and the ramp dropped a half meter to nearly touch the ground. That was good enough. He could see the trailing carrier now: it was just cresting the saddle. Curiously, its gun was still silent.

"We have to move, Captain!" said Atticus.

The turret gun roared. "Go!" shouted Rail.

The platoon, worn out and tattered, hammered down the ramp and turned right to sprint for the rocks. Fire from the Repsians in the trench cut wide arcs across the ground between them. A soldier running ahead of Atticus lost his legs mid-stride. His torso spun in the air, before falling to strike the ground in a splash of crimson. Atticus ran past it. There was nothing he could do—not a goddamn thing.

He dove for cover at the rocks. Fire from the trench line shattered stone around him. He found Grippa, Hank, and the others collapsed five meters inside the rocks.

"No, no!" he shouted. "On your feet, people! We have to keep moving! This is no time to rest!" He moved among them, kicking and cajoling, until they'd all risen to climb down through the rocks. "Don't stop until you get near the bottom!" he called after them.

A terrific crash of metal echoed in the saddle. For a moment, Atticus thought a ship had crashed on top of them. He ran back to the edge of the rocks and looked out. The Repsian carrier pursuing them had driven down the slope and broadsided their own carrier, knocking it on its side. The Captain was struggling to pull himself from the turret housing. He was horribly exposed to fire from the trench and dirt kicked up around him.

"I can't get out!" Rail shouted. "My legs are trapped!"

Atticus stood to break cover, but someone grabbed his exo-suit and pulled him down. "I'll get him, Bragg," growled Thorkin. "You go down there and work on that trench. That's our biggest problem right now."

The Sergeant was right. Atticus clapped him on the shoulder. "Glad to have you back, Sergeant Thorkin! This thing's been tough on all of us."

But Thorkin just stared at the toppled carrier. "Get out of here, Bragg," he said. "Let me go out my own way."

This set Atticus on his heels. He wanted to say more, but the Sergeant broke from the rocks to run for the carrier. He still had Walt's mech-gun and fired it at the trench as he ran. Clouds of dirt kicked up around his boots. Atticus lifted his own rifle and gave the Sergeant covering fire. There were too many Repsians in the trench to keep all their heads down, but he did what he could. It was satisfying to be fighting back.

At the carrier, Thorkin knelt beside Rail. The Captain's lower half lay beneath the turret housing. Words Atticus couldn't hear passed between them as rounds sparked around Thorkin, then the Captain lifted his arms for the Sergeant to pull. As Thorkin stood to take them, his left leg was knocked from beneath him, and he fell to his right knee. Bright blood ran from several ragged holes in his suit leg. Atticus renewed his efforts to protect the Sergeant, firing at anything that appeared above the lip of the trench.

Thorkin struggled to his feet, his left leg trembling and took Rail's hands. The Sergeant braced his right foot and pulled, drawing the Captain from his metal trap. But something punched Thorkin's left shoulder, spinning him to slam against the carrier. His left arm had swung in a wide arc to strike the hull beside him, and now it hung limp by his side.

But Rail was free. The Captain tried to scramble to his feet but his legs were weak, or injured, and he fell on his faceplate. Thorkin had fallen to his knees beside him. The Sergeant reached out with his right hand to grab the back of the Captain's suit and he struggled to drag both himself and the Captain across the ground to the rear of the carrier, out of the line of fire from the trench.

A round from the trench struck the Sergeant's back. It passed through him to blow a spray of blood from his chest. He screamed and collapsed, but Captain Rail now lay in shelter.

"Thorkin!" shouted Atticus. "Sergeant Thorkin!"

There was nothing for a few seconds, then the Sergeant spoke. His voice was raspy and fading. "What the fuck are you still doing here, Bragg? Get down to that trench or this shit doesn't matter."

"Stay down, Sergeant! I'm coming to get you! Both of you!"

"Negative, Major," said Thorkin. He coughed wetly and groaned. "Too dangerous. I'm done here, but Rail ain't, so go kill those bastards in the trench and come get him."

"And you, Sergeant."

"Forget about me, Bragg. I'm done. There's nothing back in the world for me now anyway." The Sergeant coughed, and grunted in pain. "I know I've been a damn fool, but raise a glass to me back at the station. Better still, put me in for a medal. Not likely after all this, but my little grandson is forever asking if I've got one. See that he gets it, will you?"

Atticus wanted to go get them, but Thorkin was right: assaulting the trench, not running into a hail of fire to die, was the answer. He had to let Thorkin go. "I'll do that, Sergeant," he said. "That's a promise. Any other business you got?"

"Naw, a grunt my age lives on borrowed time, Bragg. You know that. All my shit's been in a tight little ball for a long time."

"I hear you," said Atticus. "Listen, get yourself into good cover. I'll be back. You hear me?"

The Sergeant didn't respond.

Atticus retreated into the rocks to follow the others, wondering how things had gone so quickly from hopeful to hopeless. He found the rest of the platoon near the bottom of the saddle, resting in the rocks and waiting for him. He waved for them to stay where they were, then crept to the bottom of the rocks to peer out and examine the trench.

It was a formidable position. A heavy turret gun was positioned at each end of the trench, and at the point of each angle. Mounted on open-frame towers, the guns still pointed out over the plain. Their silence during the fight almost certainly meant they could not traverse far enough to fire back up the saddle, and that was the reason he and the others were still alive.

In the trench below the guns, Atticus could see thirty or more Repsians, many of whom still fired hand weapons at the overturned carrier, but they seemed hesitant and disorganized, perhaps still uncertain what they were up against.

Now was the time to strike.

Atticus moved back to the others, waiting in the rocks. "Alright, folks, here's the scoop," he said to them. "We'll move down through these rocks to the end of the trench and force a way in. Then we'll work along the trench, killing everything, or at least holding it down while I get Rail. Look sharp and move fast, and we'll take the ugly bastards by surprise, like we did at the ship."

"Hold up there, At," said Walt. "Let's give this thing a thought or three before we put our valuable asses on the line. This trench is here for a reason. There's Imperial troops over there on that feature." He pointed to the ridge line on the far side of the plain. "We have a clear road, right here, right now, while the bugs are busy trying to kill our least favorite person. Bugging out is a win-win, the way I see it."

He had said this on c-channel for everyone to hear, and now a dozen tired faces looked at Atticus hopefully. He knew escape, not rescuing Rail, was on their minds, and he hadn't been certain they would follow him even this far. He had no right to command them, and he had no claim on their loyalty. If they bolted for the ridge, he wouldn't blame them, but he wouldn't be doing that himself.

"All right," he said, "each of you has a decision to make here, and it has to go down quick." There was a thunderous boom from the saddle that drove his point home. "I have no claim to command you. If I see your backside humping for that ridge, I'll have nothing to say against you later. I'll shake your hand and buy you a drink. But I've never left anybody behind who wanted out, and I'm not starting now."

Atticus looked around at the others as he spoke. They were dirty, tired, and far too few for this kind of work, but he knew they could do it. They were fine troops.

"Look," he said, "I know the Captain is the original horse's ass, but in the Corps you go back for your own, including the Captain. That promise is what holds you together when everything's coming apart around you. I told you I wouldn't say anything against you if you scrambled out, and I won't, because you don't answer to me. You answer to each other, as soldiers. Now I'm gonna ease down to that trench and peek in, then I'm gonna charge in, plasma blazing, no matter what's there. If anyone comes in behind me, I'd love some covering fire."

There was a long silence in which Rail's carrier continued to take a beating from the trench.

"Goddammit!" said Walt. "I knew I shouldn't have answered that comm box in The Hole. Nothing but trouble since! Fine, let's do this." He shoved past Atticus to move down toward the trench, looking oddly naked carrying only a plasma rifle.

Atticus lifted his own rifle and followed the gunner, hoping at least a few others would come behind him. He knew very well he was asking them for more than they wanted to give, but it was the right thing to do, even for a barely repentant bastard like Rail.

But they all followed him, and they broke wide to either side as they approached the bottom of the rock pile, getting into position. Atticus was proud. They were good troops, and well-trained by Thorkin, but they had taken crippling losses and suffered under corrosive leadership. No unit could take body blows like that without permanent damage. But Atticus Bragg had them now, and they would kill bugs and get the hell off this fucking planet.

Attacking a trench demanded no subtle art, only speed, brutality, and maximum surprise. Atticus decided they could have all three, if they did it right. He crouched at the bottom edge of the rock pile. A three-meter gap separated him from the lip of the trench. Five Repsians were stationed in this section, all of them distracted by the firing on the carrier. He spoke the word and the platoon cut down the bugs from the rocks with a quick flurry of plasma.

Perfect. There was surprise and brutality. Now for speed. Atticus crossed the gap to leap into the trench. It was deeper and wider than a human would make, but well-dug. The sides were scraped sheer and a firing bench had been left on the side facing the plain. Atticus was concealed from the next section by an angle of the trench.

"All clear!" he said. "Everyone in!"

The rest of the platoon crossed the gap and dropped into the trench. Atticus grabbed Hank's shoulder and pointed to the gun tower above them. "Jump up there, Hank. When I give you the word, take out those other guns."

"Aye, sir!"

"The rest of you, follow me!"

Atticus moved to the angle and peered around it, keeping his helmet low. "I see five—no, six Repsians," he said. "All focused on the carrier. Hank, you ready?"

"In position, sir, with an itchy trigger finger."

A screech of metal echoed off the hills above the saddle.

"Captain Rail!" said Atticus. "What's your situation?"

Rail's voice was weak: "The carrier's just a heap of metal now. You're about to get your fondest wish, Bragg."

"Negative, sir. Hold tight."

"What else can I do?"

Atticus didn't reply. "Okay, Hank, light 'em up!"

The big gun erupted like heavy cloth tearing, and Atticus darted around the angle in time to see the gun mounted at the next angle sag on its support tower. Metal parted and the heavy weapon collapsed into the trench on top of two bugs. *Beautiful.* "Nice work, Hank!" said Atticus.

"This thing rips, sir!"

The remaining Repsians dodged wildly as the tower followed the gun into the trench. Atticus knelt to fire at them, but a dense flurry of blue plasma erupted from behind him, cutting down the helpless aliens in seconds. Walt and the others had followed him around the angle.

He stepped up on a boxy piece of equipment to put his eyes over the lip of the trench. The Repsians in the other half of the trench seemed confused by the collapse of the gun tower, and the volume of fire on Rail diminished. That was good.

"Okay, people," said Atticus, "we have surprise, now let's hold it. Walt, set up here and hold that next angle. The bugs will try it once they've stopped scratching their asses in confusion. Hank, you help Walt and watch for bugs coming from that other carrier. I don't know what's going on with that one, but I have a bad feeling about it."

"Aye, sir," said Hank. "The other guns are down."

"Good work."

"What's your plan now, Bragg?" said Rail.

"I'm coming for you," said Atticus. "Grippa, you're with me."

She stepped up to stand next to Atticus and smiled nervously. "This isn't my element."

"You're doing great," he said. "I need your help with Rail. He may not be able to walk. Follow me. Hank, covering fire!"

Hank's tower gun ripped again and Atticus climbed from the trench, helping Grippa after him. Together they sprinted to Rail's carrier and hid in the lee of fire, under what was left of the ramp. The second carrier had remained curiously inert. Maybe only its driver was left alive and ramming was the only weapon remaining to it. Whatever the case, it didn't matter so long as the carrier remained buttoned up.

In the trench, two grenades detonated in rapid succession and voices shouted on c-channel. The Repsians were trying the angle. Hank's gun tore the air again. Its heavy rounds ricocheted from the walls of the trench and the ground to scatter into the far rock pile with a sound like gravel thrown against a stone wall.

"This is chaos!" shouted Grippa.

"Actually, things are going pretty well," said Atticus, "all things considered. Let's go!"

He darted from under the ramp and moved toward Rail. But just then the second carrier's engine started with a clatter of valves. Atticus stopped. The carrier reversed gear with a *thunk,* and backed away in a wide circle to present its closed ramp hatch to the ruined carrier. Atticus waved Grippa back to shelter. The ramp on the carrier opened with a clank and it dropped slowly. Atticus decided he had a few seconds to take stock before Hell broke loose.

"Sit rep, Walt."

"Holding, At. But I'd love to get the hell out of here!"

You and me both, buddy. "Hang tough. We got an issue here."

"We all got issues," said Walt.

The ramp hit the ground, leaving a dark, open maw above it. Any moment now.

"Hank," said Atticus, "Give me a sit rep."

"I'm keeping their ugly heads down, sir, but this thing'll run dry eventually. We gotta scoot, boss."

"Understood."

Atticus raised his plasma rifle and fired into the bay. There was no time like the present. But the blue light bounced from something inside the carrier and it flew back out to blast a smoking hole in the ground to his right.

That's not good. Not good at all.

The enormous Repsian in *kravit* armor stepped from the darkness at the top of the ramp. It ducked its head to clear the hatch frame and walked down, unhurried. Stepping off to the ground, it drew itself to its full height and stared down at Atticus with multi-faceted eyes. Its four hands were empty, but clawed fingers curled and clicked together, perhaps in eagerness.

"Oh God!" said Grippa.

Atticus slammed his rifle against his helmet in frustration. This goddamn place would keep throwing things at them until they were dead. It was just that simple.

"What's up, At?" said Walt.

"Colonel Bug is here," said Atticus. "He doesn't want us in his house."

"Tell him we were just leaving."

Atticus lifted his rifle and fired another burst at the Repsian, more from anger than hope. The plasma deflected from its armor and impacted in the left rock pile. The creature spread its arms wider, inviting more.

"This bastard's laughing at me," said Atticus.

Hank came on the circuit now. "I can't read the bug writing on this gauge, Major, but I think the gun's nearly dry."

"Understood," said Atticus. "Keep it up as long as possible, then bail to Walt."

The scout responded with a rip of the gun. Atticus stepped to his right, and circled around the Repsian, putting the thing's back to Grippa's position. This duel needed to start and end quickly, before the Repsians in the trench got the upper hand.

The Colonel pointed a finger at Atticus and said something in a harsh, clacking language.

"Screw you too, buddy," said Atticus. "Grippa, are you still with me?"

"Yes, but this is going bad fast, Atticus."

"Not news," he said. "Listen up, I'm pretty sure that carrier is empty now. When he and I start this thing, run inside. Captain, get yourself in there too. Drive the carrier to the trench and get everybody in. There's probably enough room between the trench and the rocks to squeeze through."

"What about you?" said Grippa.

"I got business here. You need that carrier."

"Yes, we do," said Rail. "Do as he says, Lieutenant."

It was time to do this. Atticus put his rifle across his chest, lowered his helmet, and charged at the enormous Repsian. He heard Grippa's cry of protest, and Hank's announcement he was out of ammunition, but he pushed all that from his mind. Nothing anyone else was doing would matter unless he could keep this big, impervious bastard out of the fight.

Atticus rammed the Repsian with the crown of his helmet, striking its armored thorax where it narrowed to meet the creature's abdomen. The blow staggered the Repsian, knocking it backward, but it didn't fall. Atticus had laid a solid hit on the thing, but maybe it was impossible to knock over something with six legs.

He jumped back quickly, avoiding an embrace by the Repsian's four powerful arms. He threw away the useless rifle and fumbled at his web belt, yanking out the knife. It was a pitiful weapon, but maybe he could jam the blade into a seam between the armor plates and hit something vital. Merely enraging the Repsian would be enough, since all Atticus really needed to do was hold its attention while Grippa and Rail took the carrier. After that, it would be man versus bug: come what may.

Atticus moved in again, quick and low. He struck upward with the knife, trying to ram it beneath the chest plate, but two arms knocked him away and he tumbled hard. The Repsian was immensely strong. Atticus scrambled to his feet and backed away, but the thing hadn't moved. It stood in place, weaving its four hands through the air in an intricate pattern, then it clicked its fingers twice and beat its fists against its chest plate. The goddamn thing was taunting him.

And Grippa was only watching.

"Grippa, move!" said Atticus. "Now!"

"Right, going!"

Atticus's eyes were locked on the Repsian, but he could see Grippa moving across the space between the carriers. Tiptoeing. "For Christ's sake, Grippa, go!"

He charged the Repsian again to distract it. He tried to spin away at the last moment, but fiercely strong claws grabbed the back of his suit and he was pulled close. The Repsian lifted Atticus from his feet and turned him in the air.

Atticus swung the knife but it skidded harmlessly over the slick armor. He lost his grip on the knife and it fell away. Then he was flying. The rocky ground rose up to strike him. He hit hard and his helmet bounced. He flipped away quickly, expecting the creature to be on top of him, but still the thing held back.

The son of a bitch was enjoying itself.

"I'm in!" said Grippa.

"Get the Captain and go!" said Atticus. "This bastard's just toying with me."

"I'm coming to get you!" said Grippa.

"Negative! Get the others! Captain, your ride is leaving."

Rail emerged from the wreckage of the carrier, limping badly. He crossed the space between the carriers without being seen by the Repsian, but his heavy boots clanging on the ramp attracted its attention. It swiveled its head to look back, its body still facing Atticus.

Now!

Atticus lunged forward, ducking beneath the Repsian's unattended arms, to ram himself between its legs. Underneath, he set his back against its belly and pushed with his legs. But the goddamn thing was enormous: only three of its feet left the ground. Claws plucked at his suit, trying to extract him. The carrier's engine roared to life, and the claws began pulling frantically.

Atticus snarled. *You thought you had me, didn't you, you son of a bitch? Let's see how you like this!*

He set his feet squarely and heaved with all his strength. The three feet already in the air lifted higher, and the Repsian teetered on the other three before falling hard on its side. Atticus scrambled to climb on the creature's back while it was down. Hard, black bristles scratched across his suit. He put his feet around the Repsian's narrow waist and locked them together, then curled his fingers into the edge of its rear armor plate. The Repsian found its feet and rose to stand, Atticus clinging to its back.

The carrier's engine roared as Grippa pulled away. Good. This was working.

With the tables turned, and the carrier leaving, the Repsian seemed to panic. It bucked across the slope and chittered, reaching back to snatch at Atticus. But the angle was awkward, and its hard fingers could only scratch across his suit and helmet.

Atticus laughed with savage glee. What could be a finer end to the legend of Atticus Bragg than riding an enormous bucking exo into history? It seemed fitting, but he didn't want the legend to end just yet.

He heard Rail's voice in his ear: "Everyone into the carrier! Now!"

The carrier was at the trench. That was good.

Then another voice came: "Incoming aircraft! Looks like a bug troop carrier! Thirty seconds out."

That was bad.

"Twenty seconds to ramp up," said Rail.

It was time to end this.

Atticus took one hand from his grip on the armor plate and tugged a grenade from his web belt. He thumbed the primer and rammed the grenade into the gap between the plate and the Repsian's back, pushing it down out of reach.

He tensed to leap off, but a claw gripped his suit finally and he was yanked away to be dangled in front of the Repsian's face. The thing was black and haired, with hard lips and multi-faceted eyes in which Atticus could see his own helmeted head mirrored a dozen times. The Repsian regarded him with pitiless calculation, but Atticus wouldn't have to endure that cold gaze long because the good Colonel had about one more second to live.

Ironically, it was the Repsian's own fabulous armor that saved Atticus. It channeled the grenade's blast upward, vaporizing the bug's head in an ugly jet of yellow and black. But the armor didn't protect Atticus from the powerful shock wave. That blew him back ten meters and he hit the ground hard, throwing his head against his helmet. He bounced another five meters, then skidded to a halt.

His head rang. He heard voices dimly, as if through a wall.

"Atticus!"

"Troop carrier touching down!"

"Ramp up!"

* * *

He lay on the ground. He couldn't place himself. Strange voices spoke in his ear: some shouted, some pleaded, some had the familiar calm inflection of the professional soldier. The ground shook beneath him, and the sky above was tan with brown ribbons of dust.

One voice, above all, called to him. "Atticus!" it said. It was female. Familiar. "Get up, Atticus!"

He supposed he would. There was certainly no reason to lie here on the hard ground without a bottle to keep him company. He rolled onto his side, groaning. Voices argued in his helmet. An alien carrier rolled toward him. Someone in the turret mount waved, maybe to him, and fired a gun over his head. He looked back, over his shoulder. A great ship hovered there, disgorging tall, six-legged creatures carrying weapons.

There's no way that could be good.

He stood and wobbled for a moment before shambling toward the carrier, and the waving figure. At least it was human. He searched his memories as he ran, sifting images of people and planets, drops and fights, until the pieces began falling into place. There was a trench here. He needed to cross it. No, he needed to get into the carrier. Dirt kicked up around him. Some son of a bitch or another was always shooting at him. It was an unhealthy way to live.

The carrier stopped and the ramp dropped. People leaned out, urging him inside. He ran up the ramp, and it shut behind him. The soldiers inside looked haggard and beaten, and there seemed far too few of them to be here. He grabbed a handhold on the wall as the carrier accelerated down the slope, taking him away from what must have been something awful.

CHAPTER ELEVEN

Divisional headquarters was a cluster of pre-fabricated huts erected several klicks back from the ridge. The huts were a depressing mil-gray that some bureaucrat had identified as the color most likely to provide camouflage on the most planets. Atticus had set up hundreds of these huts while he was in the Service, but never on a gray planet. They did have airlocks, however, and were habitable without a suit.

Grippa and Rail were hustled away upon arrival, leaving the rest of them to wait in a squad bay. This would have been fine with Atticus, except a rash few had chosen to remove their helmets, freeing their suit-stink to set about its evil work. Atticus left his own helmet firmly in place and turned on his suit filters.

Walt refused to sit. He had been pacing the little room since they arrived. The gunner stopped in front of Atticus, and pointed in a random direction.

"The Captain could be in there throwing any of us to the wolves," he said, "to save his own skin. This thing was a fiasco from the start, and he knows it."

"Could be," said Atticus. Privately, he doubted it, but one never knew. The Captain might panic under grilling by his superiors and plant a knife in any back that presented itself. Now that Thorkin and Scar-nose were gone, the roster of backs was short.

"So what are you going to do about it?" said Walt.

"Nothing comes to mind," said Atticus. "Maybe take a nap. I'm beat."

"Christ, Atticus! This is not the time for your devil-may-care!"

"I'm serious. I've had a busy day."

The door opposite them opened and a young subaltern with brilliant red hair and a pock-marked face walked into the squad bay. He allowed a flash of panic to slip at the smell, but composed himself manfully to walk across the temp-crete floor and stand in front of Atticus.

"You're Bragg?" he said.

Atticus nodded.

"Follow me, and remove your helmet." The soldier turned and led Atticus from the squad bay before shutting the thin metal door tightly. Outside, the man let out a breath and looked for latches to throw, but there were none and he hurried on. Atticus followed, grinning.

At the end of a narrow hallway they stopped at another metal door, where the subaltern knocked twice before entering. Atticus had removed his helmet and now carried it under his arm as he followed the man through the doorway. The room beyond was small and gray. Grippa and Rail sat on metal chairs against one wall, and the division colonel sat behind a desk that was lost under paper and data pads.

Atticus realized he knew this Colonel. His name was Stardowski. He had been a staff officer under General Chin. It was Chin who had given Atticus's regiment the name "Bragg's Bunch," after the Sidicus affair. To Atticus's mind, it was a silly thing, but the troops had loved it. He remembered Stardowski as being efficient, if unimaginative.

"Atticus Bragg," said the Colonel. "It's been a long time."

"Yes, sir, it has. It's good to see you again."

"I heard you were down here, Bragg, doing something for the General. It appears to have turned into a mess."

"Yes, sir," said Atticus. "It was a shit-show."

"So I've heard." The Colonel put a finger under his nose. "Everybody has a story to tell about you, Bragg. You know that, right? Do you remember telling General Chin he was full of shit and needed to look at a holo-map?"

"Yes, sir, I do. And he did."

Stardowski laughed. "I've told that story fifty times. God, you were full of piss and vinegar, Bragg. Chin loved it, but then he threw you the hard jobs."

"They got done, sir."

"Indeed, they did," said the Colonel. He pulled out a drawer, and set a bottle and two tumblers on the desk. "Drink?"

"I'd love one, sir."

Stardowski poured a double and scooted it across the desk toward Atticus. "You need anything, Bragg? Medical attention?"

Atticus popped off the drink, enjoying the burn. He wiped his lips with the back of his hand. "No, sir. Only a day or two in the rack—and a hot shower."

"Indeed," said the Colonel. He poured himself a drink. "Now to the business at hand. Nearly an entire platoon has been lost, and under circumstances that demand an inquiry. There's no avoiding that. There's also no avoiding the fact this thing is politically sensitive." He glanced at Rail, then cleared his throat. "I have suggested to the Captain that blame might be made to fall on other shoulders. He has refused to entertain the idea, however, for reasons that escape me."

Atticus kept his face neutral. For all his friendliness and bonhomie, the Colonel saw Atticus as damaged goods, and therefore expendable to serve Rail. "I see, sir," said Atticus evenly.

The Colonel gestured with his tumbler. "You should do it for him, Bragg," he said. His smile was false. "Consider it another hard job. You were good at those. I'm sure there would be something in it for you."

And something taken away if I don't take the fall, thought Atticus. He looked at Grippa, who shook her head almost imperceptibly. But maybe the Colonel was right: maybe he was damaged goods. Maybe the best he could hope for now was to be thrown a scrap from the table by men like Stardowski and Warren. In return, he would take the fall, when falls were needed, because he didn't have far to drop. He opened his mouth to agree, but Rail spoke first.

"No, sir," said the Captain. "As I have said, that won't be necessary."

"I didn't ask you, Captain," said Stardowski.

"Nevertheless, sir," said Rail, "I insist." His voice now carried an aristocratic edge that transcended mere military rank. "I did not care to have Major Bragg's assistance, Colonel, and I resented General Warren's presumption. But now I will willingly admit the General proved, in this, wise. While I did not want Bragg, I needed him. Without him, the entire platoon would have been lost, including myself and Lieutenant Warren." He nodded to Grippa. "I cannot allow Bragg to accept blame that properly falls on me. I will accept General Warren's judgment on my conduct, whatever that may be."

Stardowski stared at Rail for a long moment, then said, "You do realize, my lord, that I am required to take you into custody to await that judgment?"

"Yes, Colonel," said Rail, but his eyes told a different story: he hadn't expected to be arrested like a common criminal. For a moment, he looked like the frightened boy again.

"Very well, Captain," said Stardowski, "we'll do it your way. God help both of us when your father hears of it." He gestured to the subaltern, who still stood by the door.

The man moved to stand in front of Rail, who offered his wrists to be magni-cuffed.

"Put the Captain on the next shuttle," said the Colonel. He turned to Atticus. "Goodbye, Bragg. I don't know what you did out there to get this kind of loyalty from the Captain, but you better hope your luck lasts, because General Warren is not a forgiving man. Go get that shower." He waved them away and drained his glass.

Atticus did get that shower and Walt paid for it, grumbling under his breath throughout about being overcharged for the tiny stalls in The Hole.

Atticus stood in the hot water for half an hour, replaying the last eight days and wondering what he could have done differently. He certainly could have sat on Thorkin harder in the beginning, when the platoon sergeant's opposition to Rail hadn't yet hardened into obsession, but it probably wouldn't have done any good. The Sergeant was determined to be the main player in a tragedy of his own making, and that had ended as all tragedies do.

On the other hand, the Captain remained alive, so Atticus had succeeded in fulfilling the major requirement of his contract. Hopefully, General Warren would see it that way too, but there might be a lot of explaining to do before he did. Troubled by this, but happy to be alive and on the station, Atticus stepped from the shower, dried himself with a thin towel, and pulled on a set of utilities.

Walt had bought them beds in The Hole as well, and after a spare meal Atticus laid down to rest after spreading his suit over the mattress. As dirty as the suit was, it was preferable to whatever was staining the mattress.

"Atticus Bragg?" said a voice.

Atticus raised his head. He knew he had slept, but it seemed only a few minutes. A lieutenant in grays now stood over him.

"The General will see you now," the man said.

Atticus rubbed his face. "Send him in."

"Never heard that one before, sir."

Atticus rose from the bed and followed the Lieutenant through the station, moving once again toward officer country. The corridors were quiet now: most of the troops were down on the planet, fighting or waiting to fight. In the flag section, the same wispy man guarded the hallowed precincts, but he let the two of them pass with only a searching look. At the end of the hallway, the Lieutenant knocked on Warren's door and opened it, gesturing for Atticus to enter.

There were four people in the room: General Warren, the pale admin by his desk, Captain Rail, and Grippa. They all turned their heads to look at Atticus as he entered. The atmosphere in the room was tense.

"Hello, Bragg," said the General. He pointed to a chair in front of his desk. It was placed somewhat remotely, as if to banish any thought of intimacy. Atticus sat on the chair, putting his feet flat on the floor and his hands on his thighs.

"This was a colossal cock-up, Bragg," said Warren without preamble. "Three quarters of a fine platoon lost, one of my best platoon sergeants, and nearly my daughter. You were supposed to prevent this kind of fiasco from happening. That's why I sent you."

"Yes, sir," said Atticus. "I—"

"Spare me your explanations, Bragg. I've heard a full account of this mess from Lieutenant Warren, and I have questions. Mostly for Captain Rail. I have the unhappy duty of deciding whether to prefer charges against him, and I will tell you now I have a mind to do it."

The General was angry, and Atticus didn't blame him: losing almost an entire platoon of expensively trained Imperial infantry in a noncombat situation was very nearly inexcusable. On the other hand, if Rail were convicted by a court-martial of incompetence or criminal negligence, it would be an indelible stain he would carry for the rest of his days.

Warren shifted in his chair to lean toward Rail. "Captain," he said, "is it correct you ordered an entrenchment around the wrecked ship?"

"Yes, sir," said Rail. "I did."

"In a position overlooked on all sides by high ground?"

"Yes, sir," said Rail. "I thought—"

"It's clear to me you did no such thing," said Warren. "Did you discuss this plan with Sergeant Thorkin?"

"No, sir."

Warren turned to Atticus. "Did Sergeant Thorkin express to you an opinion about this course of action?"

"Yes, sir," said Atticus. "He did."

"And that was?"

"He was opposed to it, sir," said Atticus. "Thorkin wanted to leave while we could."

"I see," said the General. "Did you share this opinion?"

Atticus hesitated. He paid his debts, or at least his debts of honor, and now he owed one to Rail. The Captain had pulled Atticus from the clutches of Stardowski, doing the honorable thing when an easier road had presented itself. More importantly, he had turned the carrier around to get Walt. Now Rail sat slouched in a chair, awaiting General Warren's judgment. Atticus decided his obligations to the man allowed him some leeway with the truth.

"No, sir," he said. "I did not share Sergeant Thorkin's opinion."

Warren raised his shaggy eyebrows. "Why would that be, Bragg? Don't tell me you're a tactical naïf. I know better."

"No, sir," said Atticus, "I'm not. We had no idea where we were, no communications, and the ship offered the only shelter possible. You or I, or Thorkin, might have made a different decision in the circumstances, but the Captain's decision was not unsound. It saved us from those insects, which might have pursued us after they discovered our presence on that first night. Without the shelter of the ship, we would have been overwhelmed."

The General grunted, looking dubious. Grippa was gazing at Atticus with an eyebrow cocked.

Warren turned back to Rail. "Captain, describe your actions at the fight with the armored creatures—the *kravits*."

Rail licked his lips. "I was knocked unconscious, sir. Early on."

"Where were you located when this occurred?"

"Near the afflicted, sir. Monitoring them."

"Monitoring them," repeated Warren. "Outside the perimeter?"

Rail nodded. "Yes, sir."

"Who did you suppose would command your platoon in the event you were disabled in an attack?"

"Well, sir, Sergeant Thorkin—"

"It was not Sergeant Thorkin's job to command your platoon, son!" said the General. "That was your job. His job was to carry out your orders."

"I understand that, sir."

"Where was your proper station at that time, Captain?"

Rail looked down. "Inside the perimeter, sir."

"That is correct," said Warren. "I'm told your absence resulted in many minutes of chaos before others were able to organize a retreat. Minutes in which soldiers died."

"Yes, sir, so I'm told."

Warren scowled at that. "So you're told," he said acidly. He turned to Atticus. "Bragg, what happened while Captain Rail was ineffective?"

"It was chaotic, sir," said Atticus, "as you said. I put Walt on the ship's cannon, and he killed one of the *kravits*. But by then the suits of the afflicted had been vented, and the hatch was imminent. The only option at that point was to make a quick exit, sir. Very quick."

"Leaving the cannon and the stores?"

"Yes, sir," said Atticus. "No choice, sir. We had to go."

Warren turned back to Rail. "Since you're sitting here now, I presume you were awake by the time this retreat began?"

"Yes, sir."

"Did you reassert command authority at that time?"

"No, sir," said Rail. "Not at that time."

"Well then, what were you doing at that time, Captain, if not asserting your authority?"

"I was—well, sir, I was running."

"Running."

"Yes, sir."

"Like a common soldier?" said the General.

Rail didn't reply.

"Who led this retreat?" said Warren.

"Thorkin, sir."

"And Bragg as well?"

Rail nodded. "He was involved, sir."

Warren leaned back in his chair and looked at Atticus. "Well, Bragg, how are you going to pull the Captain out of this one? He was running for his life, like a frightened little girl."

Atticus didn't blink. "We were all frightened, sir. Every one of us saw what those things did the night before, to those poor soldiers. It was horrific. It was the worst thing I've ever seen, sir, and I've seen a lot. It was imperative we get everyone out of that situation as quickly as possible. The more voices there are on c-channel, the more confused things become. You know that, sir. And seconds counted. When I looked back from a hundred yards out, those things were already moving around camp. I believe Captain Rail made the correct decision allowing Sergeant Thorkin and myself to coordinate the retreat from camp."

The General stared back at Atticus, then looked around at the walls of the room, scrubbing a hand over his mouth. "Captain Rail, physical courage does not come naturally to everyone. Some have more of it than others. We know that. It is expected. But it is also expected that every Imperial officer make at least a convincing demonstration of courage."

Rail stood. "Are you accusing me of cowardice, sir?"

"Sit down, Captain," said the General. He pointed to Rail's chair. "Even you know your conduct has been far less than exemplary in this matter, never mind the reason, and never mind what Bragg may say." The General folded his hands on his desk in front of himself. "So here's what I say. This platoon was lost under a combination of impossible circumstances and ineffective leadership." Rail opened his mouth to respond, but the General raised a hand to stop him. "I did not say negligent leadership, Captain. I said ineffective leadership. That is not a crime. It is, however, unacceptable. You will receive a letter of reprimand."

Atticus almost smiled. The General was punting. Atticus decided he would take credit for this one too, and he felt certain he deserved it this time. He and Rail were even.

"As for you, Bragg," said Warren. "You're a born leader. No fault of your own. How you've fallen to this station in life is a goddamn shame, but here you are. You did succeed in fulfilling the primary objective of your contract, which was to preserve the Captain here, but in the circumstances, I think it proper to reduce your compensation by seventy-five percent under the penalty clause. You did not preserve the Captain from error, as I asked. He fell into a great deal of it."

Atticus nodded. "Yes, sir."

"But Atticus led us out at the end!" said Grippa. "He saved us."

"And so he walks away from this with something," said Warren. He scowled at them. "This thing has been a goddamn embarrassment, and we've all been tarred by it, including me. Rail, I've had to look at your father's angry face on my comm screen every day. He's not a forgiving man."

"No, sir," said Rail. "He's not."

Warren flipped a hand at them. "You're free to go. All of you. Out."

"Thank you, sir," said Atticus, rising to leave.

"For what?" said the General.

"For not putting us in the brig, sir."

Warren laughed at that. "You probably deserved it. You were a good soldier once, Bragg, probably great, but you're a lousy mercenary."

"Maybe that's why I'm so poor, sir."

"Perhaps so. Goodbye, Bragg."

Grippa and Rail followed Atticus out, and they found Hank and Walt standing outside the door, dissembling.

"We weren't listening," said the gunner.

Hank shook his head. "Not even a little bit."

Atticus laughed. "How did you two get past that guard dog at the podium?"

The scout gave him an arch look in return. "Who said that was the only way in here, Major?"

Atticus laughed and clapped Hank on the shoulder, glad he and Walt had come. It felt good to have friends again. "Now that that's done," he said, "does anybody have a place I can crash? Otherwise it's the floor in the Hole again for me. That didn't end so well last time."

"I'll ask around," said Grippa.

"Not necessary," said Rail. "I have a suite in the R & R Sector.

Use it until the lease runs, Bragg. I'm leaving this benighted place, and not coming back."

"Thank you, sir," said Atticus.

"Don't get any ideas, Bragg," said the Captain. "We're still not friends. I'd be very happy never to see you again. But thank you for running interference with the General."

Atticus was certain this was the first time Rail had thanked him for anything, at least sincerely. "My pleasure," he said.

Rail didn't respond. He turned to walk down the hallway, away from them.

"Well," said Walt. "I guess that puts a bow on it. What now?"

"Bourbon in a short glass with three cubes," said Atticus.

"I concur," said Walt, "but no pilots this time."

"Agreed," said Atticus. "No pilots."

"Except me!" said Grippa, taking Atticus's arm.

He smiled. Yes, except her.

ABOUT THE AUTHOR

The Author, a lawyer by trade, lives in The Berkshires of Western Massachusetts with his family, two dogs, a cat, and a flock of chickens. John B. Cheek was his great-great-grandfather, an Arkansas farmer, carpenter, and cobbler.

Sign up at johnbcheek.com to be notified of my new releases.

Also, please consider leaving a rating or review at your favorite bookseller. Independent authors like me rely greatly on reviews by readers like you to continue writing the stories you enjoy.